Editor: Caroline Palmier—Love & Edits

Cover Designer: Melissa Doughty—Mel D. Designs

Formatting: Cathryn Carter—Format by CC

Copyright © 2024 by Erin Mackenzie

All rights reserved.

No part of this book may be reproduced in any form or by any electronic or mechanical means, including information storage and retrieval systems, without written permission from the author, except for the use of brief quotations in a book review.

This novel is entirely a work of fiction. The names, characters, and incidents portrayed in it are the work of the author's imagination. Any resemblance to actual persons, living or dead, events or localities is entirely coincidental.

the END ZONE

BOOK TWO OF THE
OUT OF BOUNDS
SERIES

For anyone who has ever been afraid to take a risk. I hope you find a way to let your faith be bigger than your fears.

You are stronger than your anxiety.

A NOTE FROM THE AUTHOR

Please note *The End Zone* does discuss mental health issues and readers who find the topic sensitive should be advised.

PROLOGUE

MIA

SIX YEARS AGO

"So, in less than twenty-four hours you're just leaving me at this school to fend for myself for the next year? That's really nice, Nate." I playfully elbow my best friend next to me as we walk down the sidewalk back to my dorm.

Nate Campbell is the best running back this school has ever seen so was I really shocked when he was drafted by the NFL to play for the Tampa Knights? Of course not.

"You can always come visit me, Smalls. Or better yet, just be my neighbor next year." He flashes his blue eyes my way as we continue on our walk.

I still have one more year of college, but I have no clue where I'll go once this is all over. I've loved living in Wisconsin. The small town atmosphere of the Midwest has definitely grown on me, but I'm more than ready to live somewhere that doesn't spend half of the year below seventy degrees.

Tomorrow, Nate heads to Florida to meet the team and coaches and get himself settled in Tampa before training camp begins. It'll be weird being on campus without him considering he's essentially my only real friend here. My roommate Natasha and I are close enough, but she has a longtime boyfriend, so the majority of her time is spent with him. I guess I could tag along with them and just be a permanent third wheel next year.

Nate opens the door to my dorm and I step inside as he follows closely behind. His hand runs through his tousled brown hair, pulling it away from his eyes as he steps into my small kitchen. This will be the last time I see these shaggy locks since he's about to cut it and it's a shame considering his hair is what drew me to him to begin with. It's prettier than mine.

Nate and I became fast friends—it was easy, we just kind of fell into sync with one another. Being drawn to Nate had nothing to do with him being a great football player and everything to do with who he is as a person. Spending all of my time with someone who constantly made me laugh, challenged me, and actually listened to the things I said was as easy as breathing.

"What about getting a dog?" I ask as I'm breaking free of the sweater I have on.

"A dog?" His eyebrows furrow as he says it and then his expression softens, as if he's actually considering it.

"Come on, you know you're a dog person. You need the company. Who are you going to talk to all the time in your apartment?" My arms cross over my chest with a knowing smile and he pulls me into a hug as he laughs.

"Fuck, I'm really going to miss you, Mi."

"If you find a new best friend, I'll sneak into your house and cut holes in every one of your beloved REO Speedwagon shirts as revenge."

Nate gasps at my threat and I throw a devilish smile in his direction.

"You wouldn't dream of it. You know you love them just as much as me. I think seeing them at Summerfest was the highlight of the summer, and Bryan was always my hair inspiration." He attempts to fluff his hair and we both laugh because Nate's hair looks nothing like the drummer's, but I won't hurt his feelings by telling him that.

When Nate and I met, one of the first things that bonded us was our love for music. I barely remember how the conversation started, but I know it ended with us doing a very off-key, yet entertaining karaoke set of "Don't Stop Believing" by Journey. That was the moment we simultaneously knew that we were meant to be friends and it's just been that way ever since. He was wearing a black Rolling Stones t-shirt and had on dark denim jeans with vans. His crystal blue eyes stood out in a dark room. Aside from his physical appearance—you know, the muscles and all—I never would've guessed he played football.

Being best friends with the star player on the football team doesn't go without its assumptions and questions though. I'm used to the side eyes and confused looks from the other girls when Nate and I are always showing up places together, but never actually *together*.

After a while, we'd gotten so tired of fielding questions about us being more than friends that eventually we just started ignoring the comments rather than always addressing them. We let people think what they wanted and we were content with that. If people wanted to think I was screwing one of the hottest guys on campus, so be it.

The night after the Homecoming game last year, Nate had quite a bit to drink. Really, anything more than a few beers is a lot for Nate since he's not a huge drinker. But the football team had just won a big game, and he knew he was going to get drafted, so he was on cloud nine all night. He had every reason to celebrate.

There was a moment where I could have let my *mild* attraction and lady bits call the shots, but I'm nothing if not a responsible adult. My friendship with Nate is too important to me and I didn't want to risk losing that. So, when we were in the hallway of the frat house and he waltzed his 6-foot frame in my direction with a look of pure lust and those baby blues staring right at me, I knew I couldn't let anything happen. And that meant turning him down when he leaned too close and touched too often.

I still remember the cedar scent wafting from his skin, the flannel shirt he was wearing, the scrunchie of mine that he had around his wrist… it's probably one of those memories I'll never forget. Our friendship could have changed drastically in just that one moment. At times, I can't help but wonder *what if?* But I know I did the right thing by pulling away.

We have never talked about that night and we've never come close to anything else like it again. We went right back into our normal routine, walking to classes together and having our karaoke nights at the local bar near campus when we could make it. We'd make pizza together the night before he'd leave for away games. We developed a lot of little habits with one another and I'll definitely miss doing all of that with him. It's going to be so different next year for me, but I'm really proud of him.

"You should come apartment hunting with me, actually. The team is setting me up somewhere for the first few weeks, but before classes start, can you fly in?" Nate asks while unwrapping a pink Starburst from the dish on my counter and tossing it in his mouth. "I'll book you a flight. Please, Mi. You know I'll need your help." He cocks his head to the side as he chews.

"Fine," I concede. "I *guess* I'll go to sunny Florida for a weekend." I tease, flinging my scrunchie at him, which he proceeds to pick up from the ground and slide onto his wrist.

Who knows? Maybe I'll go visit him down there, end up loving it and consider it as a place to live after I'm done with school. The beach is one of my favorite places and I love the warm weather, so it's actually not the wildest idea.

Before Nate leaves, he reaches his hand out and grasps mine for our tacky little handshake. It hits me that this will be the last time we get to do this—at least for now. It's something we randomly started doing when he would leave for away games.

Like most little quirks Nate and I have, I don't know how it started, but we just found ourselves doing it every time before he'd leave and it's stuck.

"Are you going to find someone else to do this with now since you're leaving?"

Clapping our hands together twice, then bumping elbows, back to a hand clap and finally a hip bump and a hug.

Nate turns the doorknob and opens the door to leave. "No, Mi. It'll only ever be you."

CHAPTER ONE

NATE

PRESENT

Focus.

Breathe.

Relax.

"Nice, Campbell!" Coach Aarons shouts from the sidelines as I'm jogging in the opposite direction with the ball in my hands.

Regular season begins soon and saying that I'm ready would be a bold-faced lie.

"Run it again!" I shout to Liam Evans, our quarterback.

"Again? We've done it a dozen times; you've got the route."

He slings the ball into the slot one more time and I make an adjustment to come away with the catch.

"Make that a baker's dozen now." Winking at him, he claps his hands at me and I toss him the ball before making my way over to the bench to have a seat.

"I'm heading in, you coming?"

Shaking my head at Liam's question, I gesture for him to go ahead without me. "I'll be there in a minute."

As I lean forward, my elbows rest on my knees and I grab the playbook to take another look over it. Studying it, trying to memorize every single x and o on this damn thing.

The football field has always been the place I've excelled. The one thing I've always been exceptional at. I never used to question my ability on the field or my contributions to the game, but as of lately, that's all changed.

Coming off of a Super Bowl winning season only adds extreme pressure going forward. All summer, any time I've stepped on this field I've felt mediocre at best. There's no telling what's going to happen day in and day out because every morning I wake up, already feeling defeated before the day even begins.

I love this game. Or at least I really used to. Deep down, I know that's still the case, but recently I just feel… miserable. Although to the people around me, they'd never know. I'm still walking into the facility with a smile on my face, dragging my teammates in the locker room and wearing the charismatic persona on the field. It almost feels like Nate Campbell, NFL running back, is a role I'm playing. As if who I am in football and who I am behind closed doors are two completely different people.

Losing your love of something that makes up your entire life is like having a fucking identity crisis at the ripe age of twenty-seven.

The warmth of the sun hits my face as soon as I get up and head inside to the locker room. Practice has been over now for about an hour, but taking time to myself to rerun plays and go over everything on my own has been needed.

After I get out of the shower, I notice a handful of texts on my phone. I swipe past the ones from the guys, but I can't ignore the text from Coach Aarons.

> COACH
> Come see me before you leave.

Fuck.

As I'm walking down the hall to where his office is located, I pass countless pictures and plaques along the walls. Reminders of all of the great players who have also worn the same uniform as I do. It makes me wonder if any of them also felt how I've been feeling.

Did Henry Kurtis wake up every morning and have to will himself out of bed? What about Jimmy Jones? Did he get so anxious some nights that he'd spent the evening on a bathroom floor rotating between the shower and the toilet?

Did they also feel the crippling pressure of the game?

Coach Aarons' door is ajar when I approach, so I tap two knuckles on the outside and peek my head in the open space.

"Come on in." He summons me with his hand before pulling his glasses off of his face. "Saw you out there when all was said and done, everything alright?"

Lie. Redirect.

"Yeah, all good." I plaster on a smile and prop my right ankle over my left knee, leaning back in this cushy office chair. There's a newspaper article on his wall from last season when we won the Super Bowl. In the photo, everyone on the sidelines has erupted in cheers, pouring the bucket of water over his head in celebration. Fuck. I still can't even believe I was part of that team, can't believe that I have a ring. It feels like such a long fucking time ago, even though it's not even been a year. Who I was six months ago versus who I feel like I am now couldn't be more different and that's... confusing.

Coach Aarons' eyes narrow at me, something tells me he isn't buying what I'm selling right now, but I don't let my face falter. I keep the bright expression; I keep the light on.

"I'm ready for Carolina." A redirect, to change his focus

from me to our upcoming game. Even though it's another lie because while I always love a division game, I have no fucking idea how I'll be on the field.

"Division game, we need to start the season off strong." He pulls himself up from his chair and I do the same.

Great, nothing like adding to the pressure that I'm already feeling. He extends his hand out to me as we both stand there. Coach Aarons is a big guy, with one hell of a mustache. He played football when he was younger, only one year in the league before he got injured and never recovered fully. About a decade ago, he became a head coach and I'd say he's found his calling. He turned this franchise from the laughing stock in the league to Super Bowl winners.

"Yes, sir." We shake hands before I turn to leave his office.

"You'll let me know if something's going on, yeah?" I knew he was questioning my answer earlier. Coach has been almost like a second father figure to me. He's good to me on the field and honestly, even better off of it. Lying to him feels wrong, but there's no way I can tell him what's going on. Fuck, I barely know myself what's happening to me so there's no way I can even try to explain it to someone else. But I nod at him before closing his door behind me.

"God damn," I mutter once I'm back outside. There's hot and then there's Florida summer hot. The wave of heat is instant the second I step outside and walk through the parking lot to my truck. Although, it still beats the brutal winters I grew up with in Wisconsin.

It's a quick drive back to my apartment, only a few left turns and a couple stoplights. Driving downtown is a colossal nightmare. No one ever knows where they're going, people dart off in the crosswalk, even when the lights haven't changed. It's been like this since I moved here and at first, I loved it. The constant bustle of the city was exciting, but lately it only stresses me out. I'd love to move outside of the city, like my buddy Ford did. But I'd want to be even more secluded than he is.

I pass rows of cars as I drive through the parking garage at my apartment, but thankfully I have my own designated spot.

The comforting smell of cedar fills my senses as I walk into my apartment and toss my keys down. My golden retriever, Hendrix, nearly tackles me before I'm even through the door. Knowing he's always happy to see me is one thing I'll never get tired of. My phone dings again so this time I pull up the texts to see what the hell all the commotion is about.

> LIAM
>
> Tee time is set for nine tomorrow morning.
>
> I have all of my golf puns ready for your entertainment.
>
> FORD
>
> Please, for the love of God, don't. I'll pay you to not say any of them.
>
> CHASE
>
> Catch me ridin' birdie. I'll be there.
>
> FORD
>
> Hunt, I'm disappointed in you.
>
> LIAM
>
> Big Caddy gets it. He's with me. Nate, you can have Anderson.

Shaking my head, I put my phone down and head towards my bedroom. The curtains are open in the back, casting a ray of sunshine directly into the living room as I walk by. When I pass the guest bathroom, I notice a pink hand towel hanging on the hook near the sink. That was definitely Laura's doing. Her and I dated briefly earlier this year, but I quickly realized it wasn't anything more than physical. When we met last Halloween, there was an instant attraction. She's gorgeous and we had fun, but that's where the connection ended.

Sighing, I walk down the hall with Hendrix on my heels. A golf day with the guys sounds real fucking good right now.

"What a tee-rific day for some golf, fellas." Liam walks up to me and Chase with a grin on his face.

"Where's Anderson?" Chase asks.

"Probably with your sister."

"Honest to God, Liam…What the hell is wrong with you?" Chase shakes his head and walks away from us. I'll never get tired of watching Chase get uncomfortable when Liam cracks a joke about Ford and his sister.

"Speak of the fucking devil," I shout as I see Ford step out of his truck.

"What?" Ford questions as he gets closer.

"Liam scared Chase off again with one of his visuals of you and Abby." I gesture my hand over to Chase sitting in the golf cart on his phone as Liam stands there with a prideful smile on his face.

"Fucking child, Evans." Ford's eyes roll and he walks over to the golf cart where Chase is so we can get started.

As the day has gone on, the heat has only gotten more unbearable. It's a swift reminder that I'm not looking forward to those over one hundred-degree temps on the field we'll be facing soon.

We're almost done, thank God, because if I have to hear Liam hoot and holler for himself one more goddamn time… I might stab him in the eye with one of these golf tees. But then we'd be out our first-string quarterback, so I need to refrain myself.

"Are we almost finished? It's fucking hot. Everything's melting. I'm sweating through this polo." Ford swipes his gloved hand over his forehead.

Liam walks up to the tee and sets his ball down before taking a practice swing.

"I'm about to take the win for the day, sit back and relax." A cocky grin takes over Liam's face.

He swings his club and the ball goes flying down the green. We all watch on as it lands feet away from the hole, causing me to let out a groan.

"Mother fucker," I say under my breath with a low chuckle.

"Woo! That's about to be a birdie, boys," Liam shouts with a wink as he walks back to the golf cart, hopping in next to Chase.

I get in the other cart next to Ford and we take off to the last hole. Being out on the golf course with the guys today, I've tried my best to maintain who they know me to be. It's pretty easy in this setting. Golf is competitive, but it's fun and the most important fact, it's not my job. So I don't feel the same heavy pressure to perform. Although, part of me thinks they already can tell something's off, considering we spend so much time together. I know my best friend Mia already has her suspicions.

"Is that an alligator?" I hear Ford's voice as I look up near the lake that's nestled within this course, and sure enough, there's an alligator sitting right on the edge of the green next to the water. That's a pretty big one, but I've seen them on golf courses plenty of times before. They couldn't give a shit about us as long as we leave them alone.

"Damn, he's huge," Liam says as he eyes the gator.

After Chase, Ford and myself all fail miserably on this hole and end up back at the carts, Liam walks over to his ball that's sitting on the green. The rest of us stay seated, watching Liam tip toe like a fucking mouse over to line up for his swing. He keeps looking over his shoulder as if he thinks the alligator is going to sprout wings and fly directly into him.

"Stay," he says with a straight face, motioning his hand in a stop position towards it and the rest of us fucking lose it. I try to cover my mouth, but the laugh just bellows out of me as I hold my side.

"Don't be so fucking loud, you're going to make it angry!"

"It's not a damn dog, Evans. Putt your ball and let's fucking go." I laugh again and shake my head as I watch Liam nervously swing the club and see his ball roll right past the hole.

"No. Redo. Mulligan. I call a Mulligan. The fucking dinosaur over here is distracting me," Liam pouts.

"Get the fuck out of here. This is not the first time you've been on a course with an alligator. You aren't calling a Mulligan for that," Chase scoffs, and Liam grips his club in his hand, flipping off the alligator with the other.

"Well, they're never the size of a goddamn school bus," Liam argues.

After another swing, he gets the ball in the hole.

"Stupid fucking dinosaur," Liam mutters to himself before getting back in the golf cart.

Chase sits down across from me at a table once we're in the clubhouse, and we both take off our baseball hats, placing them on the table. I run my hand through my hair and instantly regret it considering it's soaked in sweat. I wipe the palm of my hand on my shorts.

"Kristen has to be due soon right? It feels like she's been pregnant forever," I say to Chase.

When he mentioned that he was having a baby with Kristen Floyd, I already knew he'd be in for a nightmare. She's been a cleat chaser for years, and as far as I'm concerned, she was probably just waiting to see which one of us she could get to knock her up. A shame it's Chase because out of all the guys I'm close with, he's probably the last I would've expected to end up with an accidental pregnancy. He's responsible, smart, the 'dad' one of the group. But just another one of those things that you don't expect to happen, yet it does. After his initial panic wore off, he's been nothing but absolutely pumped to have a kid.

"Any day now. I'm nervous, but fuck, I'm so excited." He takes a long swig of his beer and then swiftly changes the subject, asking Liam about some TV show.

Some of the older gentlemen around the clubhouse come and say a few words to us before we leave. None of us are actually members at this country club, but Ford's dad is a big shot around here so we get to reap the benefits by playing this course any time. Mia always jokes that being in the NFL allows me to get whatever I want. If that were true though, I'd probably be a lot happier.

CHAPTER TWO

MIA

If I were a pair of AirPods where would I be?

The way I've just swept through my entire apartment searching for these God forsaken headphones, I belong on that old show 'Supermarket Sweep.' Although, I'd lose because I can't actually find what I'm looking for. I've been zooming around this place, trying to find them in the small window of time I have before I absolutely must leave to make it to work on time.

I'm still coming up empty as I'm rummaging through my junk drawer in my kitchen and my phone rings. Nate's face flashes on the screen and I reach over to answer, placing the phone on speaker.

"Hey," I call out from across the kitchen island.

"Hey, you okay? You sound out of breath."

"I'm currently acting as a one-woman search party. I can't find my AirPods." My voice gets louder the further away from the phone I get.

"When I get home, I'll check my place." Nate's voice sounds hollow. Something I've noticed as a trend the last couple of weeks. Actually, it's probably been that way for the last few months. His usual upbeat tone has shifted.

"How was golf? Did Liam win again?" I've abandoned my search for now, I don't have the time to keep tearing this place apart. I head into my bedroom, pulling the t-shirt off over my head and swapping it out for a bright pink tank top.

"He's a good golfer. It's probably time I just accept it. Of course, he's very humble too."

I can't help the laughter that follows that comment. "Oh, of course."

Nate goes on, telling me a little bit about his day. I catch something about an alligator but I don't ask him to elaborate. Sitting on my bed, I pull my socks on and lean back in my bed to grab my water bottle that's on my nightstand. I have a client to meet in fifteen minutes, so I'm tossing everything I'll need into my gym bag.

Becoming a personal trainer wasn't on my short list of things I thought I'd do with my life, but after my own personal physical therapy and strength training after an accident, I developed a passion for it. It would be awesome to own a studio one day, but right now, I work at a local gym downtown. I look every now and then for a studio, but so far, I haven't found anything that's caught my eye. Plus, everything is so fucking expensive these days. Three thousand dollars a month, plus security deposits, and might as well throw in my first born too. Jesus.

"Any appointments with the guys today?" Nate's question brings me back to our conversation.

"Graham's coming in for something quick, I actually need to be there soon, so I have to run."

"Okay. Hey, check his shoulder, he's been babying it." Graham's on the offense with Nate. He's one of the linemen, so I get why he wants him healthy.

"I'm not a doctor. You have team trainers for that," I quip back at him.

"I just want to see if he'll show you any weakness."

My eyes roll as I slip on my sneakers. "Oh my God, Nate."

"Well, he's my leading blocker!" A hearty laugh comes through the phone with his reply.

"I'll be sure to report back." Shaking my head, I grab my keys and gym bag before heading towards the door.

I hear a light sigh on the other end. "That's my girl."

"Goodbye, Nathaniel," I say playfully before locking my apartment door behind me.

"Talk to you later, Mi."

Just as I'm rounding the corner of Main and Marshall before I get to the gym, a bright red for rent sign in a window catches my eye. This must've just gone up because I definitely didn't see this yesterday and I know I would have remembered. Nothing ever goes up for rent down here, I've checked multiple times. Even asked one of the county officials one day. I was not so pleasantly told that I'd likely never see something publicly posted for rent down here.

I curiously glance in the windows before sticking my face up against it. Peeking in the room I can see mirrors lined up on one wall with a long bar running all along the perimeter. This had to have been a ballet studio based on that set up.

There's a phone number and name listed on the sign so I snap a quick photo of it and continue on my way. What do I want to bet this one is *also* out of my price range? Either way, I can't not call to find out.

———

"Push, Turner. Come on!" I shout to Graham as he's pushing me on top of the sled drill. His exasperated sighs are telling me he's had enough of the five-foot-two with a whistle telling him what to do.

"Okay, okay. Call it."

He stands, wiping the pooling sweat from his brow and a satisfied feeling burns in my gut. To answer Nate's burning question, Graham's shoulder seems fine—or he's just really good at hiding pain.

"You belong out on the field with this bullshit. You'd have those guys in tip-top shape, little lady." Even though Graham doesn't have a lick of an accent, he still likes to subtly remind us that he's really a sweet, southern gentleman at his core. I've seen him get rowdy, but he's really just one giant teddy bear. He grew up on a farm and always talks about going back to farm life once he's done playing football.

I used to wonder if the workouts I had planned for guys like Nate or Graham were even tough enough for them or beneficial enough, but Nate put that to rest when he told me he'd rather run over burning coals barefoot, repeatedly than work out with me. He's all talk though.

Once Graham and I are all packed up, we head out of the gym and go our separate ways. Now that regular season football is beginning, I won't be meeting with him again until next off season. During the season they're on much stricter protocols with their bodies and weight, so I leave that stuff to the professionals.

My phone rings the second I press the button for the crosswalk to head back home. It's starting to drizzle, and as luck would have it, I didn't bring an umbrella. Hopefully it can hold off another ten minutes for me to get back home. Or if it gets bad enough I can always just duck into Nate's building up ahead and wait it out in the lobby.

"Nathaniel," I say slowly, dragging out the last few letters as I look both ways once the light changes.

"Done with Graham?" The edge in his voice causes me to stop walking once I reach the sidewalk again.

"Yes, I'm on my way home."

"Want to come up?" Nate's balcony looks out over the water, but if he's looking directly below, like he is right now, he can see down on the sidewalk.

"Stalker, much?" I kid, staring up at him. His arms rest on the railing as he leans on it holding his phone in one hand and giving me a little wave with the other.

"Come on, I'm hungry," he begs.

"Oh, that sounds like a personal problem."

"I was going to make chicken marsala. Extra garlic bread. Side of pasta. Have dinner with me, Smalls." The pleading in Nate's voice isn't something I've been able to resist often. Plus, Nate's actually a really good cook. I swear if he didn't have a career in the NFL, he'd make an incredible chef. He can make mushrooms sound appetizing and I *hate* mushrooms.

"Okay, you've won me over with the promise of extra garlic bread," I tease, turning to his building and heading inside the lobby.

Once I get to Nate's door, I knock a couple times before walking right in. Hendrix comes to greet me and I drop my bag at my feet to get down and pet him. Nate's shirtless body is already standing over the stove stirring something in a pan. He wipes his hand on the towel that he has slung over his bare shoulder and I notice the outline of his cell phone in the pocket of his light gray joggers.

"Hasn't anyone ever told you not to cook shirtless? It's dangerous." But, wow. It smells amazing in here. When I get closer and take a look at the stove, Nate pulls my head to his mouth and plants a kiss on the top.

"Never heard that one before." A deep chuckle leaving his chest as his lip curls up on his face.

"You'll be happy to know Graham did not show any weakness." I dip my finger in the pan as we stand against the counter and taste the sauce simmering on the stove, throwing my head back with a moan as the flavor hits my palate. *So. Fucking. Good.*

Nate swats my hand away when I try to go in for seconds. "Really? Well, that's good. He wasn't a full participant all week in practice… so I was wondering what was going on."

Shrugging my shoulders, I walk out of the kitchen and flip on the television. Nate's default channel somehow always comes up as NFL highlights, even though he's aware he shouldn't be watching commentary on himself.

Dinners with Nate are my favorite, especially when he cooks. Usually whichever one of us cooks dinner doesn't have to clean, and nine times out of ten, he's cooking and I'm cleaning. Listen, I can throw down in the kitchen, but why should I when he actually likes cooking *and* he's good at it?

"Ready for Carolina?" I ask as we sit together at the island eating.

"People keep asking me that…" He sighs, taking a sip of his water.

Lowering my gaze in confusion, I say, "Should we not be asking you that? I mean, you have a game coming up, it seems like a fair question… Is everything alright?"

"It's a fair question. I just… I don't know how to answer it."

Nate leans back in his seat, stretching both arms behind his head, showing the valleys of muscle that run over his stomach. "I don't feel… *in it* right now. I'm not sure how to explain it."

I place my fork down and wipe my mouth with the napkin before completely turning my body towards his.

"Well, start at the beginning. What's going on?"

An obvious wave of apprehension washes over Nate's features. He gets up from his seat and places his empty plate into the sink. His hands flex out in front of him before he places them firmly on the marble surface. His hands are truly massive and if I was attracted to my best friend I would probably be obsessed with the way they look.

"Honestly, Mi... I don't know. Something's off. I can't pinpoint it. But I don't think I can manage it anymore. I don't know how to control it. I don't feel like myself. Since winning the Super Bowl, I just feel like the pressure to do it again, do it even better, is too much. My name is in every article, on every news cast and my head is just screaming that I'm not doing enough."

A knot forms in my stomach at his words. I knew something was going on. His tone. His behavior. I could tell, but I didn't want to press it. I've known Nate for a long time, and one thing I've learned is regardless of what it is, Nate won't talk about something until he's ready.

"I wake up every morning with this monster in my head. And it just builds and builds throughout the day. These anxious thoughts just creep in and it's almost becoming debilitating. I'm trying to hide it on the field, around the team, the coaches, but I don't know how much longer I can keep that up." His head shakes back and forth before he shifts his eyes to the left and then brings them back to me. "I've thrown up three times in my adult life, they all had to do with drinking. Want to know how many times I've fucking vomited in the last month?" His head rises and he looks at me with a sad, broken stare. I don't want to know, because something tells me it'll only break my heart.

"Seven," he whispers.

"Nate," I say softly, getting up and making my way around the kitchen island to his side. When I reach for his arm, I can feel his pulse jumping at his wrist.

"Hey, look at me." My hands cup his cheeks as he turns to me and I place one hand on his chest only to feel his heart beating so rapidly, if I didn't know any better I'd think he just sprinted the length of a football field. "I had no idea you were struggling this way. But you'll be okay, I'll help any way I can. It's okay." My forehead leans against his arm as we stand there and I continue whispering over and over, "It's okay" until I can visibly see his body relax, and feel his heart rate slowing back to a steady pace.

His throat clears. "Fuck, I'm sorry. I didn't plan on telling you any of that tonight... or ever." Nate's arms wrap around me, holding me close. An interaction that we have daily, but this just feels like he needs the contact right now, the closeness.

"I had no idea this was going on. I sensed a change, but I never would've guessed. Thank you for telling me, though. You know you can always tell me anything, right? You can come to me for anything."

He nods and takes a deep breath. I know there's even more where all of that came from, but instead of asking anything more, I let him rest. I realize how big of a deal that was for him to share with me.

"I'll clean up tonight." Nate reaches for my plate, but I take it from his hands.

"No, tradition is tradition. I'm cleaning."

He smiles and walks down the hall towards his bedroom.

After I have everything loaded into the dishwasher, I call out to Nate, "I'm going to head out, I'm tired." When I glance at my phone, I see it's just after eight. It's been a long day with unexpected and disheartening information and now I just want to get home and into problem solving mode. I need to know how to help him.

Nate walks down the hall and pulls me into a hug when he's close enough, the bit of stubble on his face rubs against my cheek, but the warmth of his bare chest is comforting and I nuzzle myself into him a little further.

"Trying to cop a feel, Smalls?" His head pulls back and he smirks.

"You're hot," I say without thinking of the context. "Warm. Your body is warm. Your chest is warm. I... it's just comforting, leave me alone," I pout.

He pulls me in closer as he laughs and I can feel the rumble of his chest as my head rests there.

"Thanks for tonight, Mi." His lips press hard on the top of my head and I smile before pulling away.

Entering my apartment, the silence is a nice break from the bustling outside. Living downtown has been great as far as convenience goes, but I still don't love the constant rush that it entails.

I quickly undress to hop in the shower before the chirping sound of my phone goes off. It's a tone I haven't heard in months. I could have sworn I deactivated all of my dating apps after all of my disaster dates over the summer.

Wrapping a towel around myself, I reach for my phone to see there's a message from someone named Devin. The message simply says, 'hey gorgeous.' *Great introduction.*

I click his profile and notice his picture is of him with a toddler on his shoulders. Is this guy a dad? I could go for a single dad. Once I scroll to look at his caption, it very clearly says 'not my baby' and I'm instantly annoyed. I have no problem dating someone with a kid, in fact, a hot dad sounds pretty good right about now, but why is that your picture on a dating app?

I toss the phone back on my bed and head for the bathroom.

After a shower, the couch is calling my name and I throw my feet up to get comfortable.

> His profile picture is him holding a baby, but then the caption says 'not my baby.'

SUMMER

> I don't understand that? Should I take a picture with a really hot car, but then caption it 'not my car'?

> It wouldn't bother me if a guy I dated had a baby, I just don't understand why you chose it as your picture if it's not reflective of your life? What are you looking to prove here? That you look good with babies, but still need to clarify that it isn't yours?

SUMMER

Exactly. Do you know how good I'd look next to a Maserati? Can I afford one... that's a hard no. Dating a hot single dad would probably be the best sex of your life. I just have this feeling. But no hot dads in my area though. *whomp whomp*

Actually I just googled Maserati's, I don't like them that much. I think deep down I'm just a simple gal who wants a hot guy with a big truck.

> There's something about a man who drives a truck... I can't explain it.

SUMMER

I know what you mean. *melts into a puddle* Yes, please help me up into your big truck, daddy.

> All of that. Except not the daddy part.
>
> When is your move date again?

SUMMER

In two weeks you'll have me there permanently. Make room for me until I find an apartment, you know I can't stay with Ford and Abby. The last time I could hear them from across the house and I just don't need them to rub it in my face that they're having mind blowing sex every day.

A laugh escapes me. Abby and Ford are one of those couples

who will probably never get tired of being all over each other. If I didn't find it adorable and romantic, I'd hate them for it. I never expected Ford to be such a sap, but Abby has really done a number on him. In a good way, of course. Seeing how effortless their love is gives me hope that I'll eventually find it for myself one of these days.

Dating has been non-existent for me for the last year. I've tried to find men I could make a connection with, but nothing ever sticks. I want to be in love. I want all of the romance and the comfort that comes with finding your person. But admittedly, I'm terrified of commitment. I'm terrified of trusting someone with all the vulnerable parts of myself only for them to up and leave, to decide they don't want it. So, a real, true relationship is something I've never actually had. I've never taken the chance. The only man I truly trust is Nate, and there's no romance happening there.

I send Summer a series of emojis and then lock my phone before starting another episode of *Friends*. My mind drifts to the conversation I had with Nate earlier and all I want to do is figure out ways I can help him, be there for him. I know he's under a lot of pressure. I just didn't realize it was becoming so hard on him and that he was struggling so much.

The episode of *Friends* grabs my attention when Chandler's character comes into the picture. He's easily my favorite and who I'd probably relate to the most. You know, crappy childhood, parents who are barely there, leaning on humor as a coping mechanism. Oh, and also the one who is afraid that they'll end up alone forever. That'd be me.

It's the one where Chandler tells Monica that she is, in fact, high maintenance, but he likes maintaining her and it instantly makes my heart swoon. This show constantly teeters my emotions between laughing out loud to teary eyed back to laughing all within a thirty-minute time span.

Being in love with someone who you also consider one of your best friends sounds great in theory, but what happens if you break up? Where does that leave the friendship? If you ask me, dating your best friend is just too risky… even if sometimes your mind wanders.

CHAPTER THREE

NATE

A few months ago, I made a commitment to Ford that I'd attend his charity dinner for the downtown Rec Center, and even give a speech. That version of Nate is the bane of my existence, because the me standing in my closet right now, mulling over suit options really doesn't want to fucking go.

"Should I wear black or blue?"

"Go with blue. The navy will look good with your eyes," Mia says firmly.

When I look over my shoulder at her through the FaceTime call, she isn't even looking at me or the suits. I watch her as she's leaned forward on her yoga mat, head down and arms outstretched in front of her.

"With the snakeskin tie? Perfect."

"Wait, what?" Her head darts up and she moves slightly closer to the screen.

"Aha, see, you weren't even looking." A quick smile curves on my lips. Something that's been forced lately, except for when I'm around Mia.

She sits back and rolls her dark brown eyes at me. "Oh my

gosh. But I don't need to look at you to know what color would look best between black and blue. If you want my vote, it's for blue."

I let out a sigh before turning off the closet light. Swinging the door shut behind me, I grab the phone from where it's propped up on the nightstand and look at her through the screen. Her knees are underneath her as she crosses her arms over her chest. I'm pretty sure I can see a honey mustard stain on the t-shirt she's wearing. I know it's not regular mustard, she hates the stuff. If I had to guess, I'd say she ate a turkey, lettuce and tomato sandwich for lunch and dipped it in the honey mustard. Mia's the most predictable person I know.

"And you're sure you don't mind coming with me? You don't technically have to." My hand runs through my hair before I rub my eyes with my palm.

"I'm sure. I told Abby I'd help out. Plus, you need someone to heckle you from the back while you give your speech." She scrunches her nose before reaching out towards the phone. "I do need to run though so I'll see you later. I'm not sure what I'm wearing yet, but now that I know you're wearing blue, it makes it easier so we can coordinate a little."

My eyebrow cocks up at her through the screen. "That's a little premature, don't you think? I don't remember agreeing to the blue."

"Right, of course. Bye, Nate," she says sarcastically with a smirk and waves me off.

"Change your t-shirt!" I shout into the phone, not sure if she caught it or not before the call ended.

I appreciate Mia not treating me like I'm some broken mess after the pity party I threw for myself the other night. She's acting completely normal, just how we've always been and it's somehow bringing me out of my funk slightly. I didn't go into that night with the intention of telling her anything, but Mia has this way sometimes of just pulling things out of me without even trying. Her presence alone makes me want to just open up and I always feel better just being near her.

Time has been flying this evening. Mia's standing at the bar and I watch her clink her drink with someone to her left and then her attention is stolen by a familiar face. Connor Hughes, shortstop for the Tampa Angels baseball team has pulled up a seat next to her. I watch her laugh from across the room. His hand rests on the small of her back as he guides her into the chair beside him and he orders her a drink.

Tequila. Club soda. A couple lime slices. I think to myself as I watch the bartender place the drink down in front of her.

She looks beautiful tonight. Mia always looks beautiful. Even in her workout clothes or oversized stained t-shirts with no makeup, hair in a ball on top of her head… she's a natural beauty. Mia never dresses up like this, though. I can probably count on one hand the amount of times I've seen her really dolled up, but she knows how to turn it up when she wants to. The light pink dress she chose looks like it was custom made for her small frame and with one shoulder completely exposed, you can see her sun-kissed skin.

I continue to watch her interact with Connor. He's a nice guy, he lives in my building actually. I like him, so why is my jaw clenching and my hand balling into a fist? I lift the golden liquid in my glass to my lips and take a sip, just watching Mia charm her way through their conversation.

I'm not surprised he's taken by her. Everyone loves Mia Clark, she's a ray of goddamn sunshine.

The first night I met Mia is a moment I've held onto for years. Something branded in my memory. She was wearing black leggings and a giant sweater that her body was swimming in. Her smile was contagious, but it was her familiar brown eyes that really got me. Something in them just made me feel at home.

The freckles on her nose weren't covered in makeup. Her dark eyelashes fanned over her cheekbones as she stood next to me. Her first comment was complimenting my hair, it was a bit longer at the time. I remember laughing, just full-blown belly laughing with her. She just instantly felt like someone I'd known my whole life, instead of a random girl I met that same night.

I was lucky to stumble into her friendship that night. It's something I'm thankful for every single day. Standing next to her in that living room all those years ago, singing ridiculous karaoke, felt like the beginning of something I'd be cherishing my whole life.

"She looks good." Liam's presence takes me out of my own head and I turn towards him with a stare. "Are you ever going to do anything about it?" he asks as he leans over, his voice low.

My hand grips my glass a little tighter and I feel a pinch of annoyance creeping up my throat.

"What do you mean?" My other hand works its way around my jaw, pulling lightly.

"Mia. Are you ever going to just take what you want? Or better yet, give her what she wants?" Liam's staring at Mia, and all I want to do is block his view of her in that dress. Block everyone's view, if I'm being honest.

"You both keep ending up single... if you think that's just a coincidence, you're dumber than I fucking thought." He looks at me before sipping his drink, smirking as he does.

Pinching the bridge of my nose, I turn slightly to face Liam. "It's not like that between us. Plus, she's too good for me." I say it as if I'm joking, but I'm not. Mia's too pure, too special, too whole. She deserves someone who can keep their head on straight, and right now, that's not me.

"Well, you're right about that." Liam and I share a laugh.

"She's my best friend. That's all we'll ever be." It's the sentence I've repeated to myself for a while now. There was a brief time I thought I might've had a shot with her, but it was clear that she really only wanted a friend and I wanted to be that for her. I buried my feelings for her and put all of my love and adoration for her into the friendship we've built. Mia is beautiful and amazing, but it's not like that with us. She needs me in her life as a friend and I've been that for her. Because I need her in the same way.

"So, Hughes buying her drinks and making her laugh, has no direct correlation to the state of your messy as fuck hair?" Liam questions. Instinctively my hand runs through it again at his mention before I quickly pull it back.

"Purely a coincidence," I lie. Because no, I don't exactly love what I'm seeing, but Mia's dated plenty of guys since we've known each other. Granted, I've never been friends with them or lived in the same apartment building as them, but either way, it's not my business who she spends her time with. If she's happy, I'm happy.

Liam's head shakes back and forth as he grins deviously. "If you say so, Campbell... but it's only a matter of time before someone else comes in and sweeps her off of her feet. If you're one hundred percent okay with that, then fine. I'll back off."

A frustrated sigh leaves my mouth and I run a hand through my hair. *Fuck, keep your hands at your sides!* I internally shout.

Mia Clark is my best friend. It'll never be anything more than that.

Once the night is winding down, I make my way to the bar and have a seat. Mia finds me after she's done schmoozing her way through half of the people here.

"Why are you sitting here by yourself?" She nudges my shoulder with her elbow as she takes a seat next to me. Her lavender scent wraps itself around me as she pulls the barstool closer.

"I just sat down, I've been walking around all night… you, though, you've made quite a name for yourself tonight, Ms. Clark. You're very popular." My eyes trail over her body as she shakes her head with a chuckle. She pulls the cup of maraschino cherries up between us and tosses one in her drink. I'm tempted to ask how her conversation went with Hughes, but I remind myself that I don't need to know that.

"Yeah, well the people need a reason to like you, so… enter the charming best friend. Nice blue suit by the way." My eyes trail down Mia's arm, to her perfectly polished fingernails. Light blue, a color she wears often.

"They already like me." I bark back, but I see her eyes roll and a playful smile lands on her lips.

"I've moved on to Shirley Temples," she proclaims, raising her glass before taking a sip.

"Yes, your drink of choice." I laugh and then grab one of the cherries myself and take the stem off and twist it between two fingers, leaving the cherry on the bar top.

Mia grabs the stem from my fingers and holds it up to me. "Why don't we try to tie these in knots with our tongue and see who can do the most? You know, for old times' sake."

My tongue instinctively runs over my lips. "Okay… should the winner get to pick the fast food place we stop at when we leave here?" Something tells me no matter who wins, we're going to Frenchie's.

She tilts her head and nods up and down with a smirk. Mia moves our drinks out of the way and puts napkins in front of us to wipe any of the mess. She pulls a handful of cherries from the cup on the bar and sets them down.

"This might not be the most adult thing to do right now, but at least it's fun," she notes.

"I think we've done a fuck ton of adulting tonight, so a brief intermission for some stem tying is fine." I feel the corner of my lip turn up towards her.

"I've been practicing; I feel like I might finally have you this time... Ready?" Her eyes beam up at me and she bites her bottom lip.

"You've been practicing... with who?" My eyebrows raise at her comment.

"Last week! When we were all at Louie's. I grabbed a few when I got bored of hearing Graham's story about horseback riding." Her cheeks begin to blush and it causes me to shake my head at her.

Between the two of us, we've already cleared a handful of these within five minutes. This is how we kept ourselves occupied some nights in college. We'd be out at the bar with friends, but not drinking... so we passed the time with menial things like this.

Mia only has three stems tied and I can see the frustration on her face as she's working her tongue to get the fourth one in a knot. Her nostrils are flaring, and I can tell she wants to throw something by the way she's gripping the napkin in her hand. It causes me to lightly laugh and turn my head slightly away.

"I have five here, Mi. I think we can call it." Wiping my mouth with a napkin, I pull my glass back to me to take one last sip.

"How? How the hell are you so damn good at this? Is your tongue a machine? That's the only logical explanation at this point." She throws herself back against the barstool and crosses her arms over her chest.

"In fact, it is and I know how to use it." I wink at her as I rush off the stool because I know she's going to hate that comment. In a lackluster attempt, she tosses her scrunched up napkin at me as I smirk and start to walk away.

"Oh my God, get out of here," she calls from behind me, but she can't keep a straight face and I see her smile from across the room.

"One of these days we're going to drive out here and the for sale sign will be gone and a stunning white house with a big wrap around porch and black shutters will sit on this lot and we'll be out of luck," Mia says as she sips her milkshake and we pull into the same vacant lot we've come to countless times.

We found it by mistake one day when I first moved here. It's just an open patch of land with an old battered FOR SALE sign in the ground. You can barely read the numbers on it anymore.

"Fuck, don't say that." My eyes go wide at her. I love this place. It's my one quiet escape. Somewhere I find myself often. Everything is quiet out here, especially my mind. The stars and the moon shine so fucking bright out here. Downtown, it's hard to see it like this, with all of the city lights taking away from their light.

Glancing to the passenger's seat, Mia's dress is hiked up above her knee so she can keep her milkshake between her legs, even though there's a perfectly good cup holder in the center console of my truck. My eyes drift to her legs, they're so fucking tanned right now. The scar above her knee looks more noticeable when she's this tanned, and seeing it gives my chest a burning sting at the memory.

"What do you think about going to outer space? Amazing or terrifying?" Her wrist moves back and forth as she gives her milkshake a twirl.

"Terrifying. Absolute horror," I answer without any hesitation. Going in space or deep into the abyss of the ocean are two places you'll never catch me.

"Really? I think it'd be so amazing. I mean look at how gorgeous this is just from where we're sitting. Can you imagine how amazing it probably looks up close?" She cranes her neck a little further looking out the windshield and I sigh at the sight of her out here. She loves this random patch of dirt. And hell, I do too.

My phone dings at the same time as Mia's, causing us both to reach down and see a photo of a scrunchy faced little baby with a pink bow on her head with a text from Chase.

CHASE

It's a girl! And she's so fucking cute.

CHAPTER FOUR

MIA

Last night reminded me why Nate's my best friend. Without a single prompt, after I so graciously accepted defeat in our stem tying contest, we went to Frenchie's for milkshakes and then to the old abandoned lot to sit in silence and darkness, and it was fucking glorious. There's literally no one else on the planet who gets me like he does.

Although, this morning as I lay in bed, the one regret I do have is the late bedtime. I'm usually up with the roosters no problem, so when my seven o'clock alarm starts blaring, I'm finding any excuse I can to snooze it. It works for about fifteen minutes before I force myself up and out of bed. I reach for the curtains to open the blinds just a tad to get some sunlight in as it's rising. Glancing out my bedroom window, I can see the sidewalk below and the bakery just a few buildings over. Some days I can read the specials from my window, but today isn't that day. Whoever wrote them this morning has very small handwriting, making it impossible to read, even when I try squinting.

Nate's name flashes on my screen as I'm mixing the almond milk with my coffee and I quickly answer it.

"Hey, morning," I say into the phone as I'm drizzling the caramel over my iced coffee.

"Hey, Smalls. Want to go for a run?"

The thing about Nate is, any time he has a lot on his mind, his go to form of release is pounding the pavement. I have a list of things I want to get done today, but I can spare an hour to burn off some steam with him.

"Yeah, do you want to run the track at the high school?"

"Yes. I don't want to run downtown, there are too many people, it stresses me out," he answers eagerly.

"Perfect. I'll meet you there in thirty."

"Are you wearing that in case we get lost and the helicopters need to be able to find us?" he snarks while chewing on a protein bar, and referring to my very loud colored workout set as I approach him.

"No, it's solely to embarrass you. Is it working?" I quip back. Yellow is a great color, okay.

His eyes trail up my legs and I notice when he lingers a moment before moving up to my eyes. Best friend or not, Nate's still a guy and even though I know he isn't into me, the stares and looks are sometimes a little reassuring. Ol' Mia's still got it. Whatever *it* is.

"You look like a highlighter," he teases as he walks by and smoothly grabs the scrunchie off of my wrist. My knee jerk reaction is to swat his hand away, but like normal, he's too quick and already out of arm's reach.

"Alright, a few times around this track should do it." Reaching down, I tighten my shoelaces and take a sip of water before we get started.

Nate and I don't talk as we run. We stay within a similar pace, although he's slightly ahead of me. The heat is making this a lot harder than it should be, but we power through. I force my mind to think of things other than the sweat pooling everywhere or the ache in my left knee that's starting to flare up.

The second he stops and throws himself on the grass in the middle of the track, I do the same. He's lying there, white t-shirt completely soaked in sweat as he pulls it up to wipe his forehead. I don't look at Nate with the same eyes that most women do. But I can appreciate a nice thing, and Nate Campbell's body is a true work of art. His muscles are so defined, and the way the valleys on his stomach contract as he sits up slightly definitely isn't the worst view to have on a Saturday morning.

Nate pulls his shirt off over his head and wrings out the sweat that it's collected. It's truly… disgusting.

"You guys have it so easy," I snark as I sit there across from him, wiping sweat off of my forehead and cursing myself for not bringing a towel.

"You have a sports bra under that tank top, take it off, Clark," he taunts. His arms and chest are glistening with sweat and he shakes his hair before throwing his baseball hat back on and I shake my head in laughter.

"Fuck, I feel out of shape. If Coach Aarons saw me just now, he'd have my ass." Nate's head is now resting on the grass and I'm leaning up on my elbows, facing away from the sun to look at him.

"How are you feeling about the game tomorrow?"

"It's almost a double edged sword. I feel okay, but I also feel like my chest might explode. If that even makes sense."

"Well, the fact that you can acknowledge both feelings I think is actually a good thing."

He's silent as we lie there in the grass.

"Honestly, Mi… I can't explain what's going on. I just know something's off. My mind isn't right and I'm fucking scared to get on the field and have that be a factor."

My hand reaches out and grabs his, linking our fingers

together. His thumb gently glides back and forth on my hand and I can't help but secretly kind of love that.

"How can I help?" It's more of a plea than a question.

"I don't know." He lowers his gaze as he answers.

He pulls himself up to a sitting position, resting both elbows on his knees as he faces me. His blue eyes come up to mine and I can tell he's thinking about saying more, but he doesn't.

"One more lap?" he asks, in an attempt to change the subject by jumping back into a run.

"You go ahead."

"I thought you were doing all of these runs with me."

"Ehh... I thought about it, but I'm not the one who needs to be able to run a forty-yard dash. That's you, pal." I tap his arm before beginning to walk away.

"¡Ay Dios Mio!" he shouts as he begins running again.

It makes me laugh and brings me back to an old memory. Nate needed to finish one elective but was struggling with Spanish. I happened to take it all through high school and felt pretty confident in my abilities so I offered to help. He barely scraped by, but for him it was enough. Every now and then he still drops a random phrase here or there in Spanish—he's right maybe half the time.

"Your party is all set. I just need to order the churros, but all of the grown-up food is taken care of." Abby asked me to meet her for brunch this morning after my run with Nate. She's working on a Christmas event for the Rec Center and has decided to start prepping now... in September.

"Don't worry about it, I'll grab those. Plus, if Ford ever hears you referring to his favorite food as childish he'd be offended and I don't have time to convince him that he's still a grown-up even though he likes a ton of children's snacks." My hand reaches for my mouth, covering laughter.

"Did Nate help you with any of it?"

I shake my head. "No, he has so much on his plate, I didn't want to add any more to it. Especially when I'm available to do it myself, you know?" I think it's safe to say that nobody knows what Nate's been dealing with, so I don't elaborate on my reason.

She raises her dark eyebrows as she nods.

"Oh, I meant to tell you, though. I saw a building for rent down here, *finally*. I want to call and get more information on it to see if it would work for me."

"That's incredible. Where?"

The waitress brings us our food mid conversation. She sets down both of our plates and I swear my mouth waters at the sight of the eggs, bacon and rye bread in front of me. I get this same meal every single time we come here. I'm nothing, if not consistent.

"Main and Marshall. It's not big, but it'd be great. We can walk by it on our way out."

"Perfect!"

Walking downtown on the weekends isn't for the faint of heart. There are people constantly all over the place and it's becoming less and less appealing to be down here.

"Oh, I noticed you and Connor chatting the other night, how'd that happen?" Abby asks while we wait at the crosswalk. I glance down at the two of us standing here in completely opposite outfits. I very clearly look like I just left the gym and she looks like she just left a PTA meeting after being at the Rec Center with the kids.

"Well, first he said hi… then I said hi, and—" She rolls her eyes and we both laugh. "No, he honestly just started talking to me while I was sitting at the bar. He's really nice." I shrug.

"And incredibly handsome," Abby adds.

I point my index finger at her as we continue to wait. "Yes, and incredibly handsome."

"Did he ask you out, or mention seeing you again?"

I shake my head no at her. "We didn't talk all that long. I wouldn't have expected him to ask me out after a twenty-minute conversation."

"Really? I knew I wanted Ford after twenty seconds. I got so nervous after the first time he spoke to me, I literally ran to the bathroom like a scared freshman who was just approached by the hot senior."

"Well, not all of us get to have those fairytale romances, I suppose."

The crosswalk changes and as we're close to the building, I notice a woman with keys unlocking the door while a couple stand just behind her.

"Shit," I mutter, picking up my pace and trying to ignore the fact that my knee is still throbbing from earlier.

"What?" Abby asks.

"Right there, where those people are, that's the building I'm interested in."

"Well, what are you planning on doing? Marching in there and saying it's already taken?" Abby jogs up next to me as we approach the door.

"No, not exactly. But if they're already looking at it, what's two more people taking a peek? I won't bother them, I'll be in and out." Abby's hand slightly covers her face as we walk into the building behind the couple.

Thirty minutes later and we're still here. I love this place. I have to find a way to make it work. As I guessed, it was previously a dance studio. The mirrors are perfect though, I wouldn't take them down. I'd just remove the bar that's in front of them. I'd add a couple of TVs near the giant windows that overlook the sidewalk. There's a small desk in the entrance that I'd probably have Nate take out so I can add something a little more my style.

There's plenty of space here to add the machines I'd want, too. The realtor, Quinn, didn't mind that we looked around while she was showing it to her clients. She handed me a card of hers too, so I can call if I have any questions. I basically just eavesdropped on the whole conversation she had with the couple. They asked the same questions I would have for the most part, the biggest one being the monthly rent.

Abby's standing near the entrance looking extra embarrassed by me crashing their tour, but she'll be fine. She gets to go home to someone who wants her more than he wants air in his lungs.

Let me have this.

"Okay, we can go," I whisper to Abby and we make our way out.

"What'd you think?" she asks me, standing on the sidewalk about to part ways.

"I love it. It needs some minor stuff, all cosmetic things though, that I could do or Nate can help with."

"I'm glad you found somewhere you like." Abby reaches out her arms and hugs me before crossing the street back to the parking garage.

I've never walked into a building and instantly felt like it was mine until today. Everything I've ever pictured fits perfectly in that space and I'm just praying I can find a way to make it work. *Risk taker* isn't a term that would be used to describe me, but this one seems like it could be worth it.

It'd be great if I had a way to know for sure that it would all work out, but that's not how life works. I've done everything on my own for the last ten years. I haven't had the luxury of asking for help or reaching out to my parents when things get tough, so a risk this big, a commitment like this, it's scary. But maybe never taking the chance is actually the scarier part.

CHAPTER FIVE

NATE

Liam and I arrive at the stadium at the same time and walk in together, greeting the social media team as they take pictures of us. Liam's suit is flashy as hell, and meanwhile, I'm wearing denim jeans and a white t-shirt with a baseball hat. The attention Liam gets is tenfold compared to mine, but he loves that shit. Relishes in it.

"Feeling good? Heard you were watching game tape late the other night," Liam turns and asks me as he pulls his suit jacket off.

"I'm alright." My head rolls around to stretch my neck.

"My golden boy is just alright?" He stares at me with a knowing smile before his expression softens. "You can call me, you know. If something's going on. But continuously going out and doing our jobs… that's all we can ask of ourselves." Liam's hand lands on my shoulder and he stands across from me, looking me in the eyes and I nod.

"Yeah, I know. I'm good though." Becoming a serial liar isn't something I thought I'd be good at, but apparently, I'm able to believe the lie enough myself to sell it.

"Let's go out there. Play our fucking best. Savor in the fact that we're the defending Super Bowl champs and just see where this season takes us." He stares at me, waiting for confirmation. I nod my head in his direction just before I hear Ford coming up behind me.

"I need one of these," Ford blurts out as he holds up a picture of Chase's baby. His unexpected comment causes Liam and I to pull back, looking at him with narrowed eyes.

"You *need* one of those? As if you can just go to the store to pick one up on your way home?" Liam remarks.

"You fucking know what I mean. I just can't wait to get married and have a kid. I'm ready for it. I didn't think I'd be so excited about all of it, but hell, now that I'm with Abby, I want it all as soon as she's ready." Ford shrugs as he pulls his shirt off.

"Don't fucking knock up my sister, Anderson," Chase interjects as he's walking in, catching the tail end of our conversation.

"Is it really considered 'knocking up' if they're getting married?" Chase grunts in response to my question.

"You don't want mini Andersons running around?" Liam's voice reduces almost to a baby voice as he whips his belt off of his pants.

"What's that, Anderson?" Coach Aarons walks in with his clipboard hanging from his hand. "Having a baby?"

"Jesus. No, I'm not. I made one comment about wanting a kid and these two are already on their way to naming it." Ford brings his hands up to Liam and I.

Coach shakes his head with a chuckle, his shoulders moving up and down as he walks by us and to the other end of the locker room.

The deafening sound of fans should drown out any thoughts I have in my mind as we stand in the tunnel about to run out for the home opener. Their excitement should be contagious; it should pump me up. The hype videos are playing on the Jumbotron and I should hear them and get fired up, but I don't.

I feel anxious.

I feel pressure.

I feel an overwhelming sense of dread.

It's been like this for months now. The pressure to come out and perform well feels suffocating. I stayed late more often than normal this week, looking over game footage and studying the playbook. I've been trying to think of ways to get myself out of the funk, out of my head but I keep coming up short. I spent an afternoon with a few of the rookies the other day in hopes that maybe immersing myself into everything like it's my first season again will somehow help with everything I've been feeling. Somehow bring the joy back.

This game used to be so fun for me, but the anxiety has become all-consuming and I can't shake it. I can pretend it's not there, sure. I can walk around the facility, around the field with a smile on my face and jokes ready to go, but deep down I know something's lurking.

When I think about everything going on in my mind and how it affects me on the field, I'm constantly having to find ways to bring myself back down. Somehow center myself. Honestly, the only thing that has consistently helped has been Mia. When my mind searches for peace, it's her face I see and her voice I hear. Every crippling moment has always been made better by the sound of Mia's voice. My best friend is the goddamn sunshine in my life when everything around me is dark and gray.

The offense is introduced and I run out onto the field once my name is up. Fans erupt around me, cannons fire and teammates high five me as I jog over to the bench.

"Time to work. Get in, do your job, get out. Play smart." Liam makes his rounds as the quarterback, pumping up the team. The game begins and things are off to a shaky start.

"Fuck, thought you had that one," Ford mentions as we're

walking off the field after a failed third down attempt. Getting out of the backfield today has been hard as hell. I'm sure my rush yards are going to be less than fifty for the whole game.

"I can't get a fucking gap," I shout, taking my helmet off and aggressively placing it on the bench before I sit down beside it. I can feel Coach Aarons' eyes on me, so internally, I tell myself to cool the hell off, but it's no use.

My hands start to shake as I sit on the bench and I can't fucking stop them. Jerking my head around, I search the stands. *Where are you, Mia?* My eyes land on her a moment later. Brown hair up in a high ponytail, a homemade t-shirt bearing my name and number on the back. Every home opener since college Mia's worn some version of a shirt she makes. I smile at the sight of her in the stands. She's got her eyes focused on the field, though.

Focus.
Breathe.
Relax.

I repeat to myself as I sit there before being called back into the game.

As the remainder of the game goes on, my personal struggle of making it past the line of scrimmage remains the same and I barely have a run for more than three yards. Tough games like this only add to the frustrations that I've been facing. The pressure to perform well is at an all-time high, especially since we're coming off of a Super Bowl winning season. And the monsters in my head keep reminding me that I'm not fucking doing enough.

"Fourth and inches… Get in there, Campbell." One of the running back coaches approaches me on the sidelines.

I simply nod in his direction and secure my helmet on before running into the huddle for the play. Let's fucking try this again. Head down, barrel through.

Once Liam hands me the ball, I follow behind Graham, who

pushes the pile forward and I land on his back, crossing the first down marker.

"Let's fucking go!" Liam smacks the side of my helmet as we all get up and I jog back over to the sidelines. After watching the last four minutes of the game go by from the bench, I'm quick to run into the tunnel when the game is over. Our win is credited to Liam and Ford being an unstoppable duo as our tight end and quarterback. Ford had two touchdowns, and that ultimately helped secure the win for us.

Back in the locker room, everyone's high fiving and talking about the game. The team played lights out football, it was a great win. But I can't stop dwelling on the fact that my performance was less than impressive. I feel Coach Aarons' eyes on me as I move about the locker room getting ready to leave.

"Campbell, a word?" He gestures for me to follow him out and I simply nod and head for his office.

"I'm sorry, Coach." It flies out of my mouth before I have any real idea of what I plan to follow that up with.

"Something going on you need to share?"

He leans against the desk, arms crossed with his glasses sitting on the tip of his nose. His entire body looks stiff, like he's bracing himself for something, but his eyes are softened. He's looking at me, almost in a way that makes me want to spill every last thing I've been feeling, but I don't. I can't.

"No, sir. I'll bounce back next week."

I can tell he knows I'm hiding something. He's known me too long, has seen me go through too much shit, to continue believing my obvious lies. The way he exhales lets me know he's upset that I'm keeping something from him. But how do you say what you're dealing with when you don't even know how to describe it?

Once I walk out of his office and down the hall to the exit, Mia's standing at the gate, waiting for me. An invisible weight instantly lifts and she waves as she notices me.

"You did good," she says once I get within earshot.

Her arm reaches out to hug me and I pull her in, squeezing her against my body.

"Were you watching the same game?" I cock an eyebrow at her in question.

"Oh, stop. It was a tough battle. You did your job, though. Their defense just also did theirs. But you guys won." She nudges my arm as we walk over to the parking lot.

"You guys want to grab something to eat from Louie's?" Ford asks as he approaches Mia and I.

Mia looks at me, searching my face for a silent answer before we respond. I nod my head to Ford and say, "Yeah, we could eat."

Louie's is fucking packed as soon as we walk in the door. It smells like hot pretzels and beer the further we get into the building. I keep my baseball hat pulled down over my eyes so hopefully nobody recognizes us, or if they do, they'll respect the fact that I'm just here to eat.

"I really am proud of you, Nate." Mia shrugs, giving me a nod and a smile as we sit down. She reaches for my hand and squeezes it on the table. Sometimes I think if Mia was the only person in the world to believe in me, I'd still be just fine. She gets up from the table to meet Abby over by the bar and it's then I feel Ford's hand on my back.

"Are you good?" He stares at me, waiting for a reply.

"Yeah, yeah, thanks. I'm good." This is the trending question of the day, apparently.

Ford and I talk at the table for a little while longer before Mia brings over a plate of nachos and a basket of buffalo wings.

"We're splitting all of this." Her hand gestures to the food in front of us and I nod my head, but then hold up my index finger and step away for a moment, only to return with a cup of ranch.

"Can't forget the good stuff." Mia's eyes widened with an enthusiastic nod.

Once we've cleared out the food, I bring my empty glass up to the bar and turn to walk away, but the bartender grabs my attention. Sure, I noticed her, she's good looking, has tits that would probably bring me to my fucking knees, but I wasn't planning on talking to her.

"I don't want to make a scene, because I quickly figured out you guys are in your own little corner for a reason, but just wanted to say good game." She flashes me a sweet smile and grabs my glass, walking it back to the sink. I smile back at her and linger for a moment at the bar before deciding to walk back to the table. A different version of me would have planted my ass on that bar stool and made sure I took her home for the night, but things have changed. Casual sex and one-night stands have lost all appeal in the last few months. Just another side effect of whatever the hell is going on with me, I guess.

"I'm exhausted and would rather collapse on my bed than this table, so I think I'm ready to go," Mia says when I get back to the table. Her nose scrunches up into a yawn and the tiniest little squeak leaves her mouth when she does.

"Come on." I sling my arm around Mia's shoulder and say goodbye to Abby and Ford before walking us out.

My eyes feel heavy as I keep opening and closing them, like I barely slept. Hendrix is still curled up at the end of my bed in his usual spot between my legs, so I gently try to maneuver out from underneath him to get up.

My body is sore from yesterday's game, and my muscles feel

like they need some relief so I text the only person I know who's also awake at seven in the morning.

> Foam roll me?

MIA
I'm just going to leave the one you like at your apartment from now on.

When Mia walks in an hour later, she's carrying a bag over her shoulder with the giant green foam roller sticking out of the top and a drink carrier with two smoothies. Her long brown hair is pulled back away from her bare face with a headband and she smiles at me, placing the smoothies on the counter and I grab the bag from her arms.

"Fuck. What the hell else is in here, why is it so heavy?" I place the bag on the chair and take a look inside. Mia carries a whole ass computer with her in this thing? I pull it out with a questioning look.

"Well just in case I want to stop and do some work at a coffee shop or something," she blurts with a quick laugh at the end.

The foam roller she brought over has all of these grooves and indents on it, it works like a deep tissue massage, and it's a Godsend on my muscles after hard games.

"I heard from Bree the other day. Are you planning on going to your parents' anniversary party?" She jumps up and sits on the kitchen island, grabbing a smoothie and putting the straw between her lips.

"Yeah, I need to take a look at the dates though. I am not looking forward to going and potentially having to explain why I suck at my job right now."

Mia interrupts me abruptly, lifting her hand in the air.

"Don't do that. You don't suck at your job, Nate. Everyone faces pressures at work, yours are just more extreme. There's no shame in admitting you're struggling with some of it. I'm proud of you for talking about it instead of keeping it all in. Plus, you get to choose what you want to share. So, if you don't want to share anything, it's up to you." Mia hops off the counter and wraps her arms around my waist. She nestles her body into mine.

"Thanks, Smalls," I murmur, pulling her tighter towards me. Mia's hands squeeze around my waist and I wince a little at the pressure of her tiny arms around my sore ribs.

"Shit, am I hurting you?" She pulls back.

"You? Hurt me?" I say through a strained stretch and a lousy half grin. "I'm good, Mi. You couldn't hurt me if you tried."

Her eyebrows crease as she folds her arms over her chest. "That definitely sounds like a challenge and I will be taking you up on that, but it'll have to be another time, because right now I need to get going."

I groan as she walks to the other side of the kitchen. She's dressed in a bright blue workout set with blindingly white sneakers. She really would be the easiest person to find in a crowd simply by her wardrobe choices. I'd still probably find her eyes first though.

"Have a good day," I say as she's grabbing her smoothie off the counter and puts her bag on her shoulder.

"You too, Nate." Mia turns back and smiles at me as she reaches the door.

After Mia leaves, I get to work with the foam roller. My quads are fucking killing me this morning and I know if I don't try to loosen them up, they'll only be worse tomorrow.

"Fuuuuck," I whisper as I roll back and forth over my legs, one at a time. Every muscle feels tight, every inch of my body feels like it needs a relief. It's also been too fucking long since I've touched a woman and I know I've got a lot of pent up frustration there, but that's no one's fault but my own. I made the decision to stop sleeping around. It's been months since I've had sex. When Laura and I ended things a few months ago, I wasn't upset at all—I think part of me actually felt relieved. Which is such a fucked up thing to admit, because Laura's great, but it wasn't going anywhere and my mind wasn't in it.

For the last week, Liam's voice has been playing on a loop in my mind. Being best friends with someone you used to have feelings for is a complete mind fuck. Because seeing her openly flirt with a friend of mine for the first time, feels maddening almost and then Liam says things like,

"It's only a matter of time before someone else comes in and sweeps her off of her feet. If you're one hundred percent okay with that, then fine."

And it fucks with my head.

Because *I am* fine with that.

I have learned to be fine with that. Because Mia is my best friend. And I'm hers.

I have been fine with that for years.

So, fuck off Liam. Get out of my head.

CHAPTER SIX
MIA

This morning I called Quinn and set up an actual meeting with her at that rental space, considering last time I basically just crashed her tour. I'd love to bring Nate so he can have a quick look, too. He's really handy and could probably point out a few things I may have missed. He has football practice all morning, but he's usually free after three.

I hit Nate's number in my speed dial once I've confirmed that Quinn is free later and he answers, breathlessly.

"Hey there, did I interrupt something?" I ask playfully.

"Very funny. I'm out running, about to be back home." His voice evens out just before I continue.

"Ah, okay..." I trail off as I'm trying to pull a rogue string from my t-shirt, shifting all attention from this phone call.

"Mi, you called... what's up?" Nate's voice brings me back to the present.

"Yeah. Oh, you know what, we actually should discuss Ford and Abby's engagement party."

"All I know is I need to bring some beer."

"Yes, beer. I gave you a very easy task."

He scoffs at my comment. "What do you mean? You don't think I can handle something important?"

"Well no, it's not that. I just didn't want to add anything major to your plate. Plus, it's just easier to handle it myself." It's not a lie, I'd prefer to do things on my own rather than ask for anyone's help.

"I can help. Come on, try me. Give me something good to do."

I stand there thinking of what's actually left that I could delegate to Nate. I've basically handled everything important myself.

"You can be in charge of bringing bags of ice," I say flatly. It's literally the only thing left on the list.

"Ice? Really, ice?" I can sense the bothered tone immediately. "Fine." He sighs. "I'm going to bring the best fucking ice you have ever seen. You have no idea what you've just done, Smalls."

The words rolled off his tongue in a challenge. I'm already regretting this because he's definitely going to do something obnoxious.

"Oh, great." Sarcasm heavily rooted in my reply.

"I'm almost home, so let's talk more later."

Once Nate and I end the call, I set my phone on the charger before quickly realizing that I completely forgot to ask him about coming with me to see the building. I reach for my phone to call him right back, but a text distracts me.

> SUMMER
>
> I think men are good for orgasms and killing bugs and that's all. And honestly, sometimes not even the orgasms.

Well, I need them for the orgasms. I can't give myself one to save my life and I'm embarrassed at the amount of times I've tried unsuccessfully.

> Oh gosh, what happened?

SUMMER
I'm just meeting the crappiest men. I need a change of scenery. I can't wait to be there soon.

I'm so excited for Summer to live here. Don't get me wrong, I love hanging out with Abby, but she is heavily attached to Ford. Although I can't blame her… if I had a man who wanted to devour me like a four-course meal every day, I'd be rushing home to him too.

I grab my yoga mat to get a quick stretch and set it up in front of my tripod, placing my phone in the holder just before I click on Nate's name for FaceTime.

My mind is running through a ton of scenarios right now as it rings. What if I deplete my savings account to afford this building and it fails? I'd be so disappointed in myself and not to mention, embarrassed. I've always made it on my own, but something like this… a step this big is scary and it just makes me wish I had a way to be sure it'd all work out. After doing some math earlier, I know that I have enough for the first, last and security deposit in my account… it would leave me nearly pennies, but I can always build it back up.

A heavy sigh leaves my lungs as I sit there and envision everything that building could be. I really don't know anything about owning a business, but I know I'm good at my job. I shake my head just as Nate answers, but I don't see his face, just the ceiling and there's steam in the air.

"Uh… Hello?"

"Hang on!" he shouts, his voice echoing.

I stretch my left arm across my body and then my right while I'm waiting for him to grab the phone. My body is leaned forward into the downward dog position when I hear shuffling on the other end and look up. Nate's shaking his brown hair all over the place and water is sprinkling from every angle. He's bare chested, but I know he has a towel wrapped around his waist since I catch a glimpse of it as he moves around the bathroom.

"Hey, sorry. Miss me already? What's up?" He flashes his smile at me. A freshly showered Nate is always a sight for sore eyes. He's got that whole wet hair thing going on and lingering droplets of water on his forehead. He runs his hand through his hair before he moves into the other room.

"If you were in the shower, you could've just called me back." I laugh as I twist my body to stretch my lower back on the mat.

His head shakes back and forth. "I was just getting out…" I can feel his eyes staring at me all the way through this phone, practically burning into me, before he speaks again. "How are you able to twist your body like that? I'm afraid you're going to snap yourself in half." He winces as he watches me through the screen.

"Yeah well, that's how everyone feels while watching you play football for a living. Fun, isn't it?" I laugh before continuing. "I forgot to ask when we spoke earlier, but do you remember how I've wanted to rent my own building for a personal training studio?"

He nods at me.

"Great. Well there's a place downtown, right around the corner from me and I looked at it the other day… I think it might be perfect—"

Before I can say anything more, Nate interrupts.

"Show me. I want to see it. Can we go now? I'm free."

A smile breaks free on my face. This is why bringing Nate with me to see it is important. I've never had someone as consistently in my corner as he is. He's just as eager about this as I am and that makes me feel good, reassured even, that this isn't some wild unattainable dream.

"Yeah, actually that's why I was calling, I wanted to see if you can come look at it with me. I know it's last minute, so I wasn't sure if you had plans or a date or something…"

His bright blue eyes meet mine through the screen and he smiles. "Yeah, of course I'll come see it with you. And… uh, no dates for me lately."

"Oh, okay. Well thanks. I'm not too up to speed on your dating life these days. You haven't shared anything since before Hawaii."

"Not a whole lot to share." Nate shrugs, and out of nowhere, I see Hendrix barrel his way into Nate's chest.

"Hi Henny!" My greeting causes Hendrix to get even more excited and before I know it, something happens. And I'm seeing all sorts of things that I should not be seeing.

Nate's body twists to the side and his phone falls at the perfect angle against the bed or the nightstand—I'm not sure which one—but it's giving me a view of something I've never seen before. The towel that was securely—or so I thought—wrapped around Nate's waist is now on the floor and the bare ass of my best friend is center stage on this FaceTime call.

I shield my eyes, calling out to Nate. "Towel, Nate, towel! Grab the towel!"

I might sneak a peek between my fingers as they cover my eyes because curiosity wins. So, he's got a nice ass and some killer back muscles, but that's no surprise, he's an athlete.

"Ahhh, Hendrix, buddy relax, relax!" I hear Nate's voice, and slightly uncover my eyes as he reaches for the towel to wrap it back around his waist, but he turns too soon to face the phone and there it is.

Front and center.

A full view of something that I *definitely* should not be seeing.

"Oh, God!" I blurt out and swat at my tripod, knocking it down along with my phone.

"Hang on!" Nate calls out.

"I'll just text you the address!" I yell while frantically reaching for my phone to end the call with one hand still covering my squinting eyes.

Is that allowed? I've never seen a naked Nate, and while I am impressed, I know that was a major oops. I need to erase that from memory. Do I wash my eyes out with soap now or later? I don't know what just happened, one minute the towel was there, and the next it wasn't and things happened so fast. I lean back against my bed and press my knuckles directly into my eye sockets.

Erase.

Delete.

Backspace.

Seeing Nate's bare ass... fine, whatever, we've all got one. It was firm and nice, but I could have guessed as much.

Seeing Nate's... other part... those poor women he sleeps with...Well, actually maybe not poor women, I'd say that they are probably pretty satisfied with... all of that. But how do they... I just... I have so many questions.

A faint blush feels like it covers my face causing me to bring the palms of my hands to my cheeks and cup them. My head shakes back and forth as I let out a slow and steady breath. Why is that sending tingles down my legs?

Okay, moving on. I can't focus on any of that right now. It was an honest mistake; a towel fell and it's just a body part. A body part of my best friend that I've never seen before, but again, it's the human body... nothing weird about that.

That's definitely an image I need to quickly forget. Although I'm not sure how the hell I'm supposed to do that now.

CHAPTER SEVEN

NATE

"Hendrix, my man, I think you just gave Mia more than she bargained for." My eyes narrow, looking down at my golden retriever wagging his tail at my feet. I quickly throw on jeans and a t-shirt and walk into the kitchen to grab my keys. Mia texted me the address of the building she wants me to look at with her and it's close enough to walk to. The door closes behind me and I see Connor Hughes, my neighbor, about to walk into his apartment. He just moved in a month ago, but I've known him for a while. Most recently, I saw him at the Rec Center dinner where he was chatting it up with my best friend.

"Connor, hey," I say, as I'm approaching the elevators.

"Campbell, what's up?" My hand extends to shake his.

"Nice game the other day, I caught the end of it."

"Just trying to bring a trophy home to the city like you guys did." He laughs and I shake my head.

I'm so fucking tempted to ask him about his conversation with Mia the other night, but it's not my goddamn business and I have to get that through my head. I shouldn't even care.

"Well, it looks like you're on your way," I state as I'm backing into the elevator.

Mia is waiting for me on the sidewalk, bouncing on her heels as I'm walking up to her. The leggings she has on would stand out in a crowd anywhere, they're an obnoxious hot pink and she's wearing a white Tampa t-shirt with the Knights logo on it. Pieces of her brown hair shape her bare face as she waves me over.

"So close to our apartments, right?" She points out with excitement.

"So close," I say, mimicking her enthusiasm and she smiles at me.

As soon as I walk into the building, I know I can picture Mia here. I can see this place being hers. She floats around it so seamlessly already.

"Mi... this place is great. It needs a little work, but it's all easy stuff I can do for you." My eyes scan the room we're standing in. It's not huge, but Mia doesn't need a massive space. She's beaming as she walks around. It's like I can see the wheels turning in her head, planning where she would put things, envisioning her days here.

"It is, isn't it?" Her eyes meet mine and I smile at her, watching her cheeks perk up into giant apples as a smile just overtakes her face.

The realtor is a football fan, so while Mia walks around, this woman—Quinn, I've learned is her name—has me cornered.

"When is the team extending you for an enormous contract? They know you're due for it..." She smirks at me while peeking her head around to see where Mia went. She's made her way somewhere near the back and is poking around back there. I'd like to go find her so I can see the rest of this place, but I politely continue listening to Quinn talk.

"They need to make you a Knight for life." Her arms cross over her chest, pushing her tits up and I won't lie, they're nice, but I've seen this game too many times. I know what she's doing and I'm not falling into this. This meeting isn't about me. This is about Mia and I won't be distracted.

"I'm just happy to play the game I love," I lie to get her off my back before excusing myself to go find Mia. When I see her, she's looking something up on her phone and then she stretches her arms out, as if she's measuring something.

Why do women think that's how you accurately measure things that need to go on a wall?

"Use this." I lean over her shoulder and hand her the measuring tape I brought with me because I knew she'd need it once she was here and all of her ideas started running rampant in her mind.

Mia smiles at me and pulls it open while she continues to measure whatever she needs. When Quinn walks in, she asks Mia what she thinks, which in turn Mia squeals with excitement about the place.

"I'll definitely be in touch. Thank you so much." Mia grins as we exit the building.

"I really liked it... I think it'd be great for what you want to use it for."

"I know. I've been looking casually for over a year and nothing has made me as excited as this one." The way her chest moves up and down with big, excited breaths makes me want to offer to help, offer to do whatever I can to give her everything she wants for this.

"Is the financial part stopping you?" Her head does a little tilt back and forth as we walk down the sidewalk.

"Technically, I can afford it... I'd be living off of ramen noodles and frozen waffles for a while, but it's probably worth it."

It bothers me that she won't ask for my help when she knows I can help her. Any time I've ever offered, she's turned me down before I can even finish my sentence. I've always respected Mia's independence. She's the most self-determined person that I know, but I wish she also knew that it's not the end of the world to accept help. She's always taking care of everyone else—always. She goes above and beyond for the people in her life, I just wish she'd let someone take care of her for a change.

"Mia, you can't live off of ramen noodles and waffles, this isn't college, I won't allow it. I'm drawing a line." My finger draws a line in the air as we walk.

"Well, then I guess my best friend will just have to cook for me every day for the next... year." She nudges her body into mine, looking up and staring at me.

"I'll cook for you any day, Smalls."

The streets are busy this afternoon and the constant weaving in and out of people on the sidewalks is aggravating.

As we approach the dog park ahead, the wind picks up and Mia's chestnut strands of hair start blowing all over the place. She stops for a second, gathering it together and twisting the pieces into a ponytail on top of her head before she changes the subject.

"So, Summer will be here just before Ford and Abby's party."

I notice the gray clouds start to move, casting a shadow in the area we're walking. If it starts to downpour right now, we're fucked.

"Really? That's great. I didn't know she was actually moving up. You probably can't wait to have someone to go out with." I smirk at Mia as we continue down the sidewalk.

"What do you mean? I go out... sometimes. *You* don't even go out a lot," she questions, almost sounding offended.

"No, I just meant with Abby spending all of her time with Ford... I just assumed you missed going out and doing girl things." I take a deep breath and lead us down towards the river trail. There are a few restaurants down there and as long as they don't have an endless wait time, I could go for some food.

"Oh. Well... I'm excited for Summer to be here, but not

because I miss going out all the time. She's more of a homebody than I am, actually. But I guess having another close friend to call will take some of the burden off of you." She shrugs and I place my hand out in front of her, stopping us right there in the middle of the sidewalk. I turn my eyes towards her, making sure she's looking at me before I speak.

"That's not even close to what I meant and you know it." I stare at her intensely, making sure she understands that I never intended for my comment to make her feel like I wanted a break from us, from this. "Spending time with you is my favorite part of any day. I'll actually take offense if you try to replace me." I squeeze her shoulders and let out a subtle laugh.

Mia's throat moves up and down, and I watch her take a deep breath. Her eyes meet mine and we hold a slightly burning stare for a moment before she nods her head and shrugs herself out of my embrace.

"Oh, you're not getting rid of me. I'll still be calling you for every minor inconvenience." A flash of humor crosses her face and our steps fall back into rhythm as we continue to walk. Mia maneuvers her body in front of me to let a woman with a stroller pass us and then tries to move to my left. My fingers instinctively grip the sides of her arms gently and I guide her back over to the inside of the sidewalk.

———

"How are you, Campbell?" Coach Aarons asks the second I step into the weight room this morning. His clipboard tight at his side, black and white windbreaker securely fastened as if he's expecting rain. Again with this question.

"Morning, Coach. I'm doing alright," I answer, reaching for more forty-five-pound barbell weights to stack on the end of each rack.

His stare follows me as I walk from either side of the weight rack, I can feel his eyes on me. A suspicious line formed at the corners of his mouth. Almost like he wants to say something, but he's holding it back. When I glance over at him, his expression stills and grows serious.

"Something wrong, Coach?"

"Campbell," he says my name with depth and authority. And it has me on the edge of my seat for what's to follow. But then, just as quickly as his expression becomes serious, it softens and he shakes his head. "I just wanted to check in. I want to make sure you're alright." His hand slaps my shoulder and he turns to walk out.

I know that I hit the jackpot with my head coach. He gives us space, but also makes it clear he's there if we need him for personal issues, and on top of that he's just a fantastic football coach, what more could anyone ask for? Even if I haven't exactly taken him up on his offers to talk, I know if I really need to, if I get to that point, I can.

Focus.

Breathe.

Relax.

I repeat those three words over and over through the entirety of my workout today. I don't know how to admit that I'm in over my head. I don't know how much longer I can keep up the facade that everything is just fine, when I can feel that it's not. Everything just keeps building and building—the anxiety, the pressure… I feel it all physically. The pain in my chest, the tremors in my hands, I'm trying to hide it all, but truth be told, I'm fucking terrified that I won't be able to hide it much longer. Especially the physical parts. And my job relies entirely on me catching a ball.

Not knowing how to deal with all of this isn't just angering, it's scary. Everything I once loved about the game is a distant memory because of how clouded my mind has become. The pressure disrupts my performance, it makes my heart race, makes it hard to breathe sometimes. I can't think clearly in situations where I need to and that impacts how I play on the field. Football is such a decision driven game. I have to be on the same page as my quarterback. I have to be in sync with my team. And the pressure lately has become so overwhelming, the anxiety nearly paralyzing.

Just as I'm finishing up, one of the rookies grabs me before I leave. Alex Farr is a great player. I watched his combine and he did well enough in training camp and the pre-season to secure himself a spot on the fifty-three-man roster.

"Fuck, man. Learning this system is so much harder than when I was at college." Alex sighs, gripping the bar in front of him.

"Yeah, no shit. It's the big leagues," I bark out.

"This is incredible though." He exhales with a long sigh of contentment.

"It is. A lot of it is. But don't get too distracted by the fairytale. It's not easy, there will be chatter. People who constantly root for you to fail, or at least always mention your failures or shortcomings. The game can get to you. Hell, life can get to you." He glances in my direction. "Fuck, I probably don't sound too motivational right now." I chuckle, internally recognizing that I don't belong in a conversation right now where a rookie is looking for encouragement. I'm not the guy for that job.

"You're being realistic. I appreciate that. Whatever they say about you is just noise, though. You're not just good at what you do, you're great at it, man. I don't doubt this shit is a mental load just as much as it is physical. Either way, it's got to be rewarding. Do you know how many kids I saw in the stands with your jersey at the last home game? If I can have half the admiration and career you've had in just six years, I'll consider myself lucky."

I stand there with both hands on my hips, thinking. When's the last time I took a moment to look around in the stands and take everything in? I've been so distracted by my own battle that I've barely given a second thought to anything else.

Farr's new to all of this. Everything he's seeing and experiencing is all with a fresh set of eyes. He's still walking onto the field awestruck. Still battling for his spot. But when he mentions the kids in the stands, that's something I've overlooked for a while. I know it. I used to be those kids. Wearing my favorite player's jersey every Sunday, even if I wasn't at a game, and I was just watching it in the den with my old man.

I laugh, shaking my head. "You know, it's funny... or maybe it's not actually, but I used to be that kid. We all were at some point, right? Living and breathing for our favorite player, our favorite team. The rush and the highs, the lows and heartbreaks. I still remember when Joe Deer dropped that pass in the Super Bowl with Green Bay. I was ten. We lost and I was fucking devastated. I think I even cried." Another laugh reaches the surface. "But the next day, I was still out there wearing his jersey, proud as hell."

"That's the thing about kids, man. They're resilient. They're going to come back rooting even harder the next time. They teach us how to love it. All of it. Even the shit parts." Alex slaps my back as he heads towards the door.

Even the shit parts.

When I was seventeen, I was on the Varsity football team my junior year of high school. We were in the state championship game. I wasn't a starter at the time, but our starting running back got hurt on a play. A bad hit right at his knees, he had to be carted off the field. He ended up tearing his ACL. My coach called me up to him at the sidelines and I remember feeling excited. Nervous since I hadn't played a lot that season, but so fucking excited. He placed his hands on my shoulder pads and looked me in the eye when he spoke. He told me it was my turn, that I was being called up.

He said, *"A lot of the greats are guys who've come off the bench. Go be great."*

Since that game I've always been a starter.

I have everything I've ever wanted, I've reached all of the professional milestones I've set out for myself, but I'm still struggling. I'm miserable in a game that I love down to my bones.

CHAPTER EIGHT
MIA

"Hey, morning, Dad. Is everything okay?" My voice is laced with concern as I answer. I haven't heard from him in months.

"Fine, fine. I just thought I should check in."

Hearing my dad's voice for the first time since last Thanksgiving makes my eyes sting. I always know there is a possibility that he might disappear again, and unfortunately after the holiday last year, he did.

"Oh, okay. It's good to hear from you," I say, bringing the phone up to my ear. Last time we spoke, it was simply a text from him saying he was doing fine, just working a lot. I try really hard to be patient with my dad, to be someone who doesn't judge him and still loves him no matter the stress or heartache that he may put me through.

At fifteen, my parents separated after my mom's affair, and I haven't seen her since. My dad had no idea how to cope or handle raising two teenage girls, so he found ways to distract himself from the reality around him. He spent nearly every penny we had and owed bookies money every single weekend. His nights were spent at the poker table, betting on any game or race he could squander up money for, or gambling away his paychecks. Even on the nights he won, it was never in his pocket for long. More than once I'd come home from school to my room left in chaos after he'd torn it apart looking for my stash of money from my part-time job. Ever since, I've always been the adult in the relationship. I check on him more than he checks on me. I'm the responsible one, the reliable one.

My younger sister has basically given up on him and I just can't bring myself to do that. He's still able to hold a job for the most part, but he secludes himself a lot. He moved here to be closer to me during a time I finally thought he was getting himself back on track, but shortly after, he fell back into old habits again.

I know he has an addiction. I know that if my dad could turn back time, he probably never would have placed that first bet. His heart was broken, his world was shattered and he just wanted a way to distract himself from all of it. I'm able to empathize with him, even though I don't agree with it. Maybe it makes me naïve to believe in him every time he tells me he's getting better, but my heart won't let me give up on him.

"I was going through some things and found stuff here that belongs to you and your sister… I, uh, I don't know if you still want any of it, but you can come take a look at everything one of these days."

"Yeah, of course," I answer eagerly.

His words are clear and sure. He doesn't sound exhausted like he's been up all night or irritated by a bet gone wrong. He sounds rejuvenated almost. But I won't let myself get my hopes up.

"How have things been, Dad?"

"Oh, you know. Busy… same old stuff."

I sigh, same old stuff. After a few more minutes of small talk, he has to go and we end the call. Our conversation wasn't anything monumental, but at least hearing from him gives me some small sense of relief.

As if on cue to lighten my mood, Nate shows up at my door to go get something to eat.

"What's with the face?" He lets himself in and immediately heads for my candy dish.

"Eventually, I'm going to collect a reimbursement on all those pink Starbursts. And as for my face... I just spoke to my dad."

"Shit. Really? How is he?" Nate's the only person who really knows about my family life. The less people who know my baggage, the better.

"Says he's good." I shrug. "You know; I take everything with a grain of salt... we'll see. It was nice to hear from him. I just always hope he's doing okay, you know?"

Nate's head nods up and down as he follows me over to my bedroom while I grab my shoes out of my closet. He lifts his arms, grabbing the top of the door frame and leans forward a little. His shirt lifts up as he does and I glance down, noticing the V shape where his shorts are hanging low. Knowing what's down just a little further, I shift my eyes back up to his face before any involuntary blush happens.

"Well, let's go eat our feelings. I could use the distraction too." His lips move into a straight line.

"What's on your mind?" I ask, grabbing my crossbody bag from the closet.

"Just stuff."

"Wow, you're so detailed," I joke. He tugs my ponytail playfully as I walk by and then follows me as I side-step him in the doorway to the living room. "Let's go, Mr. Mysterious."

Nate and I begin walking downtown and over to a sushi restaurant on the river trail near the water. It's pretty busy down here, so we have to wait a little while for our table.

"So, are you going to tell me what you needed the distraction from?" Nate's features almost look tormented when I ask him.

"Honestly, I just didn't want to be home alone. I worked out this morning and ended up hanging back to talk with Alex Farr a little bit. He's a good kid, he's excited… he reminds me of myself actually." He shakes his head laughing.

"He's come to me a few times for advice on things and I just… I want to help him, but I don't feel like I'm in any position to be handing out advice or mentorship. I'm afraid I'll just suck the life out of him."

"You're great at giving advice. You had help when you first entered the league, remember? One of the veteran players took you under his wing. You looked up to him and talked about him constantly. Be that for someone else." I lean myself against the railing as we wait for our table.

Nate's hand runs through his hair for at least the third time in the last few minutes. If he doesn't tell me with his words, I can always read his body language. He's stressed.

"I'm an idiot and searched for my name online. Before you tell me I need to stop doing that, believe me I know. It's never good and even if it is, the next sentence is ten things I've done wrong. I'm constantly just being judged for what I'm doing or not doing, and I know it's getting to me. I can feel it invading every last corner of my mind. I'm trying to shake it off, to just let things roll off my back, and give off the impression that outside chatter doesn't affect me, but when is enough, enough? Every ounce I have, I'm leaving on that field, Mi. Even on days I'm not sure I even want to be out there. So that's why I needed the distraction today. I needed you."

"Well, you've got me, you goober," I say softly, tapping my sneaker against his.

We're standing against the railing near the river trail as the humid breeze hits our backs. There are a few boats passing through and countless people sitting outside at the restaurant next to us, but right now, it feels like it's just the two of us. It's always been this way with Nate. Easy. Comfortable. We're constantly in our own little bubble and it's always felt like my safe place, his too I think. His hands grip the railing as he stands there.

"Nate, there will always be people out there with something to say. You could never make a single mistake, miss a pass, or miss a block, and someone will complain that you're too perfect. I know you feel the constant pressure to perform well. I know you have a lot you're dealing with internally. But who you are as a man, the greatness in here"—I tap his chest—"your value isn't tied to how well you play on the football field. Remember that. People are always going to throw stones. Instead of letting those stones knock you down, collect them and build yourself up." Nate wraps me in a very tight, very needed hug—for both of us.

"Fuck," Nate breathes out. "Sorry I turned this into another fucking pity party. My head's all over the place."

"Don't apologize. I needed a hug," I say, smiling. "I've been giving things some thought and I want to try and help you in any way that I can. I have an idea and just… hear me out. If you really hate it we don't have to but—"

"Mia," he cuts me off. "I won't hate it."

The buzzer vibrates in his hand, letting us know our table is ready. Once we are finally inside, Nate pulls out my chair and looks at me with amusement as we take our seats at the restaurant.

"I know the things you're dealing with are confusing and hard to manage. I don't know how to completely fix that, but I want to help you."

"You help me all the time, Smalls. That won't be anything new."

The waiter comes over and takes our order, where we decide to split a stupid amount of sushi rolls, but sometimes you just need to go a little wild, right?

"We can do things that are specifically focused on relaxing you and getting away from the pressure. Like best friend dates, but solely focused on you. Things that make you happy and relaxed. Things that calm your mind and your body, so nothing competitive." I have no idea if this is actually an idea that he'll go for, but it's where I'm at. I can tell Nate's not in a good headspace. The way Nate has described the things he's been dealing with hurts to hear. He's usually upbeat and charismatic and I want so badly to help him work through everything he's facing. I want him to know he doesn't have to face it alone.

"Well, I like competition." He smirks at me.

"Well, your nervous system doesn't. So, you need some separation from that when you aren't on the field. I know you're struggling, Nate. You don't need to hide it from me. You aren't alone, let me help you the best way I know how."

"We could—"

"Not golf," I cut that train of thought immediately and he lets out a laugh.

"You've been going at full speed since I've known you. You don't slow down and you don't take breaks. You've put this immense pressure on yourself to be the best, and I get that. I really do. I understand how important your job is, but not at the cost of your mental health. That's too high of a price and I love you too much to not try and help you. The power of just taking a pause is vastly underrated, Nate. So, what do you say?"

His smile broadens in approval. "Okay. I trust you." His arms spread out, showing his wing span, which is pretty impressive.

"Perfect." His infectious smile only causes my own to take shape.

Making sure the people around me are happy and feel good is practically my life's calling, and if anyone deserves to be undeniably happy, it's Nate.

Tonight is Ford and Abby's engagement party and I'm honestly just dying to know what Nate's got planned for all of the ice he's bringing.

"Wow," Nate says as I'm walking out of my room and he's standing at my kitchen island. I run my hands over my stomach on the champagne colored dress I'm wearing and look up at him. I've had this dress for years, it's probably the fanciest one in my closet. It's got an open back and has a low-cut V in the front. Not that I have a lot of cleavage to show off, but this dress is comfortable and I've always loved the color.

"What?" I ask, confused.

"You just… You look really fucking beautiful, Mia. Damn." Nate's never complimented me like that. And he rarely uses my actual name. Sure, he's told me I look beautiful before, but something feels different in that one. He works his eyes up and down my body as he says it and I watch his throat move as he swallows.

"Oh, thank you. Is Summer ready?" I ask.

"She is!" Summer shouts from the doorway as she stands there in a short black dress with big loose curls.

"You look great, Summer," Nate simply states.

See. That. That's how he's supposed to react to me. Normal, with very few words. Not wide eyes and a hanging jaw with two swear words in his sentence.

She smiles and I grab my bag and walk all of us out towards the door. Once we get into Nate's truck, I see he very clearly did bring his A-game with the ice. He has bags of it. Different kinds of it. Cubed, crushed and the small nugget pieces of ice. I'm looking in the backseat where Summer has squeezed herself in next to one of the coolers.

"This is ridiculous," she mutters and gives me a dirty look.

Nate's wearing a giant fucking grin with his stupid adorable dimple on full display. He's sporting a perfectly tailored pair of burgundy pants with a matching jacket and a white button up underneath it. But he has the top few buttons undone. He's always been really fucking good at dressing to impress. I feel like it's some kind of requirement for athletes because these men all clean up nicely.

Number one, run fast. Number two, be able to look like a GQ model.

"Ask me if I ordered an ice sculpture," he says as we're pulling into Ford and Abby's driveway and I see a large white truck unloading something on wheels covered in a tarp. My hands cover my eyes, carefully not to ruin any of my make up, but damn him. He really had to get an ice sculpture? This ought to be good.

"I cannot believe you," I say with a laugh as he turns off the truck and gets out to help Summer and then comes around to my side.

"You gave me a challenge, Smalls. You know I don't back down from a challenge," he whispers as he helps me down from his truck.

"What the fuck is this?" Ford asks when he sees the giant bird made of ice.

"It's a fucking swan, what does it look like?" Nate stands next to the sculpture as if he carved it himself. Beaming with pride. Ford shakes his head and holds up his hand before he just walks away.

Everything has gone smooth tonight and it's nauseatingly clear how well matched Ford and Abby are by their constant public displays of affection all night.

After three hours, a lot of speeches, and endless glasses of champagne poured for everyone, I'm ready to clean up and call it a night.

"Everything looked so good. And the food… oh my God. Thank you, Mia." Abby hugs me and holds onto me tighter than necessary. "I don't really get all that," she says, gesturing to the half-melted ice sculpture. "But I love it anyway." Abby's had enough champagne and I'm expecting Ford to whisk her away any time now, even if we're all still here, it won't make a difference to him.

"Clarky!" Liam shouts from across the room. I've barely seen a lot of the guys all night. I've spent most of the evening making sure Abby and Ford had everything they needed.

"Liam," I say back to him once he's closer. He wraps me into a hug and then pulls back, holding me. "Everything looked great tonight, everything went well. Overall, great job." He kisses my forehead and releases me as I turn my attention over to Nate.

"Nate, are you ready? I'm going to pass out."

He nods and we walk out the front door after saying goodnight to everyone. Summer is still out back chatting with Chase and Graham, but she said Chase would drop her off so I don't think twice when I throw myself into Nate's truck without her. I'm exhausted and can feel my eyes already closing.

My eyes flutter open and instantly I know something is different. This isn't my bed. Why am I not in my bed? Where's my body pillow? Why don't I hear soothing sounds playing on my sound machine? I smell cologne. I feel around in the dark room and find that I'm wearing the same dress I had on last night and I realize I'm waking up in my best friend's bedroom. I spring up, almost giving myself whiplash. The bedroom door is closed so I gently pull it open and walk down the hall to find Nate's big body hanging off the couch still wearing his pants from last night, just no shirt. He looks really uncomfortable. Poor guy. Hendrix nuzzles up beside me and I bend down quickly to pet his head.

"Morning, Henny," I whisper.

Nate's kitchen light has a dimmer, thankfully, so I turn it on to the lowest setting—just enough so I can see as I make a pot of coffee. My best guess is I fell asleep in Nate's truck and he just put me to bed here. The last thing I remember is pulling away from Ford and Abby's house.

I'm leaning against the counter, waiting for the coffee to finish brewing when the Google Home device sitting on his counter grabs my attention. It has a picture slideshow playing that I don't think I've ever really watched before. Pictures of him and his family make up most of it, but there is a surprising amount of him and I in there. One of the pictures that flashes on the screen is from the first weekend he moved to Tampa. I had just flown in since I was still in college, but he needed help apartment hunting. We looked at a handful of apartments that day, but when we were in this one, I took a mirror picture of us in the master bathroom. I jokingly told him this bathroom had the best shower sex mirror since the shower and mirror were directly across from one another. I'm sure that's not what sealed the deal, but it's the apartment he eventually signed with and still lives in.

Then, I see a candid photo of Nate and me at Summerfest five years ago. I'm on his shoulders, my hands are in the air and we're both smiling from ear to ear. I smile, reminiscing on that weekend. When I first met Nate, there was just something about him that drew me to him. It had nothing to do with his talent on the football field and everything to do with the man beneath the helmet. He's so many wonderful things. I hate how hard he is on himself. I hate how easily he lets outside opinions get under his skin. He's incredible and easily the best man I've ever known.

It amazes me how deep of a sleeper Nate is. I most definitely haven't been the quietest while trying to make a pot of coffee, but he's slept right through the clinking of coffee mugs and the whistle of the coffee machine.

"Do you need a walk, Hendrix?" I ask, as if he can actually answer me. Walking back in Nate's room, I grab a t-shirt of his and throw it on with a pair of his sweatpants and slippers. I look ridiculous, but I'm not taking this dog out in the clothes I wore last night.

I fasten the leash on his collar and turn towards the door to head out and lock it behind me. My phone starts ringing as soon as I turn to walk to the elevators so I put the phone to my ear and move the leash to my other hand. I really underestimated the strength of Hendrix at this moment, because the second he can, he runs towards the end of the hall and the leash jerks out of my hand, causing me to almost topple over. My phone falls on the hallway floor just before I'm able to even get two words out.

"Damn it!" I yell as I catch my balance.

"Jimi Hendrix, you come back here!" I leave my phone on the floor where it fell and jog over to where he is now sitting in front of someone's door down the hall.

"That was not very nice, mister! Here I thought we were about to go have a nice morning walk and you're already misbehaving?" I pick up the leash and bend down to scratch his head.

The door in front of me opens, and a very tall bare-chested man stands above me with a confused smile on his face. As luck would have it, the very tall and handsome, half-naked man standing in front of me is Connor. The man I met at dinner a few weeks ago. And naturally, I look like a homeless troll. This is perfect.

"Not what I was expecting at eight in the morning… but I'll take it." Connor smiles.

"I am so sorry. He never darts off on me like that." Hendrix's tail continues to wag as Connor reaches down to pet him on the head.

"It's okay. It's nice to see you again, Mia. Who do I have the pleasure of meeting here?" he asks, in a voice that's as smooth as god damn whiskey.

"Oh, this is Hendrix," I say, pulling his leash and motioning for us to leave the doorway and get on with our morning.

"I had no idea you lived here… near Nate," I add.

Connor flashes me a smile that looks like it belongs on a billboard for perfect teeth.

"Were you coming from Campbell's place?" he asks with a slight accusatory tone.

"Yeah, I fell asleep there. We're just friends though. Nothing going on there," I say, awkwardly. I have no idea why I feel the need to explain myself to him.

"Just friends?" he questions.

"Just best friends." I laugh, gripping the leash tightly.

"Have you always lived here? I've just never seen you around here before," I ask.

The dinner at the Rec Center was the first time I'd met Connor and I'm certain I would have remembered his dirty blonde hair and dark eyes if I'd seen him before then. Plus, his height and build alone is memorable.

"No. I just moved in recently. I play baseball. I've known Nate a while though… professional athletes tend to run in some of the same circles," he states.

My eyes widen and I nod my head up and down as we stand in this hallway.

"What?" Connor laughs. "Got something against baseball players? What if I said I'm a shortstop? Will that convince you to get dinner with me?"

Get dinner? I'm too stunned at his forward request to answer right away.

"It doesn't have to be tonight… but I'd love to take you out some time." My cheeks blush at his proposal. I'm intrigued and cautious at the same time. I'm tempted to say yes, but nothing comes out.

He nods his head up and down as I start to back away from his door while he stands there.

"I'm sorry, you just completely caught me off guard… but um…" It can't hurt to get dinner with him. Before I can talk myself out of it, I make a quick decision. "You know what? Yes.

Sure. Dinner would be great." A smile forms on my face as he hands me his phone and I give him my number.

"Nice to see you again, Mia. I'll talk to you soon."

"Yeah, you too," I say steadily.

Like any normal girl, the second I walk away, I google him. Between the dinner where we first met and this morning, I feel like I just got surface level information. I need the nitty gritty if I'm going out with him. He never actually gave me his last name, but he plays baseball here so how hard can it be to find him?

Connor Hughes. Twenty-nine years old. Shortstop for the Tampa Angels.

A date can't hurt. Hell, I've been on countless bad dates, what's one more if this one goes south?

Hendrix and I walk for a while before I see the dark clouds rolling in and that's when I begin to pick up our pace. The phone call earlier was Summer, so I make a mental note to call her back when I get a chance.

I feel the light patter of rain just as we're rounding the corner to Nate's building and as soon as we get inside, the floodgates open and all hell breaks loose from the clouds. A beautiful morning turned into tropical storm force weather within minutes.

"I was hoping you'd make it back before the rain," Nate's voice startles me as I'm walking in.

"Jesus!" I say, dropping my phone on the floor creating a loud thud in this quiet apartment. "Warn a girl next time. Why are you standing in the dark, you psycho?" I bend down to take Hendrix off the leash and he darts off into the other room.

"I'm not standing in the dark, that light is on." He gestures to the dining room light that's dimly lit, casting a small shadow across the floor.

Nate's leaning his shirtless body against the counter as he stares at the outfit of choice I have on.

"Not a word. This is because of you." I point my finger at him, noticing his brown hair is going in a thousand different directions after probably getting the worst night of sleep possible on that couch.

"You passed out in my truck. It was just easier to toss you in my bed. You're welcome, by the way. My fucking neck and back are killing me from tossing and turning all night on that couch." His fingers graze the small of my back as I walk by and I arch myself forward in response. Nate and I have always been touchy, feely, but that right there sent goosebumps down my spine. And that's not something that's happened in a long time.

Flipping on the kitchen light, I pour myself another cup of coffee after handing one over to Nate.

"Fine. Thank you," I say sarcastically into my coffee, as I watch the rain pound outside.

CHAPTER NINE

NATE

"First down, Tampa!" I hear the game day announcer as I'm standing on the sidelines, gasping for air. They just had to bring out the chains to measure the spot of the ball from my last run.

"Every time they do that shit, I hold my breath." Chase comes up beside me. I haven't seen much of him lately outside of games and practice, but he has a good reason. He's busy being Super Dad.

"Every damn time." I sigh just as I'm called back into the huddle.

After another quarter of the game gone, we're still down by two scores, and if I'm being honest, it's not looking good. Philadelphia gives us a run for our money every damn time and this new quick quarterback they have is a fucking magician with his footwork. Last year's draft class was stacked with talent, not that they aren't every year, but these guys seem to be playing on a whole new level.

Once we're down in the red zone and close to scoring, I get up and stand next to the offensive coordinator to get a better view of what's going on. After the ball is snapped, Liam gets it out of his hands immediately. He throws towards the end zone where Ford is sprinting for his life to make it there in time for the catch. I pump my fist at my side when I see Ford come up from the back of the end zone holding the ball in his hands and the crowd erupts.

After a quick three and out by our defense, the offense is back on the field.

But something's not right. My vision is spotty. I'm set up in the backfield behind Liam and instead of hearing the play he's calling or seeing the ball he's holding out for me, I hear ringing in my ears and I tense up. My body then moves like it's on autopilot, but my mind isn't focused one bit on what it's doing. The only thing that snaps me back into the game is the powerhouse hit I take from Philly's defense, knocking the ball out of my hands and laying me flat on my back.

My worst fear has officially come to a head.

It's affecting my game. It's affecting my focus. My concentration. To the point where I can't even explain what just happened other than my body locked up and my heart started racing.

I lie there, hearing the echoing oohs and aahs from the fans as the play unfolds.

I'm not hurt. Nothing hurts.

But I'm done. At that moment, I know it. There's no more hiding it. No more pretending like everything's fine.

When I get back to the bench, all eyes are on me. I don't need to look around to know it, I can feel it. I can feel the stares. Liam slaps me on the back and sits on one side of me while Ford takes up residence on the other.

"Don't sit here and beat yourself up over it," Ford says.

I don't respond and neither of them say anything else, but they do sit there beside me for the remaining few moments of the game. It's pretty fucking clear to everyone in America right now that something's wrong with me. Too bad I don't know what the hell it is.

The game ends with us on the losing end of it and I can't stop blaming myself, even though the whole team has approached me since I've been in this locker room, assuring me that's not the case. There's no big speech for the team from Coach Aarons, but that doesn't mean he isn't saving one specifically for me. Lucky for him though, I'm already planning to meet with him. Because what happened today can't ever fucking happen again.

"Coach!" I shout as I'm walking down the hall after him.

He slowly turns to face me, but doesn't say anything. He just gestures for me to go into his office.

"Sit," he says in a commanding tone.

"I'm sorry." Throwing out an apology is the only way I know how to start this conversation.

"I don't need an apology Campbell. I need my starting running back to be man enough, to be the leader I know he is, and admit when he has personal matters going on." He paces his office, and fuck, I just feel bad.

"You could have been injured."

"I know." I sigh. "Coach, I don't know what's going on. That's the truth. But something is off. I'm not feeling like myself, I haven't for a while. This monster inside my head… in my chest… it keeps growing and I can't shake it. I wish I could explain it better, but it's just this weight I constantly feel on my chest. Like someone dropped a building on it and I can't breathe. I wanted to go out there and be the best this season. I tried to just shove it all down, ignore it, play through it. The pressure has been killing me, though." My eyes are burning as I stand up and continue talking to him.

"I–I can't fucking believe I'm about to say this, but I need to step away. I need to get my mind right. And right now, I'm a liability to the team. I love this game, Coach. I love it, but I'm miserable and I need to figure out why."

Pretending that you're fine is easy until you actually accept that you aren't.

And I've accepted it. Or better yet, it came slamming into my chest, opening my eyes to the realization that I can't continue like I have been.

His head falls back and he lets out a shaky sigh. "I knew something was bothering you, I wish you would've told me sooner, but... I understand. Pride's a funny thing when it comes to athletes. Take the time you need. Get your mind right. Your spot will be here when you're ready. We have an in-house team therapist too, if you want to talk with her. And Campbell, I suggest you do." Instead of a handshake, he pulls me into a hug and we just stand there for much longer than normal.

When I walk out of the facility tonight, Mia's standing by the gate, her hands fidgeting with one another in front of her. Her eyes remain on me the entire time I walk over to her until I'm close enough to give her a hug, and she all but throws herself at me when she grabs a hold of my middle, pulling me into her.

The calming scent of lavender wafts off of her as I stand there inhaling the most familiar scent. I take slow, deep breaths while we stand there, replaying the game in my mind and the moment I told Coach that I need a break

I never in a million goddamn years thought I'd be the guy who has to take a break from football. Yet here I am, standing in the parking lot after admitting just that. If I can't find a way to control this, it's going to eat me alive, I know it. It'll ruin every good thing I've ever accomplished professionally because that'll be the conversation piece.

"I'm staying at your apartment tonight. I'll take the couch, it's fine, but I'm not leaving you alone."

"I'll be fine, Mi. I promise."

She's already walking me to my truck and grabs my keys from my hand, hitting the remote start button on it as soon as we're in range.

"And you aren't driving my truck," I add.

She gives me an unamused look as we approach the driver's side.

"I wasn't planning on driving, and also, it's not up for debate. I'm staying over." Her voice is soft and sincere, calming, but with a hint of authority. It's what I need to hear right now. I just need to be surrounded by the sweet and soft voice of Mia.

She hops in the passenger seat and I put the truck in drive to get us back to my apartment. She's not sleeping on the couch. She can have the bed, I'll make it work on the couch if I have to, or we can try to share the bed, even though that's something we've never actually done.

The truck is silent the entire drive. Mia doesn't put on music, she doesn't start a conversation, she just sits there, checking on me out of the corner of her eye every few seconds. I'm tempted to tell her to stop, but I know that'll be a losing battle. Mia's a helper to her core, it's just who she is. She's also stubborn as fuck, so telling her to do something that she doesn't want to do is useless.

"Hi, Henny," Mia greets Hendrix as we walk in and she grabs his leash, taking him out for a quick bathroom break in the dog park within my complex.

Having a few moments to myself, I hop in the shower. The warm water rolls down my back and I wince at the way my chest aches from the hit I took. A hit I needed though. My phone's been blowing up for the last hour and I haven't had the energy to check it. I didn't say anything to the guys when I left the locker room, I just went right into the coach's office and then left the stadium. I glance at the mirror filling with condensation, and the Post-it note from Mia with a giant smiley face on it stands out. She left it there on my birthday three years ago and I never took it down. It's way at the top, so I'm sure she had to climb on top of the counter to even get it there. It was one of twenty-four she put all around my apartment on my 24th birthday.

Mia's always been the person who goes above and beyond, does the little things that most people would overlook, she pays attention to details and remembers even the smallest things about people. She texts my mom every time she hears a Celine Dion song because my mom mentioned one time how much she loves her. Just little things like that, it all reminds me why Mia's my best friend and the best person I know. I have no desire to see or hear from anyone right now, except for her.

I hear the front door close and take that as my cue to turn off the water and get out. Mia's standing in my kitchen, mashing up bananas and the oven is preheating as I walk out, drying my hair with a towel.

"Banana bread with walnuts and chocolate chips?" Hendrix wags his tail at Mia's feet as I approach them both.

"As if there's any other way to make banana bread." She smiles, pouring a hefty amount of chocolate chips into the mixture.

"So, do you want to talk?" Her demeanor shifts once she places the bread in the oven and sets a timer. She pulls her hair up into a scrunchie and takes a seat on the loveseat across from me.

"I told Coach I need a break. I don't know for how long, but there's something going on, and I need to figure out how to control it before it destroys me. I thought I could handle it by just hiding it or running for my life every morning to try and sweat it out, but I'm going to have to face it and find a way to manage it. So I'm taking a leave of absence from the team. They can't have me out on that field when I know my mind isn't right, my body isn't right. I thought I could handle it, Mi… but I can't. I'm just afraid it's going to ruin me." My hands run down my face and then I feel a hand on my thigh as Mia takes a seat next to me.

"Then we'll figure this out." Her tone is sure and sharp, like she's already in problem solving mode. "Being afraid of something is usually all the more reason to face it. You're tough and resilient, you know you belong on that field. Let me help you get back there." She nestles her body closer to mine and I nod my head against her, wrapping my arms around her. Holding Mia like this feels... right. Like she's just supposed to be right here, right now, and maybe always.

Texts from the guys have been sitting unread on my phone since I got home. I'll want to talk to them about all of this eventually, at least give them some type of explanation, but I just don't even know what to say.

> **FORD**
> Coach addressed the team. Nothing specific, but said you were taking some time. Here if you need anything, man.
>
> **LIAM**
> We're just a phone call away. Call anytime.
>
> **CHASE**
> Prayers, man. Let me know how I can help.
>
> **LIAM**
> Let Mia be there for you.
>
> And I don't mean that in any way other than let her help.

I know I lucked out when it comes to the people in my life, because fuck, I don't always deserve all of their grace but they sure do show it.

"Abby texted me, they're all thinking of you." Mia places her phone down at the same time that I do.

"I don't even know what the fuck to say to the guys. I let them down."

Her head shakes back and forth as her tongue swipes between her lips, "You didn't let them down. Stop telling yourself that. It's okay if you don't know what to say yet. They aren't going to judge you for it, if that's your worry."

That's exactly my worry, even though I know it shouldn't be. I can't help but sit here and think about how fucking weak I am for letting things get like this. Like a mind reader, Mia sees my thoughts written all over my face and reaches for my hand.

"I'll talk to them," she whispers as her dainty fingers squeeze mine.

"Hand me that blanket up there, please." Mia is standing in my closet, gesturing to the extra comforter on top of my closet.

"No, you aren't sleeping on the couch. Just sleep in my bed."

"Are you sure?"

"Yes. We can put a pillow barrier or whatever you need, but you aren't sleeping on the couch. If you insist on staying here, you can sleep in here." I point to my bed from where we're standing as she gives me a conflicted look before nodding her head in agreement.

When she comes out of the bathroom, she's wearing one of my shirts and an old pair of sweats that she has tied tightly against her skin. Mia wears my clothes all the time. Wears my name and my number on her back every Sunday, but somehow, the thought of her wearing my shirt right now and hopping into my bed next to me is stirring emotions I didn't expect.

"You're going to burn up in those sweatpants."

"Well, I didn't exactly think this through and I don't have shorts and I can't just get in bed with my best friend in my underwear." I tilt my head at her with a contemplating stare and it makes us both laugh. She's right. It's a better idea if she wears sweatpants.

I watch as Mia lays herself on the bed and pulls the comforter up over her as she turns on her side to face me. My bedside light is still on, casting an ambiance lighting in the room, and I can see the freckles scattered across her nose and the warm chocolate tone of her eyes as she lays there next to me.

"Are you okay?" she whispers.

"No." I sigh. "But I will be."

CHAPTER TEN
MIA

The heat from Nate's body is radiating off him as we lie here. His side of the comforter is resting at his waist and I can see the way his bare chest is moving up and down in rhythmic breaths as he sleeps. His square jaw is relaxed, not clenched, his eyebrows don't show creasing, his ocean blue eyes are resting. He's calm.

When I saw Nate standing on the field as if he was frozen in time, I knew in that split second that something was about to happen. Philly's lineman just pummeled right into him, and usually you'd see some resistance, some fight, but there was nothing. Nate went down as if he was fast asleep, standing on that field and wasn't expecting the hit. I guess all things considered now, he wasn't. He was out of it the moment the ball was snapped, probably even before that.

I don't know a whole lot about professional athletes and their mental health struggles, but having someone so close to me experiencing it, all I want to do now is to learn more about it and figure out the best way that I can help him.

I sigh, looking at my phone to see it's just past one in the morning. I've been lying here, chasing one train of thought after the other for almost three hours. I need to force myself to get some sleep, but part of me just wants to watch Nate all night, to make sure he's okay. He moves a little as he shifts from his back to his side, and with the movement it brings him even closer to me. The pillow barrier was useless because with the way I sleep, I just end up using it as something to hold onto.

As I lie there a little while longer, Nate's hand moves and when he touches the pillow, his pinky grazes mine. I haven't shared a bed with someone in so long and even though we're just friends, it still feels nice. The contact. The closeness. I finally close my eyes and keep my hand there, just barely touching his, but it's enough to allow me to rest.

The hushed voice of Nate talking to Hendrix drifts through my ears as I'm waking up. The room is still dark, he didn't open any of the curtains, allowing me to sleep which I appreciate, even though he should be the one getting extra rest.

"Hi," I say softly, rubbing my eyes as I walk down the hall from the bedroom to the kitchen. Nate's standing at the kitchen stove, spatula in one hand as he scatters shredded cheese into the pan.

"Smells good." I smile, grabbing a coffee cup from the cabinet.

Nate looks over and smirks at me. His sleepy smile looks lighter today. Like maybe he needed yesterday. As awful as that sounds, maybe admitting that he needs the break and actually asking for it is the beginning of his healing.

"Figured the least I can do for you is make an omelet, considering you were stuck here all night."

"Yes, held against my will and now being force fed an omelet. The horror." I blow on the top of my coffee to cool it off a bit before taking a sip.

"What are you doing today?" I ask as I sit on the bar stool, bringing both of my feet up to sit criss-cross.

"I want to call my parents. I have missed texts from both of them since I'm sure they saw the game. I just don't want them to keep worrying. I'm probably going to go for a run, too. I texted Coach to let him know I'll be taking at least the next three weeks off. It'll give me time to myself, time to get a break and hopefully figure out how to manage this going forward."

"Yes, call your parents, please. I'm sure your coach is more than fine with that, Nate. I'll go for a run with you, if I'm done with work in time."

Nate places a giant omelet with cheese, tomatoes and spinach in front of me and I'm tempted to whip out my phone and snap a picture of this masterpiece. Because this looks so damn good and smells incredible. I drizzle a tiny bit of sriracha sauce on it before diving in.

———

"Is that all for today?" Rose, the front desk associate at the gym asks as I'm behind the counter loading up my gym bag.

"That's all. I keep it light on Mondays," I reply.

"Any news on opening your own studio?"

I shake my head at her. "Not yet, hopefully something will be in the works soon, though."

Rose smiles and hands me my client folder that I left next to her and I place it into my bag. Just as I'm about to leave, I hear my name from behind me.

"Mia, hey." Laura's blonde ponytail swings as she approaches me. Big, blue eyes and a body that most women would do anything to have.

"Hi, Laura," I say, reaching out to hug her.

"I saw the game yesterday... Is Nate okay?" Sharing Nate's business with his former hook-up isn't something I plan on doing, but it's nice that she's asked. I've always liked her.

"He'll be alright, thanks for asking." It's the truth, because he will be. Eventually.

"Good, good, I'm so glad. At least he has you, right." She

laughs as she says it, and I can't determine whether it's sarcastic or a meaningful remark. My head tilts slightly at her comment, causing her to pick up on my uncertainty behind her words.

"That's what friends are for," I add before pulling my bag over my shoulder.

"Right. Yes. That's what I meant." I nod slowly at her and begin to start saying my goodbyes, but she hesitantly takes a few steps closer to me. "It's just… did you know Nate keeps a collection of your scrunchies in his bathroom drawer? He wears one every game during warm-ups. I asked about it once when we were together, he didn't even try to hide the fact that they were yours."

I figured Nate had to be doing something with all the scrunchies of mine he's stolen, but I figured they were probably just scattered all about, not in a drawer.

"There's a Post-it note with a smiley face in his bathroom on the mirror dated three years ago from you. For three years, he's held onto an emoji from you." That, I did know. I saw it this morning. I just assumed he's too lazy to reach up and take it down.

"Well, that was for his birthday…" I say, realizing how stupid I sound.

"You still don't see it." Her head shakes back and forth as a small laugh escapes her. "You two have a handshake that you do every time he leaves for an away game. It's silly, but sweet. I had a lot of fun with Nate, but I never held a candle to you."

"What are you talking about?" There's a sudden jump in my heart rate at her words.

"You and Nate. I wanted to actually *not* like you when we first met, but it turns out you're a freaking delight, so there went that idea." We both turn to start walking towards the door. "Honestly, Mia. I'm glad that Nate and I stopped seeing each other. I don't ever want to be someone's second choice, and that's what I'd always be after you."

"We are just friends though. We're close, yes, but only friends."

She shakes her head back and forth as she opens the door and we walk out. The wind is blowing and the sun is shining, there isn't a cloud in the sky as we stand out here. It's a beautiful day and all I want to do is to end this conversation because it's throwing my mind into a tailspin.

"I know you are, but..." she pauses, inhaling a deep breath. "He never looked at me the way he looks at you. I was a placeholder for you, Mia. I think every woman will be until he finally admits his feelings for you."

At that, Laura gives me a hug and walks over to her bright, shiny BMW that's perfectly parallel parked in the spot to my left. I turn my head back, watching her get in, completely dumbfounded by that entire conversation.

Comments like this aren't new to me, but it is the first time I've heard it in a while. We dealt with this in college, and I remember constantly rolling my eyes at the thought of Nate actually wanting to date me. We had our one almost-kiss, and even that I convinced myself was a fluke, just due to him having a few drinks.

The women that Nate dates look like Laura. They're blonde and have curves in all the right places. They dress up and wear makeup all the time, they drive fancy cars, and probably don't wear the same leggings twice in one week.

Good thing I have a solid fifteen-minute walk back to my apartment to overthink everything she just said to me.

I had planned on taking Nate to the state fair that's in town this week. I bought tickets after I declared that Nate needs to take a pause and do more things for himself outside of football. Of course, I didn't expect him to then take a break from football itself, but life has a funny way of showing you exactly what you need.

My phone dings with an email as I'm walking back to my

apartment and I see it's from Quinn, the realtor. I emailed her the other day, letting her know I was interested in discussing rental options, the term, amount, things like that. It's a long shot, being able to go through with this, but I want to try. I haven't heard if any other renters have been interested, but I asked her to let me know in the email if it was being pursued by anyone else.

> I just got home, do you want to go for a run or have you already gone?

NATE
We couldn't be more in sync if we tried.

Not even a minute later, there is knocking at my door. Did I tell him a time this morning? I don't even remember. But this is purely just out of familiarity. We know each other's schedules. He's here at the exact right time because that's just how it's always been. It has nothing to do with anything that Laura mentioned.

———

"How are your parents?" I ask Nate once we've stopped to take a breather in this heat. He's running himself into the ground today and I can barely keep up.

"They're good. I didn't say much, just that I have some things going on and needed a break. I could tell my mom wanted to ask more questions, but she didn't. She did ask if I was coming to their anniversary party though." The way Nate's standing right now, hands intertwined on top of his head as he paces, emphasizes the force of his arms as they're displayed.

"Going home might actually be good for you. It's a much slower pace, you'll be surrounded by your family. I think it would be beneficial for you." Nate spending time back home in Wisconsin is probably just what his mind and body need. He needs the time, space and freedom to be able to process everything he's going through. A quiet town in the Midwest sounds good for that.

He rubbed his fingers near the crease of his lip as he stared at me, like he's considering what I suggested.

"Come with me." He says it with such command, as if there's no other answer than okay.

"What?"

"Come home with me. Come to the party."

"Well, technically I got my own invite so I don't really need to be your plus one."

"So, you're going?" He steps closer to me as we're standing on this trail, right where the grass meets the gravel. His black sneakers kick a couple pieces up as he slowly takes another step.

An idea flashes in my head. Growing up, I loved taking road trips. Open spaces, different scenery, it was always so refreshing. Something like that might actually be good for him.

"Okay, but I have a suggestion. If you'd rather not, we don't have to. This whole break is completely your call. We'll do whatever you want, okay? But…what do you think about making it a road trip? It might be a good change of pace for you… a good change of scenery. Having some time to slow down. Country roads, fresh air… you know, all the stuff John Denver sings about."

Nate lets out a deep, warm laugh at that. Using music to convince him of anything works the majority of the time.

"You really pulled out the John Denver card, didn't you?" His head shakes back and forth at me, smiling as I wait for his reply. He nods his head towards the sidewalk for us to start walking back and I follow his lead. We walk a handful of feet before noticing there are people stopping holding their phones up and cameras, not so discreetly, and snapping pictures of him as we stroll down Main street. Nate keeps his head down as we walk, and again, I do the same. I sometimes forget that he's technically famous. And even more so now that he had everything happen at the game yesterday.

Once we're back in the lobby of my apartment complex, he continues.

"It's not the worst idea. But do I want to spend eighteen hours stuck in a car with you? That's the real question." He smirks and I reach out to punch his bicep before he grabs my hand to stop me. We both stare at my fist in his hand and then he brings those blue irises to mine. "I'm going to catch this every time, Smalls."

A weird heat flows through my body.

Why? Why did that just happen? Is it because of what Laura said? Is it because I saw him... uh, towel-less the other day? Did that turn on some feminine switch and now that I know what he's packing, it's making me sweat? I take a big gulp before speaking again.

I perk up. "Then it's settled. We'll drive."

"Yes. *I* will drive," he corrects me, causing my middle finger to find its way in his direction.

CHAPTER ELEVEN

NATE

"Nate Campbell, running back for the Tampa Knights has stepped away from the team to deal with mental health concerns."

"Golden Boy Campbell is taking some time off from the Knights to handle some personal things. Anyone who had him on your fantasy team, sorry about your luck, looks like you just lost your running back."

"We wish Nate Campbell well on his personal journey and the entire league will undoubtedly stand behind him and support his decision to prioritize his mental well-being. He's a great asset to the league and to Tampa's organization, but after Sunday's event, he made the call himself to step away. He's expected to return to the team for the home game against Chicago. Whether or not he'll play will likely be a game time decision."

I've turned off my television. Deactivated social media. I'm holding off on communicating with anyone from the team. I know what's out there in the press. I saw the fucking vultures with their phones and the cameras. I'm well aware that's their job, but it doesn't make it any less invasive. I know the narrative that everyone's likely going to run with. "Golden boy, Nate Campbell can't handle the pressure. He's not the same as he was. He's lost his spark."

Golden boy. That fucking nickname got thrown around in high school, followed me to college, and then somehow reared its head in the league. I think people consider that a compliment, but I've always used it as a driving force. A nickname I despised to help me make it through the bullshit. Somehow, in my mind, it worked at motivating me. I didn't care that anyone called me that. But now, it's the last thing I feel like hearing.

Ever since telling Coach Aarons that I need to remove myself for a while, I've felt like this weight has been lifted. Albeit, a small fucking weight, but it's something. Saying out loud to someone other than Mia that I'm struggling was just the first piece.

I haven't had uninterrupted sleep in weeks, maybe months. But the night that Mia stayed over, I slept like a log. All my demons go to bed with me, usually wake me up in the middle of the night, and then again in the morning. They were still there when I went to bed, and when I woke up in the morning. But somehow with Mia lying next to me, it allowed me to sleep through the night for the first time in a while. I almost wish I could ask her to stay over more often.

"Where are we going?" Mia had me meet her an hour outside of Tampa in some small town with a manatee on every other billboard.

"I'm still committed to finding ways to relax you. You're going to peacefully float down this river in an inner tube and let your mind and body relax, not thinking about a single thing having to do with football. Got it?" Mia's been awfully bossy lately, and I have to admit, I'm a fan of this side of her. The sweet and caring Mia is who she is at her core, but these glimpses of sass and fire are something else.

We walk down to a small shore area and there are inner tubes and canoes lined up along the sand. Mia walks over to a small building and comes back wearing a giant smile.

"No rain expected. Pick a tube."

I follow her along the sand and into the water as she stands there for a moment in ankle deep crystal water. This spring is beautiful. You can see right down to the bottom and it's pretty shallow. Maybe waist deep for Mia if she were to walk all the way in. She lines herself up in front of a tube, ready to let herself gracefully fall backwards into it. Her hair is up and she's wearing a denim baseball hat with a black two-piece swimsuit. We both left our clothes in the car, assuming we'll be spending the whole day in the water before ending up right back here.

"Well, get in," she says once I see her already starting to drift with the current.

I do just as Mia did, lining myself up and getting into the tube the way she did. Although her body is a lot smaller and a lot more graceful than mine. So where her entrance was seamless, mine is anything but. When I lean back and let myself ease into the tube, the weight of my body sends the tube bouncing back and bobbing in the water for a moment before evening out. Mia's a few feet ahead of me covering her mouth with her hands to stifle a laugh.

"What's the situation with snakes?" I ask as we float next to one another. Our tubes are strung together with a rope so we don't end up too far from each other down this river.

"If you see one, just leave it alone." She shrugs.

"That's what they tell you?"

"Same for the alligators, just ignore them."

Alligators on a golf course where I can run if I need to… no problem. But in the water? In their territory? No… just no. I hang my head back and say a silent prayer that I don't need to show Mia what a fucking baby I am when it comes to water monsters.

"See any headlines this morning?" I ask, clenching my jaw in annoyance.

"No, and you shouldn't either."

"Eventually, I'm going to have to make a statement." My fingers graze the water as we float and I splash some of it on my chest.

"Why? Who says you have to make a statement?"

A low laugh rises in my chest. "My publicist," I reply, and Mia just shakes her head and waves her hands in the air.

"Well, today we're floating and unavailable. She'll have to wait."

"Today we're floating," I repeat casually.

I'll give it to her, floating down this river is actually really fucking relaxing. The trees hang over the water for the most part so we're not in direct sunlight the entire day, but we still get the warmth of it as it peeks through. The water is cold, but feels good on this late summer afternoon. A few small boats have passed by and a couple canoes and paddle boats. We've seen a handful of other people floating in tubes and some just flat out swimming in the water. There's a big open area up ahead and a rope hanging off of a tree. Reminds me of growing up and using those ropes to swing from trees into the lakes.

The only sounds we hear are our own voices when we talk or the voices of others passing by, but for the most part, it's quiet. Birds every so often, or the movement of the water from the current or a splash of our feet or hands.

"Do you want to stop up there? I read about this spot. There's a tree you can swing from and a little area where we can sit and get out for a while if you want to. It's your day, so whatever you want to do." How do I tell her that I want to do whatever she wants to do? Mia somehow always knows what I need, when I need it. She takes me out of the chaos and brings me somewhere that's peaceful and refreshing. Literally and figuratively.

"That sounds good." I stand up from the tube and quickly realize it's definitely deeper here. The water almost hits my chest, but it's still clear as day to the bottom. "Stay in the tube, it's deeper here. I'll walk you to the shore." Mia stays seated in the tube before it's clearly shallow enough and slides herself through the center, letting herself go under the water quickly.

"Oh my God, it's cold. But that felt so good." She splashes a bit of the water towards me and drops land on my chest and shoulders.

"Are we playing that game?" I taunt. Ready to play whatever kind of game she'll let me.

She takes the baseball hat she has on and flips it backwards on herself.

"Cute," I say, standing there in waist deep water as I stare at her. But damn, she really does look cute– she looks more than cute, she looks gorgeous, she looks desirable. A light went on the other night for me. A light that for years I've tried turning off, or at least dimming… but it's getting too strong for me to control anymore and it's shining like a spotlight over a stage. And it's shining bright. Being best friends with Mia is everything to me, but my God, do I need her to be more.

Seeing her all dressed up at the dinner and at the engagement party, she was stunning, but this is how I know Mia.

No makeup. Hair a mess. Simple. But effortless. Breathtaking.

Mia grabs her tube and pulls it up onto the sand, tossing her hat next to it before she heads for the tree with the rope attached. She stands near the trunk, assessing the tree she's about to climb like a twelve-year-old and swing off of a rope.

"You coming?" she asks before she reaches her hands up to a

branch and practically does a pull up to swing her legs up with her.

"I'll wait down here in case you need saving."

Mia can't help letting out a hearty laugh as she stands up in the tree gripping the rope with both of her hands.

"I'm a better swimmer than you are, pal."

And with that she lunges herself off of the tree and the rope takes her small body flying across the water. She's screaming with happy laughter as she lets go and falls into the cold spring beneath her. I gently push myself into the direction where she lands only for her to pop up behind me, lifting herself up on my shoulders with her hands in a feeble attempt to dunk me under the water.

"Oh, please don't tell me you thought that would work." I turn around grabbing her and wrapping her in a bear hug as I stand there. I can tell it's a little too deep here for her to comfortably reach the bottom so I walk us over to a more reasonable spot before letting her go.

"Worth a shot," she whispers.

She's kneeling in the water, making it so that her chin is just at surface level and I'm standing next to her just taking it all in, looking around.

"I'll be right back," I say, grinning down at her as I make my own attempt at climbing this tree and swinging from the rope.

"Off I go!" My body swings and the rush that I feel as I jump into a river like a child is freeing. I shout before letting go and splash into the water. When I reach the surface, Mia is further into the water treading as I swim up to her.

My hand instinctively reaches out for hers and I pull her closer to me.

"It's too deep for you here, Mi." My fingers grip her hips, holding her in place, but not against my body even though every part of me wants to feel her legs wrapped around me.

A bit of water gets in her mouth as her chin dips and I watch her tongue part her lips, spitting it out. A piece of hair falls closer to her face and I take it between my fingers, briefly feeling the coarse strands as they're soaked in water and tuck it behind her ear. My eyes don't move from her lips the entire time.

Because for the first time in years, I really want to fucking kiss her.

CHAPTER TWELVE
MIA

Nate's eyes are focused like lasers right now. Except they aren't staring directly into mine, he's solely focused on my lips as they shiver in this cold spring. The idea to come floating down this river was something I saw in an online forum for relaxing things to do. Hats off to whoever suggested it because it's definitely served its purpose.

"Come on." Nate leans in, gently grazing his fingers against my hips as he whispers against the rim of my ear. "Let's get you back in your tube so we can finish." Apparently this spring has a bunch of different avenues, and eventually could lead you out into the Gulf, but as long as we keep making right turns, we'll end up right back where we started.

There's been a serene feeling all afternoon today. I've seen it on Nate's face too. A few times I've watched him close his eyes and let out slow breaths, something I've noticed he does while trying to calm his mind.

"I needed this," he says, pulling me into a hug before I get in my car. "It's something I'd never do on my own. And we survived the snakes, so win-win." His chest rumbles in a deep laugh against my ear before we go our separate ways.

THE END ZONE

If I cry one more time before ten in the morning, I might lose it.

The other day I stopped by my dad's to pick up some things that he said were mine or my sister's. Alongside the box with all of our belongings was an open folder sitting on the counter. Normally, I wouldn't invade his privacy, but the paper had the words past due written in giant red letters, so it caught my attention. Water bill, past due. Electric bill, past due. Rent, short almost six hundred dollars.

Growing up, I was the one making sure things were taken care of so Hannah didn't have to worry about having a roof over our heads or food on the table. My dad worked, but spent so much of his money elsewhere, I had to make sure we had something to fall back on.

Looking at all of this stuff scattered across my counter just takes me back to being that scared teenager who had to become the adult when she definitely wasn't ready, but had no other choice.

I've been trying to figure out how I can help him. Even though he didn't ask, I can't just sit back and let him become homeless because he didn't pay his rent. The majority of the things in that box were actually Hannah's and I have no idea if she wants any of it, but I'll offer it.

"Morning," Nate answers my call on the first ring.

"Do you want to come with me to my sister's to drop off some of her things I found when I was cleaning my dad's apartment?" No hello or good morning. Just straight to the point today.

Nate and Hannah don't get along. They never have. He consistently refers to her as Satan's spawn. Hannah and I are nothing alike. I'm friendly, warm… she's cold and distant.

"Do I want to go into the Devil's den? Let me think…"

"Ugh, please. If you come with me, it'll be quick. You two

can't stand each other so she'll want you out of her house as quickly as possible."

"As long as we're out before she can put a curse on me," he agrees. We're going to be leaving for our road trip in a couple of days, so I just want to get this done before that.

"Thank you."

"Let me shower, I'll be right over," he says.

"So, when did you grab this stuff?" Nate calls from the kitchen as he peeks his head inside the box. I'm still in my bedroom grabbing my purse, but I can see Nate notices the papers covering my counter top. Once I do come out of my room, Nate's eyes go wide immediately. I didn't exactly try to hide the fact that I spent the previous hour crying, it would've done no good.

He's at my side before I've taken more than two steps. "Why are you crying? What happened? What is all of this?"

"I'm fine. It's just a bunch of shit I found at my dad's. When he called me the other day, he said I could go look through some things and take whatever I wanted that may have been mine or Hannah's…" My voice cracks. "He owes so much money, Nate. He's behind in taxes, bills, everything… I'm sure he didn't mean for me to find this, but how am I supposed to ignore it now that I've seen it? He apparently has a job… so where is all of his money going?" The question is rhetorical because I know the answer, but I fucking hate it. I reach for the papers on the counter and gather them into a pile to place in a manila folder and then shove it in the drawer.

"How can I help?" He looks at me, pleading.

I exhale a deep breath. "You can drive me to Hannah's so I can give her this box, but please don't mention any of this to her. I don't need her to have more of a reason to hate him."

My fist bangs on the door of my sister's apartment, hard and repeatedly, until I hear her yell from the other side that she's coming. I didn't tell her I was stopping by; she probably would've ignored my call anyway.

"What are you doing here? And why is he here?" Hannah asks as she opens the door. Her hand gestures up to Nate standing beside me like a vicious guard dog. Her fingers grip the corner of the door like she's hesitant to open it all the way.

"Always a pleasure to see you too, Hannah," Nate says with an overly exaggerated smile that makes him look like an absolute sociopath.

Hannah and I could pass for twins. She's two years younger than me, but all of our dark features are the same. Her brown hair hangs over one shoulder as it's spilling out of a ponytail. She looks like she hasn't slept in weeks. Not sure what could be keeping her awake at night though, it's not like she has a thousand things she's worrying about constantly. I made sure of that. Hannah has never had to worry about a thing.

"These things were at dad's, I thought you should have them," I say, passing the box off to her and trying to muster up a smile as a peace offering.

"Did he die?" she asks coldly, her hair falling into her face as she leans forward, peeking into the box.

"What? Of course not. I was at his apartment… These things are yours. God, Hannah what the hell?"

Nate and I are still standing in her doorway like we're unwanted salespeople. Hannah doesn't have the common decency to invite us in, but it's probably better this way. Just drop the things off and leave.

I've had a hard time accepting the way my relationship is with my sister. I've tried, against my better judgment, to accommodate her, to go out of my way to be there for her and do things for her, but it's never enough. She barely talks to me when we are in the same room. Her snarky comments and uninterested attitude make it hard to even be around her lately. I wish we were closer. When we were younger, she was at my side for everything. And one day, that just stopped.

"Oh. Okay." She turns to shut the door, but Nate's hand stops her.

"You can thank your sister for coming all the way over here to drop this stuff off to you. She could have tossed it all in the fucking trash. I know I would have." Even when Nate has his own battles he's facing, he's never shied away from helping me with mine—even if they are incredibly less important than his.

Hannah rolls her eyes at Nate. "I probably will," she says, swinging the door closed.

I'm completely shocked as I stand there in her doorway. The lock clicks after she closes the door in my face, and I'm dumbfounded by her reaction and that whole interaction. She's so goddamn enraging and downright embarrassing. My jaw hangs as I look up at Nate shaking his head.

"You okay?" Nate questions as we walk back to his truck. "I hate that she fucking talks to you like that. Just know if she was a guy, I would've knocked her teeth in."

A small laugh roars in my chest and I get in the passenger seat of Nate's truck.

"I think it's time I just really start taking Hannah for who she is and accepting it. I have to stop hoping that she's going to change and just accept that she hates me. The worst part is, I don't even know why." I stare out of the window as we drive back towards downtown.

"It's her fucking loss, Mi. You know that, right? It's her loss. Just like your mom. It's their loss. Anyone who doesn't see what a treasure you are has no right being a part of your life." Nate reaches over the center console and squeezes my hand before whipping the truck around and my right hand instinctively braces the door.

"Where are we going?" The sleeve of my old NWU sweater

is covered in snot and I look like hell, so a public outing really isn't something I want at the moment.

"You need a milkshake." He looks over and smiles at me, still squeezing my hand and for a moment, I just feel... relief.

———

I've had this fair idea planned all week. Something fun, lighthearted, an outing that I know will bring a smile to Nate's face, so I'm not going to let my current situation in my personal life deter us from having fun tonight.

"The state fair? Fuck, I love you, Smalls." Nate pumps his fist as I hand him the wrist band for our outing tonight. I lucked out that the fair is in town this week, and I know how much of a kid Nate feels like when he gets to ride those rinky-dink carnival rides and eat elephant ears for dinner.

"Bumper cars first. Come on, come on!" he shouts as we're walking up to the gate to get in.

"Okay, my little legs are going as fast as they can." I jog up beside him and he grabs my hand, pulling me up to him. I swear I'm looking at a seven-year-old in a twenty-seven-year old man's body right now.

The happiness burning off Nate tonight is hard to ignore. He's having fun, he's cracking jokes, he's talking to me about everything and anything. It feels so good seeing him like this. I'm no magician, I know this isn't the fix to all of his problems. But between the river and this, it's a start. It's a place where he doesn't have to be 'on,' he doesn't have people commenting on everything he's doing. No one is sitting there with a stats sheet telling him he went left when he should have gone right. I think the road trip is also going to help him a lot too. Being back with his family will bring a sense of comfort to him that I think he's been missing for a while.

"Can we get on the Ferris wheel now? I've asked you thrice."

Nate stands in front of me, towering me. His blue eyes shining in the carnival lights all around us.

"I'm not a heights person, you know that. They freak me out."

He pulls both of my hands into his. "Mia, if you think I'd ever let anything happen to you, then you must not know me at all. Come on, please." He squeezes my hands and I cave to the sincerity of his words as he leads me to the line.

"I think I'm going to pass out. Vomit first, then pass out." I'm gripping Nate's arm like my life depends on it, and frankly, right now in my mind it does.

"Open your eyes, Mi." His voice is softer, strong and low, but soft.

I've felt us slowly rising for the last couple of minutes and had to close my eyes as we got higher. I can feel a breeze on my face, even though part of it is practically buried in his chest. I might as well be sitting on his lap at this point with how much I'm clinging to him. The mossy green shirt he's wearing has a small spot of powdered sugar from the elephant ear and it makes him smell sweeter than he normally does.

"Open em', Smalls."

I take a small breath in and out before opening my eyes. We've come to a stop and we're just at the top. The wind is blowing my hair back and I look around at the sights below. Lights, the water nearby, the smell of cotton candy and popcorn somehow drifting all the way up here.

And then I look over at Nate, but he's not staring at all the wonder around us. He's staring down at me. His blue eyes take on a more navy tone as his chest pumps up and down against me. These little boxes we're sitting in aren't made for people that are six feet tall, so we're sitting awfully close and touching longer than normal. His stare right now feels different– it feels… real. Too real.

"This view really is beautiful," I say quietly as I look up at him and then back to my surroundings.

His throat clears and I can feel the heat coming from his body as we sit next to one another, thighs tight against each other, his arm draped around my shoulder holding me close to his side.

"Stunning," he answers.

I get caught on the word he uses, slowly sending my gaze back up to him. I can hear people down below chatting and their laughter, the sounds of the rides nearby, but the loudest thing I hear is the pounding of my heart in my ears. Nate's stare is intense, it's consuming, I barely know how to handle it.

Within a moment, the Ferris wheel begins to move again. Except this time, I don't close my eyes.

CHAPTER THIRTEEN

MIA

"So you offered to drive across the country with him? Are you sure that you want to do that?" Summer has officially moved to Tampa and is now part of Saturday morning brunch with Abby and I. Normally, we're at Marker's Café or somewhere else downtown, but since I still have a shit ton of packing to do, I offered to have them over at my place.

"He wants to spend some time at home and asked me to come with him. It'll be good for him to have time back up there. Everything is a slower pace there for him, he needs it. I only offered the road trip because airports are stressful and driving would be more relaxing for him." I grab the waffle from the toaster, tossing it on a plate quickly. Summer reaches for the peanut butter and lathers up her waffle in that before adding honey and cinnamon to the top.

"How is he doing? When did all of this start? I feel so bad for our sweet baby Nate. I honestly wanted to just hug him the second I saw him go down." Summer's face turns into a frown as she takes a bite.

"He's going to be okay. Making the decision to step away

was hard, but needed. He'll be okay." *He'll be okay*, I repeat in my mind.

"Well, are you sure that going on a road trip—just the two of you—is a good idea?"

"Why wouldn't it be? Nate and I are together all the time as it is. That won't be new." I shrug off Summer's concern.

"You're okay with sharing a bed with Nate? What happens if things start to… tingle?"

"Excuse me, who said anything about sharing a bed?"

"Knock, knock!" Abby taps on the door and walks in. She's carrying a binder in her hands, which I can only assume holds countless ideas for her wedding that she wants to go over.

"For you." I gesture to the coffee as Abby comes and greets me.

"You're a gem." She winks at me and takes a seat at the bar, next to Summer.

"Back to our conversation. Mia was just sharing how she and Nate will be taking a romantic road trip across the scenic Midwest."

"Oh my God, I most definitely did not use half of those words," I say with an annoyed laugh.

Summer's hand waves in front of me as I'm standing on the opposite side of this kitchen counter feeling like I have both of their prying eyes on me.

"Is he doing okay? Ford said he hasn't heard from him. I figured he wanted some space from everyone. Well, except you obviously." Abby brings the coffee cup to her lips and takes a sip.

"He'll be okay." I may as well record myself saying that just so I can replay it anytime someone asks.

"But what I actually said earlier was, Nate's parents invited me to their 30th wedding anniversary weekend. They're having a party and staying in cabins. Nate asked me to go with him and then I offered the road trip. You know how I love road trips, and I just figured it would be something good for him. Honestly, road trips can help reduce stress, and I've read that they can help restore your mind-body connection. He needs this." I don't go into too much detail, but they're all aware that he's been struggling.

"I've heard that too. I mean, I get it. But are you going as his plus one or they personally asked you? How is it going to work in hotels? You know he won't let you stay in a room by yourself in a strange town off the interstate. He's wildly protective of you. Remember in Hawaii, he literally wouldn't let you take a separate Uber than him when we were going five minutes to a bar." Abby makes a good point. I guess I didn't consider that last part about the hotel, but hotels do have rooms with two beds.

"Well… he was just being safe. But anyway, his mom sent me an invite and hotels have rooms with two beds," I shoot back, feeling proud of my rebuttal.

The two of them exchange glances and just nod at one another with knowing smiles.

"Don't do that." My index finger wags in their direction. "Your little smirks and smiles. I know what you're doing."

"I'm all for this. Maybe some forced time alone will help awaken your burning desires." Summer sits back in the chair, confident in her statement.

"There are no burning desires. Nate has a lot going on, that's all this is about. I'm his best friend, this is what I do. I help." Leaning my elbows on the counter, my mind can't help but drift to Laura's comment, and then the Ferris wheel moment.

"You do. You help and you give and you prioritize everyone else all the time. Just sit for five seconds and think of Nate. Is there not the smallest piece of wonder about being more?"

I close my eyes briefly after what Summer says and my memory betrays me as the FaceTime fiasco is the first thing to pop in my mind, causing me to bite my cheek in an attempt to hide a smile.

"What is that look? Are you blushing?" Summer's hand slams on the counter.

"You are. Why? Why are you blushing?" Abby stands from the chair she was in.

"Did something happen? Something happened!" Summer shouts.

"Oh my God." I sigh, realizing how unbelievable this story probably sounds so who knows if they actually will trust me on it. "Nothing happened. He was… we were on FaceTime, he just got out of the shower and Hendrix came barreling in like a wild bull…" I pause, and they both gesture for me to keep going. "Hendrix somehow pulled the towel down and the phone kind of landed…" I trail off, hoping they will see where I'm going with this to save me from speaking the words out loud that I saw Nate's larger than life penis.

"You saw it, didn't you? God, I feel like a high schooler right now, but I'm so fucking giddy." Summer bites her bottom lip as she smiles.

"It was an honest mistake. I don't even know if he knows I saw it."

"Oh, he knows. He knows and he's probably perfectly fine that you saw it. He probably even likes that you saw it. Guys are weird like that." Abby takes a seat and sips on her coffee. "They know what they're packing… they have no shame when it comes to their body. Ford walks around naked a lot of the time." Good grief. A visual I didn't actually need.

"Okay, okay, last thing I'm going to say because I know he's going through it and I don't want to make this road trip about anything other than that…"

"I think that ship has sailed, Sum." I roll my eyes at her.

"It's okay to have feelings for your best friend, Mia. If you think you can't because you shouldn't, then that's not a real reason."

"Jesus, you are starting to sound like Laura now."

"What? When did you talk to Laura?"

A tired sigh flies from my chest. "At the gym the other day. We talked briefly and she made a comment about Nate realizing he has feelings for me and something about her being a placeholder for me."

Summer and Abby both stare at me with widened eyes and parted lips.

"I always knew it," Summer whispers to Abby.

"Listen, I'm not saying it's impossible, okay? I'm just saying it's incredibly unlikely, and most importantly, this week is not the time to try and find out. Nate's vulnerable and there are things he wants to work through. I'm there solely to support him in that." My hands are flailing all about as I talk, hoping to put an end to this conversation.

"Does he know Connor asked you out?"

I shake my head at Abby. "Connor hasn't technically asked me out, he just asked for my number. And who I date has never been something Nate's cared about. So if I do go out with Connor, I don't see him having much to say."

"I bet you're wrong," Abby says as she gets up and grabs her phone as it rings.

"In college, I always kind of kicked myself for not just giving in for one stupid kiss. But thinking about it now, I did the right thing. Nate and I have an incredible friendship and who knows if us kissing back then would have messed it all up? So to set the record straight, is Nate attractive? Of course. But there are no romantic feelings between us. If you need hard proof, just look at the women he's dated. Blonde. Big boobs. Tall. Curves. I'm so far out of that description, you might as well put me on my own island."

"I think that's just it though." Summer's remarks are usually laced with sarcasm and innuendos, something I love about her. But right now, she's being earnest.

THE END ZONE

I turn my head back to Summer as she drags her final piece of waffle through syrup.

"You're in a league all on your own in his mind. You are an island. You're the one person all this time he thought he missed his chance with. All the women he's dated have been polar opposites of you because he knows they aren't what he wants in the end. I know this week isn't about you, I'm not saying you should do anything. I'm just saying, maybe allow yourself to think about it for a change."

My lips press into a line as I nod my head at what Summer had to say.

"Plus, when's the last time you had sex anyway? Maybe you should use him as a visual for your own pleasure. There's nothing wrong with that. If you think he hasn't pictured you while practicing some self-care, you're delusional," Summer shouts the last few words as I'm now walking away into the other room.

I'm internally screaming, but to answer her question, it's been a really, really long time.

I'll admit it, I'm the most annoying person when it comes to time management. I do everything in my life according to a time or a date, some kind of schedule. So, when it's six thirty-five and I told Nate we should leave at six thirty and he still isn't here, I'm annoyed.

> **NATE**
>
> Don't lose your marbles. I had to drop Hendrix off at the doggy daycare. They accommodated me by opening up early so I could still have him home last night. I'm almost there. Send. Fucking send.

I laugh out loud reading the end of his text knowing that it was a voice message.

Okay, toothbrush, hand lotion, makeup and headbands. All my last minute items to throw in my overnight bag. Summer's little add on to the conversation yesterday crosses my mind. I do have something, uh, fun in my nightstand, but I'm too nervous to bring it with me. Chances of me using it are slim and even if I did try, the chances of it working are even less. I've never been able to give myself an orgasm. No matter how many times I've tried. I've even very vividly tried to picture Chace Crawford in his *Gossip Girl* prime… and still nothing. So much for a celebrity crush.

Nate knocks on my door before it swings open and he's holding his hand out to me.

"I even come bearing gifts."

My fucking AirPods.

"Where were these?" I excitedly reach for them and cup them in my hands as if they're gold.

"In my truck, not sure how long they've been there. I'm sure they need to be charged." He smiles and walks over to my suitcase on wheels and pulls up the handle to walk it out.

"I'll be back for that bag." He gestures to the overnight bag I have on the counter.

"Oh, I can carry this one." I wave him off and grab my charger out of the drawer.

"I'll be back for that bag," he repeats, back already turned to me as he's walking out.

In a split second decision, I toss my vibrator into the overnight bag, stuffing it underneath everything else. When Nate walks back in, he cocks an eyebrow at me after my fingers suspiciously pull away from the zipper as soon as he makes his presence known.

"What do you have there, Smalls?" His lips curve into a tiny smirk as he stands there. I walk right past him into my bedroom to grab a sweater and he follows me. His hands grip the top frame of the door as he stands in the doorway and leans forward. His shirt is hugging his biceps and I'm slightly distracted by the way the muscles flex every time he shifts himself.

"I'm all set, are you ready?" I ask.

"Deflecting. Okay. Now I really need to know what's in that bag." I stand in front of him, arms crossed over my chest. Nate's tongue slowly edges out, coating his lips before he pulls away from the door frame allowing me to pass.

"Feminine products," I lie, but also know that will likely make him stop asking.

His head shakes back and forth at me as he grabs the bag from the counter and I turn off the light, lock my front door and follow him out.

CHAPTER FOURTEEN

NATE

"Alright, Clark, what kind of playlist did you make for us?"

Leaving before sunrise wasn't my idea, but it turns out that getting on the road and out of downtown before any traffic was a wise choice.

"We have options. First, singalongs. A musical compilation of songs with two singers so we can each have our moment. I also searched through my old files on my laptop to find the playlist we made before you left to move. Thankfully I found it because it has some serious bangers on there that we love."

"Nice." I nod my head, merging onto the interstate.

"And… I downloaded some podcasts. I know you don't listen to them a lot, but I spent a lot of time researching podcasts for athletes. Specifically, where they openly talk about their struggles or things they've gone through and ways they were able to come out the other side. We don't have to listen to any of them, but I just want you to have the option… if you wanted it." From my peripheral I can see Mia shrug her shoulders to herself.

"Thanks, Mi."

With it being mid-October, I'm expecting Wisconsin to already have a chill in the air once we get there. Even if Mia didn't get her own invite, I still would have wanted her to come with me. Being alone makes everything heavier, harder. And when I'm with Mia, when I'm talking to her, I just feel like she slowly chips away all of the broken pieces.

Coach Aarons' comment about seeing the team therapist is intimidating to say the least. I'm not sure that I want to sit in a room with a stranger and talk about my issues. If I can't tell my family or my closest friends, how could I share it with a complete stranger?

I've seen Dana around the facility a lot. I'm not sure if anyone else on the team sees her, but she's been in team meetings and I've seen her around the building and in passing. Having team therapists is still new in the league, teams only recently started adding them to organizations. I remember the meeting we had when she came on board. The coach let us know that she's available for something as simple as a monthly check-in, all the way to weekly visits if we felt like we needed it.

"If you want to just talk, too. That's always on the table." Mia opens the glovebox and pushes papers to the side as she reaches her arm to the back. When she pulls her arm out, I notice a handful of Starburst.

"Did you stash Starburst in my glovebox?" Unable to keep the laughter in, I let it roll out of my chest.

Her head bobs up and down as she sits there in my passenger's seat wearing her signature leggings and giant sweater. It's one of mine, so it hangs off her body everywhere. I let her borrow them whenever she wants. I think I secretly like that when she ends up giving them back, they smell a little like her.

"I wasn't sure if they were still here." She laughs through her words. "Here."

She unwraps the only pink Starburst and hands it to me.

"Okay, so would you rather have finger-sized nipples or nipple-sized fingers?" We've been driving for almost seven hours already and Mia ended up with the idea to do a ridiculous 'would you rather' question game. Although some of the things she's finding on her phone are hilariously bizarre.

"What the hell? I definitely couldn't have nipple-sized fingers. I use these babies a lot." I say, wiggling them in the air.

"Really, Nate? Mature."

"I meant to catch a football, Smalls. Get your mind out of the gutter."

Mia scrunches her face up as she looks over at me trying to disguise the smirk forcing its way through her lips. Her really fucking full, pouty lips. The only lips I've wanted that I've never actually gotten to taste.

"Penny for your thoughts?" I ask as we're parked after stopping at a quick drive-thru. Mia's been quiet the last couple of hours, on her phone typing away.

"Sorry, I've been emailing Quinn… the realtor for that building." She shakes her head and sets her phone down, taking a French fry and dipping it into the honey mustard.

"Did you sign a lease?"

Her face turns towards the window, glancing out into the sunset up ahead. She doesn't answer my question for a solid thirty seconds before she turns to face me, finally, and lets out a sigh.

"I'm not leasing it. It's not the right time. It's okay."

"What? What do you mean? Why not?"

Mia crumples up the empty French fry container and tosses it into the bag with the rest of the trash.

"I've been trying to help with my dad's things. I can't just ignore everything I saw, Nate. I can't let his water get turned off, or his electricity… he can't become homeless."

Being selfless is one of Mia's best qualities. But it's also one of her weaknesses. She puts everyone else ahead of herself. I can feel my hand clench the steering wheel a little tighter. I'm so... just so fucking frustrated for her. I hate that she's in a situation torn between two things she loves—two things she wants more than anything. A mended father and her dream.

"Mia... None of that is your responsibility. I know you're too good of a person to idly sit by and watch bad things happen, but... did you use all of your savings on this stuff?"

Her eyes come up to mine with water pooling at the rim. The way the sweater is hanging off her shoulder right now, her bun is falling all over the place... she looks like a mess, but my God, she's beautiful. And all I want to do is be able to tell her that.

"To be honest, maybe it's for the best. I mean, I was nervous to do it to begin with and I was terrified of failing. Maybe this is just a sign that it's not the right time. There will be other buildings."

"Why do you think you'd fail?"

"What?" she asks.

"What on Earth gives you the impression that you can't do this? Because the Mia I know can do anything."

"I–I don't know, it's risky. And it's a lot of money to put into something that may or may not work and maybe I'm just not meant to do it right now."

I call bullshit. The way she lit up when I went to see that building with her, she could have set the whole place on fire. She was confident. She was sure. She's nervous, I get it... but if anyone can do it, it's Mia.

"Well, let's start with the fact that you're even brave enough to have this dream to begin with. Do you know how many people don't even dream like this? How many people just give up on things and settle for less even though deep down, they know they want more? Know they deserve more? I know you want to succeed. And I know the thought of not succeeding scares the hell out of you. But you can do this. Sure, it'd be hard work, but if anyone is cut out for the job, it's you. Come on,

Smalls. Have some faith in yourself. You believe in me endlessly. I believe in you the same way."

Her lips begin to tremble as she laughs softly, keeping her eyes on me.

"Before all of this stuff with your dad, did you think you were going to fail then? Was it the money? Let me help you if it's that. Please." We sit silently for a moment and I move my hand to set the truck in drive.

"I'm just scared." It's a whisper, but I hear it. She's picking at her nail polish now; a nervous habit she's had for years.

I calm my tone and bring my voice down. "You know, I once heard a very smart woman say that being afraid of something is all the more reason to face it."

She closes her eyes briefly, before she smiles at me again, it's one that reaches all the way up to those chocolate coated eyes of hers.

The setting sun hits her freckles perfectly as she speaks, "Oh, so you were paying attention?"

"To you? Always."

CHAPTER FIFTEEN
MIA

"Should we stop soon?" My eyes are feeling heavy; I can only imagine Nate's must be burning at this point after so much driving.

"I'm looking for a familiar hotel name. We aren't staying at the Budget Inn."

Nate's hands flex on the steering wheel. The headlights from surrounding cars cast a shadow across his face as we drive. Nate's profile is so sharp, and confident. His square jaw is just slightly tense as he continues to drive. From the outside, you'd never know he's struggling. I guess that's why for so long he was able to hide it from everyone.

Since Nate first shared he's been struggling with his mental health, I've spent every night researching. Even if it was just ways I could help him as a friend. I know he doesn't expect that from me. He'd probably tell me I don't have to do anything, but I can't just sit back, knowing he's hurting, and not try to help. Even if the only kind of help I can provide is simply a listening ear, I want to be that for him.

"Here we go. Franklin Hotels." Nate flips the blinker on after he sees the interstate sign with a familiar hotel name.

"Franklin is always so expensive, Nate. We're just sleeping here."

I know he hears me, but he doesn't reply. We pull off the interstate and into the parking lot of a gorgeous hotel not even five minutes later. Don't get me wrong, this isn't the Ritz, but Franklin Hotels are pretty nice compared to most you'd find off the interstate.

"Come on," he says, grabbing both of our overnight bags from the backseat.

When we walk into the lobby, the smell of popcorn hits me immediately. I don't actually see a popcorn machine though, only raising my suspicions.

"Hi there, welcome to Franklin Hotels," a receptionist greets us as we walk towards the desk. I watch her eyes do a full journey from Nate's feet literally up to the hair on his head. Even after a twelve-hour day of driving, he still turns heads.

The conversation with Summer and Abby sparks in my mind, and before Nate can say anything past hello, I'm butting in.

"Hi, we just need a room with two queen beds please."

Nate doesn't move his body to look at me, but I see his eyes shift in my direction.

"Yeah, one room, two beds please." He hands her his credit card and as I'm reaching in my purse to grab mine, Nate's hand pulls my wrist down to my side, holding it in place. His fingers are firm on my skin. Warm to the touch, slightly rough and calloused, but still so gentle.

Nate and I touch all the time, neither of us are shy in that regard. But his hand holding mine down right now feels somewhat possessive. Just the authority in which he's gripping it. Not too hard, but not loose enough for me to slide out of it. Not that I even want to.

"Wait right here," Nate says once we get into the hotel room. I'm standing by the door, arms crossed over my chest as he places both bags down and walks through the hotel room. He opens the bathroom door and peeks in there, slides the closet door open and does the same. He flips on every light in the room, causing me to bring my arm up to my eyes at the intensity of the lights. He pulls back the comforters on both of the beds, even tries to move the one piece of wall art but that's attached.

"What are you doing?" I ask.

"Just doing a check… I need to make sure this place is safe for you to sleep here, undress here, you know…" He shrugs as he gets on all fours and looks under the beds. I press my lips together to suppress a smile at that because it's something I didn't expect.

"No monsters?" I tease as I take a couple of steps forward.

"No monsters," he confirms as he rises to a standing position again.

"Thank you," I say quietly as I pass him on my way to the bathroom to take a shower and change for the night. I know my abrupt interruption in the lobby caught him off guard. But he doesn't seem fazed by it now as I watch him throw himself on the bed near the window.

By the time I walk out of the bathroom, Nate's already passed out on the bed. Still fully clothed. Poor guy, he's probably beat from driving all day long. I shut off the nightstand light and the lights in the bathroom before climbing into the other bed. When I turn on my side, I'm facing him and something just pulls in my chest. He's not under the covers, his shoes are off, but he's still laying on top of the comforter and I can't help myself as I get up and pull the comforter off my bed and drape it over his body. I tuck the edges in around his body, kind of like my mom used to do for me when I was a little girl.

"G'night, Nate," I whisper before getting back into the other bed and pulling the sheet over myself.

"Morning." He smiles down at me and I pull the sheet over my face.

"Hi," I groan out.

"Want to grab coffee and something to eat before we get back on the road?" Nate's freshly shaved face and bright blue eyes bring me out of the sleepy haze I was in with the thought of coffee and food.

As we walk out of the hotel room, the air here feels crisp. Fall is definitely approaching and it brings a smile to my face. Nate is walking just a few strides in front of me and I notice his hand flex at his side before he reaches for my overnight bag and hauls it into the backseat of the truck.

"Wait in the truck, I'm going to grab us some food and coffee." He closes the door behind me once I get in and I hear the truck beep as he locks it behind him and walks into the restaurant next door to this hotel.

When Nate gets back, he's carrying a tray of coffees—one iced and one hot. Plus, a bag with some food inside. When I take a sip of the iced coffee, I let out a slight moan at the way it tastes. It's exactly how I like it. *Exactly.* A little almond milk, no extra sugar, add caramel. His hand reaches into the bag and he hands me a fruit bowl with a small breakfast sandwich. I smile as he crumples up the bag and tosses it in the backseat.

"Thank you," I say quietly.

———

"Okay, I can't do any more sing-alongs right now, I'm going to lose my voice and I told my parents I'd do a speech," Nate says through laughter.

We just finished our fifth duet, this one was Halsey and The Chainsmokers, "Closer."

"Okay, okay fine." I laugh and pull up my phone, seeing a text from an unknown number. I open it.

THE END ZONE

> **CONNOR**
> Hi Mia, it's Connor. I would love to take you out this weekend if you're free.

My eyes go slightly wide at the unexpected text message from him.

> Hi Connor. I'm actually out of town for the week, but I can let you know when I get back.

> **CONNOR**
> Sounds great, where are you headed?

> Wisconsin.

I leave out the part that I'm taking a week-long trip with my best friend who he happens to be neighbors with.

> **CONNOR**
> America's Dairyland! Have fun!

I try to hold in a giggle at that, but it comes out like a snort, drawing Nate's attention to me.

"What's so funny?" he casually asks.

I don't know why telling Nate that I might go out on a date with Connor feels like some form of a betrayal. I'd hardly call them close friends, but they at least know each other and are kind of friends and that somehow makes it feel that way to me.

Nate's never known any of the guys I've dated–they've all always been so far outside of Nate's realm that it just never mattered to either of us. But Connor's part of his world, in a way, and that just feels different.

"Um, well... Connor Hughes just asked me out."

Nate's smile vanishes and all I see is surprise and confusion in his features.

"When did you give Hughes your phone number?"

"He lives next door to you. The morning I took Hendrix for a walk, I ran into him." I leave out the part where it's technically his dog's fault for making a ruckus outside of Connor's apartment, causing him to open the door to begin with.

"And he just asked for your number? Are you going?" His questions are coming out like rapid fire. It feels like I'm being interrogated and I'm hesitant to answer anything further, but I'm not going to lie to him.

"Yes, Nate. He asked for my number and I gave it to him. I told him I was out of town." I lock my phone and set it down on the seat beside me.

"When we get back, are you going to go?" Nate's third-degree is really confusing. Who I give my number to or date hasn't ever been something of interest to him.

"I don't know, maybe." I shrug. It's not a lie. I did tell Connor I'd let him know when I was back in town, but I never committed to a date. Nate's reaction combined with everything Laura and the girls said before we left is really making me question everything I thought I knew.

The windows are down and the breeze is ripping through the truck as we continue our road trip. We're halfway to Wisconsin already, but we are making a quick detour for a couple of hours to stop somewhere. Before we left, I did some research trying to find at least one thing off the beaten path that Nate and I could do.

The car ride for the last hour has been shaky, at best. Ever since Nate found out that Connor texted me, he's been short. I'm doing my best not to overthink it and to just stay on our plan.

"We have five more miles, and then we turn left, and it'll be up ahead. According to this website, we can't miss it." Nate nods his head and signals to get into the far right lane.

The sign for "Collier Cave National Park" is big, bright, and orange as soon as we get off the interstate. Travel blogs were right about not being able to miss it.

In my research, I found a lot of online articles saying to do things outdoors as a way to help with mental stress. Hence our floating inner tube day. Simply being surrounded by the calming atmosphere of the outdoors can reduce your stress levels and just bring you instant joy. I read that it's almost immediate to your brain. I figured something like this can't hurt, so why not try it? Plus, a chance to hike through a cave, climb some cliffs, see waterfalls or wildlife… It all sounds really beautiful.

"Okay, right up here, I think. There should be an entrance." I sit up straight in the seat, now getting excited about the day we're about to have.

Nate pulls into the parking lot and I kick off my sandals, throwing on my sneakers and grabbing my jacket out of my overnight bag. Nate gets out of the truck and I watch as he pulls the blue shirt over his head with one arm and then opens the back door to grab a fresh one out of his bag. His hands rifle through some of the clothes on the top before he pulls out a black shirt and pulls it over his body.

We stop at the information center first and grab a map so we know where we're going. Even though it seems like there's a pretty clear trail, I'm not taking any chances.

The trees around us are losing their leaves due to the changing season, but I still love the way it looks out here. The ground is covered in leaves, but there's still a very clear outline of the trail we're supposed to be on. As we walk, I can see a giant rock up ahead and it looks like this is probably where the entrance to the cave is.

"Okay, I'm pretty sure that's the cave. But we'll follow this map. I'm not confident enough in our memory and don't want to get lost just marking trees or something crazy."

Nate scoffs at me with a sarcastic smirk. "Men have navigated ships in the night with nothing more than the sky, I think we'll be fine in a small state park." I just roll my eyes at him and

I take a pen out of my small backpack and make notes and circles on it.

It's beautiful here, the way the trees hang over the opening of the cave, just enough to give it an almost fairytale look. Nate's walking slightly in front of me and turns back every few seconds, making sure I'm still behind him. As the path narrows a bit, I move myself a little closer to him. The moment we enter the cave and look up, I'm completely mesmerized. It's like a scene from a movie, and I can barely believe this place is real.

Everything echoes in here as we slowly walk through. There's a small waterfall where we can hear the water gushing from one side. Our steps stay in sync as we both look around in complete amazement.

"Wow," Nate breathes out, looking down at me with a smile. "Fucking incredible," he says. His words echo and I nudge his shoulder, tilting my head behind us where there's a family with kids just a few feet away.

"Kids are going to learn it some time," he whispers down into my ear.

My teeth bite into my bottom lip to stop a smile, but it's no use. We walk down the path through this cave, marveling at every intricate detail that the Earth has created down here. Each ridge and groove of the rocks look like they've been perfectly carved out to fit in the spot they're in. It's a good thing neither of us are claustrophobic because this would easily send someone into a panic if they were.

Once we walk all the way through the cave, we get to a large opening near another running waterfall. I look up, letting some of the warmth from the sun hit my face after being in a cold cave for the last thirty minutes.

There are a few trails that seemingly go off in different directions, so Nate and I take the less crowded route and begin walking.

"Can I ask you something?"

"Of course," he answers without hesitation.

"If you weren't playing football, if you weren't insanely talented and had to do something else, what do you think it'd be?"

"To be honest, I've never really given it much thought. I... I took bullshit classes in college just to get by. I always saw myself playing football. I guess I never really had a plan B, which hindsight now was pretty fucking dumb." Each stride Nate and I take is in fluid motion.

"What would you be doing if you weren't a personal trainer?" His voice is slightly hoarse.

There are black stones only slightly submerged in the water of a stream up ahead. I noticed them from a few yards back, and once I'm close enough, I step on one and then another, going in a circle as if I'm a child learning how to balance for the first time.

"I don't know specifically, but I know I'd be helping people somehow. Maybe doing social work? A non-profit? Something where I'd make a difference." I see Nate has stopped near the edge, just watching me. Probably waiting to see if he'll need to perform a water rescue.

"You'd be a chef. Or, you'd be doing something like that, too. Helping people," I add.

"I don't know, Mi." Nate's hands land in the pockets of his shorts as he paces a few steps back and forth.

"I do. You've got a bigger heart than you let people see. You're more considerate and caring than you lead on. I know the optics of being a professional athlete means you need to be tough and manly, but you can be those things and also show that you're soft and gentle. Plus, I wouldn't be able to be best friends with someone who didn't also find the wonder of a night sky magical. You're a helper, Nate. Even if you don't think you are. You've helped me a lot more than you probably realize."

"Yeah, well, you're a hell of a lot better at it than I am." His hand reaches out to mine as I stand there and I take it before stepping off the rock.

"That's debatable." I smile up at him from the ground once I've taken a seat to get a break. Nate grins down at me and I swear, a genuine smile from Nate Campbell is one of the most beautiful sights.

CHAPTER SIXTEEN

MIA

"Are you getting tired yet? Little legs about to give out?" he teases as I trail behind him on this walk. The air is cold and the sun is shining and everything just feels so comforting out here, so peaceful and serene. I really hope Nate feels the same, this whole thing was to keep up with my initiative to help him relax and reset.

"I'm doing just fine back here," I pant out. A lie I know he quickly catches on to when he stops abruptly in front of me.

"You've got dirt on your face, Smalls." He laughs, reaching his hand up to my cheek and swiping it away. Ugh, that's embarrassing. How the hell did that even get there?

"Tell me what's going on with your dad." Nate's words don't come off sharp in his request, he's sincere.

"I've been going back and forth in emails since yesterday. I gave his landlord the rest of last month's rent, plus some to help cover this month. His electric company said they'd work with me on a payment plan, so at least that's good. I paid his last three water bills though. I still have no clue what's going on with his taxes." I shrug as we stand there between tall trees towering over us.

Nate reaches for his bag, grabbing his water bottle and takes a sip. I notice the way his forearm grips the bottle; the way it squeezes so the water can shoot directly into his mouth from the nozzle. His throat moves up and down as he swallows with his head tilted back, mouth wide open and I suddenly feel the urge to jump into that cold lake a few yards ahead.

He sighs. "I wish you would've let me help you."

"I just... I don't like the idea of owing you anything. I'm independent. I have always gotten by on my own dollar, and I just can't ask you for money."

"I'm offering, you're not asking. If anything, I'm forcing my money into your hands." His voice is patient, it's calm, tranquil even.

"I know and I love you for it, but I can't take it."

He grunts in frustration. "You're infuriatingly stubborn, you know that, right?"

I begin to walk again. "I'm independent. And independence is something that a lot of people would find wildly attractive, you know," I joke.

"I'm sure there are plenty of things people find wildly attractive about you," he answers with a quiet emphasis, leaving silence between us for the next half-mile.

This entire trail is roughly five miles if we were to go all the way to the end and then back to the beginning, but we've taken a few detours and have stopped quite a bit taking a look at our surroundings. Nate's stayed silent for the most part, something I feel like he probably needs. Allowing himself to just get caught up in the calming atmosphere around us was kind of my goal for the afternoon.

The quiet, peaceful walk ends once I hear a scream in front of me. "Oh my God! Holy shit!" Nate yells from just a few feet ahead of me. His large body jumps in the air and nearly falls backwards as he regains his balance and runs off to the side of the trail.

"What?" I ask, confused by his sudden outburst.

"A snake. I almost stepped on a goddamn snake!" He rushes off even further into the trees.

Biting my cheek, I'm trying to hide the laugh that wants to erupt from my chest. Seeing this tough, manly guy leap into the air and squeal like a little girl is something I didn't know I needed to witness, but that really made my day. I inch myself closer to where Nate was walking ahead of me to see if I can see the snake he was referring to, but nothing is there.

"It's more afraid of you than you are of it."

"I highly doubt that." He slowly walks back to the trail, cautiously looking all around him.

"So, you can handle an alligator on a golf course, but a snake in the woods is where you draw the line?"

"Actually yes, that's exactly it." He playfully pulls the strap on my backpack, nearly pulling me down, but I fall right into his side. His arms cradle my own and I glance up at him before I pull myself back up to a standing position.

We share a brief moment of eye contact before the air feels too thick.

"Any idea what you're going to say for the speech for your parents?"

"Aside from congratulations, no." A trace of laughter in his voice.

"Look at you, two speeches within a month." Teasing, I run up ahead of him and out into the open field ahead. The sun shines bright out here in the open. There aren't any trees standing among the flowers, and although it's not as green as it would be in the spring or summer, it's still a beautiful sight. Something about a field like this just makes me want to take off running like I'm eight-years-old.

Nate's watching me as he walks towards me, hands clasped on the straps at his shoulders. The way his muscles ripple under his shirt is sending my heart into palpitations as he saunters closer to me. I've looked at Nate for years as just a friend, but lately when our eyes meet, I'm seeing so much more. So much possibility. And it's confusing.

"This suits you." Nate's husky voice carries across the distance to me as he approaches. "The whole outdoors, nature, open spaces thing." He raises his hand and waves it out in front of us.

"I think it suits you, too. The calm… quiet. You need to be able to escape to places like this when you aren't on the field. Your soul needs it."

"Being out here with you is definitely something I needed. Thanks for this, Smalls." Nate pulls me into him without hesitation. Like it's the most natural thing in the world to hold me like this, and I guess, realistically, it is natural for us. We've never shied away from physical touch, but it's never felt intimate until recently. I let my head rest on his chest, inhaling his cedar scent mixed with the fresh air blowing through. His arms only tighten the longer we stand there together and it's such a moment of safety for me, a moment of sincerity, things I've felt with Nate for a long time, but never allowed myself to feel them on a deeper level.

"Let me see the map that you raved about." Nate reaches his hand out to me once he lets me go. We got a little turned around with all of the detours we took.

"Oh, Mr. 'Ships in the Night' needs to see the map? You can't just stick your finger in the air and tell me where to go based on the wind?"

A grunt leaves his chest as he turns away from me and I smile to myself, placing my backpack on the ground beside me.

"Let me see the map, Mia." Nate's commanding voice brings my attention back up to him as he's taking slow steps in my direction. My hands slowly fold the map as I take a stuttered step backwards.

"This attitude lately." He stands in front of me, blue eyes working their way all over me.

"I don't have an attitude." There's an eager affection radiating off of him as he reaches his hand up to my face, running his thumb just barely over the skin on my cheek. I can feel the goosebumps rising on my neck, and it's in no way because of the cold.

He opens his mouth, but before he speaks, a loud rustling distracts both of us. A flock of birds in the tree near us flee from the branch, disrupting whatever was happening or about to happen between us.

He clears his throat, backing away and dropping his hand as he grabs my bag from the ground.

"Come on, let's make our way back."

My body stands still for the briefest moment. There's a dull ache between my thighs and in my chest as I watch him walk away.

CHAPTER SEVENTEEN

NATE

I've seen a lot of beautiful things in my life—different places, spectacular views. But nothing beats the way Mia looks today, and I almost just kissed her because of it. Well, her beauty among a thousand other fucking things that have come screaming back to me in the last couple of weeks.

It's obvious she didn't want me to know about Connor asking her out. The way she tensed up, barely made eye contact with me and her words were unsure. I have no right to tell her not to go on a date with him, but every fiber inside of me wants to tell her—no, plead with her—not to go.

"Would you look at that? We made it back using the map." Mia's hand sits firmly on her hip as we stand at the entrance to this park again. Today's been a good day. I feel good, I feel relaxed. Hell, I've enjoyed every part of it. Mia started off today by saying how research shows that nature and being outdoors can help relieve or reduce stress and I believe her, but it's not lost on me that doing this with anyone else wouldn't have been as perfect as it was with her.

"Well, it's basically one big circle."

She swats her hand at me, and I let it go this time. Her

fingers graze my stomach and it sends a throb just below the belt. A throb I didn't realize I'd be experiencing again from the touch of my best friend, but here we fucking are.

"Come here." Mia takes her phone and holds it out in front of us for a picture in front of the sign that says Collier Cave National Park. "Say cheese," she says. And just before she hits the button, my face turns to her as I smile.

I told my coach I likely wouldn't be in contact with anyone from the team during my leave of absence, but I don't count my close friends as a part of the team because right now, I just feel like I need them to talk me off a ledge so I don't just lean over the center console of this truck and kiss Mia.

> Connor asked Mia out.

LIAM

And I have a feeling you don't like that.

For all of the shit I give Liam, he's the only one who ever really calls me out on my bullshit. I'm sure Chase and Ford think all of it, but they're usually too mature to make endless comments about it. Not Liam though. He'll meddle his way into anything he can.

FORD

How are you doing?

> I'll be alright. We're in Kentucky, Mia's in the bathroom changing, and then we're going to get a hotel for the night.

CHASE

You know Connor's a good guy; he'd be good for her.

LIAM

Not better than our boy.

CHASE

I didn't know 'our boy' was in the running for Mia's affection. What happened to just friends?

LIAM

A man and a woman can't be just friends, I've said this hundreds of times. If he finds her attractive, deep down he wants to sleep with her, that's just science.

FORD

I don't understand the logic, but based on Liam's analysis, I hope you all find my fiancée hideous because you'll end up six feet under if you ever make a move on her.

LIAM

Relax. No one is after little Hunt.

Mia and I have been friends for years, men and women can definitely be just friends.

CHASE

They can, just not when they look at each other the way you two do.

My hand runs down my face as I see Mia walking back to the truck. My jacket wrapped around her body, bright red leggings and black and white sneakers. Her hair is twisted into some kind of bun on the top of her head. Fuck. Why'd I bury this for so long? Why'd I convince myself that I wanted anyone else?

Because she needed a best friend, jackass.

The thought hits me in the face in the same way that the wind does as she opens the door and the wind takes it flying, almost pulling her little body with it.

"Sweet Jesus!" she yells with a laugh as she hops in and pulls the door closed. "We're leaving just in time."

"Yeah, looks like it." I glance at the last text from Liam before I shift the truck into reverse to pull out.

LIAM

> Call if you need anything. We're all thinking of
> you and want you back when you're ready.
> And about Connor... Yeah, he's a good guy,
> but you have history on your side. You need to
> prove you can be more than just friends
> without actually losing the friendship part. Now
> go get her.

It feels like I'm drowning in feelings for her and I have no idea where she stands. I'd have to assume she stands firmly in the friend zone. Where she placed me years ago and I happily took up residence. Can she just fucking evict me now, though?

"Did you see that car back there with a thousand bumper stickers? I've always wondered why people want to put a bunch of bumper stickers on their car."

Instead of stopping for the night immediately, we take an extra few hours to drive since there isn't a lot of traffic.

"The aggressive ones are always my favorite," I answer.

"One of them simply just said 'go around me.'" Mia blurts out a laugh.

The sound of Goo Goo Dolls hums through the speakers in my truck as we drive a little further for the night. I can see Mia out of the corner of my eye nodding off every so often though. There's a buzzing in my door handle where I placed my phone and I see my agent's name flashing on the screen as an incoming call. When I glance at Mia, her eyes are completely closed so I grab my phone and answer it.

"Hey, Phil." I've had the same agent since I entered the league. He's been good to me, gets me deals I need and sponsorships. He called me after I decided to take a break and told me that he already spoke with my brand partners and they all shared messages of support, which I appreciate.

"I finalized everything you emailed me. That realtor was a real chatterbox, Campbell. Had a lot to say about you. Did you sleep with her or something?" A hearty laugh rumbles in my throat.

"No, I definitely didn't. She's just a big football fan."

"Alright, well hey take care of yourself. Keep in touch. Take the time you need. Make a statement when you come back, don't worry about it now. I'll talk to Bex." Bex is my publicist. She's emailed me twice asking if I plan on making a comment on my departure, and I do plan on it, but I want whatever I say to hold value, to have meaning… not just that I'm stepping away to fix myself.

"Thanks, Phil."

Once I place my phone down, I take the next exit to a hotel for the night. We only have a few more hours until we're in Wisconsin, but it'll have to wait until morning. I'm barely hanging on and Mia's already out. We'll both be better off getting at least a few hours of sleep in a bed tonight.

"I've been added to a group chat with your sisters," Mia tells me this morning as we get back into the truck, about to make the last few hours until we're at the cabins. "Bree said that they're taking me to some bar tonight."

Gretchen and Bree just turned twenty-one, so they're in the phase of life where they want to go out all the time. Well, Bree mostly. Gretchen tags along.

"Oh, what bar?"

"They didn't say, but they did say there is karaoke." Her eyebrows wiggle in my direction and I turn off the GPS since I know where we're at.

"I'll chaperone, but I'm not singing karaoke, thank you." I smile.

"We don't need a chaperone," she bites back, a little edge in her voice. Something that I'm actually beginning to love. She's been showing a little more attitude lately and while I love my sweet and innocent Mia... this little side of her is such a fucking turn on.

"I think you do."

She rolls her eyes as she sends my sisters back a voice memo, in which she refers to me as a buzzkill.

Shortly after, we pull up to where we're staying. I get all of our things out of the truck and my sisters run up, hugging Mia and then me. I see my dad walk out of the cabin with my mom trailing right on his heels, and they both come over, giving us a hug.

"How are you?" my mom asks as she pulls me into a hug. She stands there gripping my waist for longer than necessary, but this is what moms do.

"I'll be alright, Mom. Spending the week here should be good for me." I smile at her and shake my dad's hand.

"Well, your cabin is just down there." My mom points out. "It's the last one at the end, right next to where your sisters are staying."

In a couple days, my parents are having a big party where a lot of family and friends will be coming and staying in some of the small cabins on the other end, but they rented out these few for just us. I grab the rest of our things and walk us down the trail, taking in this gorgeous view. I love Florida and the beaches, but there's something special about the Midwest. You experience all of the seasons, things just feel different here.

"Here, your mom handed me the key." Mia hands me a single key attached to an old keychain, it looks like one from an old motel. Our cabin looks right out over the lake, in the back there's a fire pit and chairs, a patio with a hammock on it, and a hiking trail is supposed to be nearby, too. I walk around the whole cabin, doing my usual quick check as Mia meanders around the kitchen.

"So, uh, everything is good, except one thing..."

"What's the matter?" She comes walking towards the bedroom as I stand there in the doorframe.

"There's only one bed."

For me, it's not the end of the world. But Mia very clearly asked for a room with two beds when we were at the hotels and I have a feeling she isn't going to go for this.

"I'll run over to my parents and see if we can get a different cabin. Maybe something with two bedrooms, or I'll just get my own cabin. We'll figure it out." I'm already moving through the room when Mia stops me.

"No, it's... fine. It'll be fine. There's a couch I can sleep on right here."

She points down and I turn to walk out again, she's not fucking sleeping on a couch.

"Nate, I said it's fine," she demands.

"Mia, you aren't sleeping on a couch."

"Well you aren't either. So, it's fine. We can share a bed—we've done it once before. I don't bite." She laughs.

But will you?

Fuck, Nate. *No.*

With the way my body has been reacting to her lately, I really fucking hope I can hold myself together sharing a bed with her.

"Oh, unrelated, but tomorrow if you want to have a day to yourself—you should. Bree and Gretchen want to take me shopping. I think it'd be good for you to have some alone time. Or maybe time with your parents." Mia's unpacking a few things since we'll be here all week, there's no point living out of a suitcase when a perfectly good closet and dresser are right here.

"Yeah, maybe," I reply, watching her drift from one end of the room to the other.

———

"Don't go all dad mode, you're supposed to be our fun brother," Bree warns as I walk behind the three of them heading into this middle-of-nowhere country bar.

Mia borrowed a pair of my sister's cowgirl boots and now, the image of Mia in cowgirl boots is tainted because they're technically my sisters, but fuck, if Mia doesn't look damn good tonight. She's wearing cut-off shorts with a red and black flannel wrapped around her waist and a black tank top and then the boots… I had to look away when I saw her walk out of the room, it was too much. It was almost as jaw dropping as seeing her in that goddamn dress at the engagement party, or the dinner, or on the Ferris wheel… or any other time, as of lately.

She's completely oblivious as to how stunning she is. I've always thought Mia is beautiful, but with recent developments… I'm wanting her in a way that I haven't let myself in years.

"I *am* the fun brother, but I'm also responsible for you tonight and I'd rather not ruin mom and dad's weekend by telling them you did something stupid."

Bree is really the one to watch, Gretchen will likely sit at this table with me all night sneaking in pages of whatever book she's reading.

Mia brings me water and she walks up with a Shirley temple.

"You can drink tonight, you know. I'm driving. Go nuts."

"I'll have one soon, but Shirley was calling my name first." Mia smiles and I watch as she moves around the dance floor with Bree and some other girls.

"Mom and dad love her, you know." Gretchen's voice pulls my attention away from the dance floor and over to her.

"Yeah? Is that why they gave us a cabin with one bedroom? Trying to force us together?" My eyebrows crease, and Gretchen just shrugs.

"How are you? I know it's probably pointless to ask this, but we all saw the game."

"I'll be alright, Gretch. Don't worry about me," I say, holding my fist out for a bump.

Taking care of my younger sisters has always been my role. Being their big brother is a job I don't take lightly and I need them to know that regardless of whatever I'm dealing with, being there for them will always be a priority. I don't need them worrying about me.

"I know you like to act tough, Nate. But it's okay to let yourself rest."

"You sound like that one," I say, gesturing my finger to Mia. "I am resting though. This is me resting. Believe me, the last week has been filled with rest and relaxation."

Gretchen tucks a piece of blonde hair behind her ear and pulls out her book, placing it on the table in front of her.

"Also, it wouldn't be the worst thing to settle down, Nate. You're almost thirty… have you considered it at all?"

I sigh. My sister may have just turned twenty-one, but she's already on the fast track to middle-aged. Gretchen wouldn't know a fun, wild night if it was staring her in the face, which coincidentally, it is right now.

"And you just turned twenty-one, why are you sitting here like a bump on a log, hanging out with your brother when you could be doing that?" I ask, pointing to Bree and Mia now on a stage.

Wait, what? Why are they on a stage?

I stand up to see why they're the only two women in this whole bar standing on a stage, only to realize they're actually standing on the bar and some guy just handed them microphones. Are they… singing?

"What the fuck are they doing?" I ask myself, but Gretchen, of course, hears me.

"Tell me again how I should be over there, doing that?"

I roll my eyes at her and toss a napkin on the table as I get up and walk over, close to the two of them.

Music starts and it's a song I recognize. I'd bet one hundred dollars Mia requested this one. I walk a little closer to the bar where there are now too many men staring at my sister and my best friend and my mind is confused as fuck. Mia struts down the bar holding the mic in one hand and a beer bottle in the other while another few girls hop up there too. I'm going to let Mia have her Coyote Ugly moment, but then I am yanking her off of this bar so goddamn fast. Maybe coming out tonight wasn't the best idea. Now that I'm having to face these feelings for Mia, I can't stand the thought of someone else even looking at her.

Mia laughs through lyrics and then whips her hair around, causing her brown strands to fall over one shoulder and she seductively bends down, spreading her legs at the end of the song. Like every other man in this room, I'm completely mesmerized by what she's doing. She blushes as she stands, covering her face with her hand once the song is over and bends down to hand the mic to a bartender behind her before she spots me and waves. Fuck, she looks so happy. Like she just had the time of her life up there for three minutes.

Bree hops off the bar at the other end while I see Mia bending down again to talk to the bartender, her ass would be hanging out of those shorts if not for the flannel around her waist. I'm walking up closer to where she is when I see a hand reach up towards her thigh, nearly touching her. I move towards her and shove my body against his, not enough to cause a scene, but enough so that he knows to back the fuck up.

"Hands. Off," I say, causing him to falter a few steps back. I grab Mia's waist, pulling her down in one quick motion.

"You can't just hop up on bar tops, Mia," I grumble.

"They said we could for the song. You know, it was part of the whole vibe." She shrugs and tries to walk away, but my hand reaches around her waist, holding her in place.

My lips are centimeters from her ear as I tilt my head down

to whisper, "Don't bend over like that on this fucking bar giving everyone down here a show."

"I have this around my waist." She pulls at the flannel.

"I don't care if you were wearing a goddamn tracksuit and wrapped in a Snuggie. Don't bend over like that again."

Mia stares at me for a second, almost tempting me as she leans in just a tiny bit closer. "Is this you being protective or possessive?"

"Both," I growl out beside her ear.

Mia's chest lifts up and down as she pulls back and looks up at me. I watch her lick her lips and at this moment, I want nothing more than to just kiss her. To take what I want and hope like hell it's what she wants too. Something in the way she's staring at me tells me she might let me. But we're interrupted by my sister as she comes up next to Mia and then whisks her away. Mia turns back and glances at me and I just stare at her, watching her move further away as if she's the only damn woman in this bar. And at this point, she might as well be. Mia is all I see.

Walking back to the table, I pinch the bridge of my nose. I need to collect my fucking thoughts before I do something impulsive like kiss my best friend. Because every instinct in my body is telling me to, but I tried this once with her. I thought she wanted it back then too and when I leaned in, she pulled away.

God, the fucking temptation these past few days is killing me, though.

A good night's sleep is needed. I just need to sleep this off right now so I can wake up feeling refreshed, and get the image of my best friend's legs out of my head.

I can feel myself drifting as I lie in bed once we're back at the cabin. Mia passed out in the truck—no surprise there—so I carried her into the bedroom and she's still fast asleep. My mind is racing and my palms are sweating.

One hundred, ninety-nine, ninety-eight...

"Hi, is this Nathaniel Campbell?" *I don't recognize this phone number or the person's voice on the other end, but it's a Wisconsin area code.* "Yes, speaking."

"Hi, this is Doctor Westfield, at Great Lakes Memorial Hospital... you are listed here as the emergency contact for Mia Clark."

"What's the matter? What happened?" *Nothing but sheer panic floods my voice.*

"She was in a car accident. She will be going in for surgery shortly if you would like to come up here. The nurse's station can fill you in and direct you to her room."

"A car accident? When? Is she okay? Surgery for what?" *I can't get my questions out fast enough. I had called her earlier today and she didn't answer, but I figured maybe she was studying. She has that fucking final tomorrow so I decided not to keep bugging her. I figured she'd see my missed call and just call me back when she could.*

"Sir, like I said, you are welcome to come to the hospital. Do you live nearby?"

I lie. "Yes. I'll be there as soon as I can."

I called Coach Aarons immediately after hanging up with the hospital. I tried to calmly explain what was going on, but who the hell knows if I even made sense. All I know is I told him I had a family emergency and needed to fly back home. I have no idea how he still kept me on the team, but I couldn't let Mia wake up in a room with no one.

Between getting to and from the airport and the flight alone, four hours have already passed since I spoke with the doctor. I'm running on no goddamn sleep, but I couldn't care less at the moment. I'm standing at the nurse's desk at Great Lakes Memo-

rial Hospital, begging someone to tell me what's going on with my best friend.

"Ma'am, all I know is that Dr. Westfield called and said Mia Clark was going in for surgery... please, please, tell me where I can find her?" My voice pleads with the woman sitting at this desk. My eyes feel heavy and on top of being sleep deprived, I'm fucking starving, but I'm not doing a single thing before I know Mia is okay.

"Yes, I'm so sorry, she's out of surgery, but she is still asleep. You are welcome to wait in her room, follow me."

I trail closely behind a small red-headed woman as she leads me to a hospital room. A giant lump forms in my throat at the sight of Mia laying in this bed. Her right arm is in a cast. Her perfect satin skin is all scraped and bruised. And what the fuck is going on with her leg? They have it lifted in some goddamn contraption and it's all bandaged, all the way up to her thigh. I move backwards and bump into one of the chairs, trying to maintain my breathing, but I can feel it getting out of control. Fuck, Mia... What happened? My eyes sting and my body feels tense and yet it feels weak at the same time. A nurse walks in and places her hand on my shoulder.

"She will be okay, dear, try to calm down. Can I get you anything?"

I look at her, but I don't think I'm actually even seeing her. My vision becomes blurred and all I'm thinking is how did this happen? I've been gone only a few months and now my best friend is bandaged practically from head to toe, asleep in a hospital bed. I don't answer the nurse, but she comes back in with a cup of water for me and a blanket.

"Have a seat. She should be up soon. Her surgery went well."

I take a few deep breaths, trying to regain my composure and my sense of awareness. The nurse pulls up a chair right beside me and takes my hand in hers and just holds it. She doesn't say *anything, but the presence of someone else right now is calming me down. My eyes focus on Mia. I stare at her lying there, and tears well up in my eyes. She's okay. Or at least she's going to be. This could have gone so differently.*

A knock is at the door and I turn to see a face I recognize, but can't quite pinpoint, standing in the doorway with a bandage on his shoulder, but that looks to be about it.

"Campbell?" the guy asks, and I stare at him with a fucking fire burning inside of me.

"Is she okay?" he asks.

"What the fuck does it look like?" I ask, standing from my seat.

The nurse gets up and excuses herself, but not before saying, "Don't wake her, boys. If you need to talk, step outside of the room."

I follow the nurse out and he turns around to face me in the hallway. Mia's door isn't closed all the way and I don't take my eyes off her, even as I'm standing outside of the room.

"Hey, look I'm sorry..."

"Were you drinking?"

"What? No."

"Were. You. Fucking. Drinking." I have no patience for this piece of shit standing in front of me. I know I recognize him from when I was in college, but fuck if I know his name or even care to ask it. I know Mia well enough to know she wouldn't get in the car with someone who had been drinking, but what if she didn't know? I'll fucking kill him.

"I said no. I lost control on an icy road. Fuck." He stands there staring at me, but the rage I feel is enough to pummel him across this hall and into the next room.

"Leave," I say as I walk past him to go back into Mia's room.

"I want to make sure she's okay," he says, standing his ground.

"What you want is the least of my fucking cares right now. Leave this fucking room, leave the whole goddamn hospital, and if you ever come within a foot of Mia again, I won't show as much restraint as I am right now." The hairs on my arms are standing up and everything inside me wants to knock him on his ass, but before my rage takes over, I hear rustling behind me and I turn to see Mia's eyes fluttering open and closed.

I swing the door shut in his face and rush to the side of her.

"Mi, open your eyes," I say softly.

The second I see Mia's giant brown eyes, the ones that drew me in the second I met her, my shoulders fall in relief. I let out the deep breath I'd been holding for the last four hours and tears fall from my eyes.

"Are you crying?" she croaks, and a laugh rumbles from my chest.

"Fuck." I sigh. *"Thank God you're okay, Mia. I should have been here."*

The sheer pain shocks me awake and I sit up drenched in sweat.

I haven't thought about Mia's accident in years, at least not to the extent of having a nightmare about it. The whole dream felt so real, like I was reliving the whole thing all over again for the first time. The fear, the uncertainty, the rage. That was the first time I think I truly experienced an anxiety attack. The night Mia had her accident and broke her leg, fractured her collarbone and had endless scratches all over her perfect olive skin.

Once she was cleared to travel, I all but forced her to move to Tampa to be closer to me. It didn't take an awful lot of convincing since that was her post-school plan anyway, but from that moment on, protecting Mia became my sole priority.

CHAPTER EIGHTEEN
MIA

Well, being pulled off a bar by my best friend was not on my bingo card for this trip, but that seems to be the trend anyway. So many—*too many*—baffling things are happening lately. Little moments or little actions, situations…things I never anticipated.

After Nate pulled me off the bar last night and whispered into my ear, the goosebumps spread like wildfire all over my body. He looked at me in a familiar way, and if Bree wouldn't have interrupted us, I have no idea what would've happened.

My phone's been going off all morning and I've ignored it for a while, but the messages just keep on coming. I know it's the group chat with Summer and Abby. My only other friend is five feet away from me.

> ABBY
> I can't watch shows with blood.
>
> SUMMER
> It's fake for the love of God. I would be more understanding if you just couldn't be around actual blood in real life, but fake blood on a TV isn't a big deal.

> **ABBY**
> You're numb to it, you're a nurse.
>
> **SUMMER**
> Speaking of numb, why don't you just put ice between your legs? Numb the pain away.
>
> **ABBY**
> It's not painful. I'm just sore.

I didn't scroll all the way to the top of the messages, but now I guess I need to in order to understand the context of Summer's text.

Nate walks into the room carrying a cup of coffee and he sets it on the nightstand beside me. His eyes look heavy, like he barely slept and the way his hair is darting off in different directions tells me he's run his hands through it at least a dozen times.

"I heard you moving around in here, figured you were up." The deep V of his stomach practically hits me in the face when I sit up because he's standing so close to the bed. I gulp at the sight and unintentionally lick my lips.

"Thank you," I rush out, grabbing the cup and taking a sip. "Are you okay? You look like you barely slept."

"That's because I did barely sleep," he mumbles as he walks into the closet and grabs a shirt from the hanger, pulling it over his head. His muscles contract every time he moves, and I'm caught in a daze before I shake myself out of it.

"Anything you want to talk about?" The warmth of the coffee feels good going down my throat. The cooler Midwest air has been a nice change from the humidity I've grown accustomed to though.

Nate sighs and there goes his hand again, pulling through his brown hair.

"If you don't want to, you don't have to," I assure him.

"I dreamt about your accident." His voice is low and hoarse

as he stands at the edge of the bed, staring at me. Pain pulls at my chest, briefly remembering what I can from that night.

"Ma'am, are you okay? Can you hear me?" My eyes flutter open and shut as bright lights are shining in my face. A man I don't recognize is standing above me. Fuck, my leg hurts. Wow. It really fucking hurts. What's going on? "Ma'am, you've been in an accident, we're here to help you."

The year that Nate left to come play football in Tampa, I was in a car accident. There was a party off-campus that I went to. Which isn't something I'd do often, but I thought, what the hell, you know? I was the passenger. It was a single car accident, the guy I was casually seeing lost control and we ended up hitting a tree. I broke my leg, dislocated my shoulder, and had quite a few bumps and bruises. Josh had a lot of cuts and scrapes too, but ultimately, I got the brunt of it.

"It felt like it was happening again. Like I was right there. All the rage and fear I had that night came rushing back in that dream, Mi. I swear I could feel it all as if it were repeating itself. I woke up sweating, trembling, full of all the anger and frustration all over again."

He walks over to where I'm seated on the bed and just hugs me. His strong arms wrap around me as we sit there in silence for a moment.

"I'm sorry you had to relive it," I whisper.

"I don't think I'll ever be over it. I wish I could have protected you from it." His grip gets tighter as his breaths get deeper.

"There isn't anything you could've done. It's okay. I'm okay." I take his face in my hands, focusing on his tired and sad eyes. The blue in them looks dulled down and it's heartbreaking.

Nate clears his throat and nods his head at me as he presses his fingers into his eyes.

"You're okay," he confirms.

I nod at him, offering a smile. His hand grazes my cheek as he takes a seat on the bed next to me and quickly changes the subject to something lighter.

"Are your feet sore? You were dancing quite a bit last night."

"No, thankfully. I feel good. I only had one beer too, so no hangover."

Nate leans back against the headboard and brings his arm behind his head, displaying the perfect definition of his biceps.

"Good. I think maybe I'll go on a solo hike today," he states, confidently.

"I love that."

When I bring my attention back to my phone and scroll up a little further, I see the text Summer and Abby were referring to. I can't help laughing out loud at what Abby says and then Summer's reply.

"What?" Nate asks.

"Nothing, I was just reading a text from Abby." I shake my head and lock my phone, placing it in my lap.

"What'd little Hunt have to say?"

I take another sip of my coffee, shielding my face from his for a moment, allowing myself to gather my thoughts.

"She was just saying how sore she is from all of the sex her and Ford apparently have been enjoying." I can't even say it with a straight face. Nate shakes his head laughing.

"Must be nice," I say under my breath, but it's still loud enough where Nate hears me and replies instantly.

"Having sex is nice."

"Yeah, but not the sore part." The admission flies out of my mouth and I realize I've opened a door to a conversation that Nate and I have never had before.

"You've never had so much great sex that you still felt it even after it was over?" Nate's question catches me by surprise. This conversation just took a hard left from the emotional memories we were just working through, and now I can feel the heat rising up my neck.

"What do you mean?"

"I just mean, you've never had so much good sex, to the point where you're desperate for them, craving them?" The way Nate's voice has lowered is making my heart race. It's barely nine in the morning, I can't be thinking of things like this right now. "Needing it constantly. It's not a bad kind of sore, but just a reminder of how good someone makes you feel."

"I've had good sex. I'm great at sex if you must know." My defenses turn on and I don't understand how this conversation got here or where it's going, but I know I absolutely did not intend on talking about sex with my best friend this morning.

"I'm sure you are, Mi. That's not what I'm saying." There's too little space and clothing between us right now to be having this talk.

"I'm saying you should be throbbing, even after it's done. Your legs should shake and you should be aching from the way someone fucks you. If you're being fucked often and properly, you should feel it, even after you're done."

My breath stutters as I breathe in. Nate and I have never talked in this kind of detail. Sure, we both know the other has had sex, but we never talk about it.

I know my face is red. There's no hiding the heat that's making its way through my body as this conversation progresses. Based on what I saw and just my general assumptions, I have no doubt that Nate is *very* capable of properly fucking someone.

"Oh." I have a giant gulp. "I can't say that I have…" Even though I'm telling the truth, he makes me wish I was lying.

"Shame." His stare is stoic and almost longing. His steel blue eyes stare at my legs before making their way up to meet my eyes. I didn't actually want this conversation to take place to begin with, but now I just want to hear more. Nate's entire tone changed, his demeanor, his words… it was commanding.

I clear my throat before speaking. "Well, I guess your friend is doing a great job with my friend then."

Nate's eyes wash over me like a cold dark blue wave before he gets up from the bed and heads into the bathroom. He's never said anything like "if you're being properly fucked" to me before and it made things... tingle.

Maybe all the words I used to describe Laura were wrong and she isn't crazy after all.

I've just finished getting myself ready for the day, and Nate's standing by the front door of the cabin about to leave for his day, but turns to me first. "Hey, can you, uh... share some of those podcasts with me? The ones you found about mental health."

His right arm stretches back and grips the back of his neck as he stares at me. He almost looks hesitant to even ask the question.

"Of course. I'll send you everything you need." He tilts his head and I smile at him just before he walks out the door.

———

After spending an entire day with Nate's sisters, I've reached my quota on Justin Bieber songs and need to spend some quiet time with me, myself and I back at the cabin before Nate returns.

The cool breeze feels relaxing as I sit out in the hammock near the lake. I have to kick myself for never doing things like this when I actually lived up here for college. I close my eyes, basking in the warmth of the sun as the wind passes by and let my mind drift, until I hear footsteps and lift my head up to see Nate making his way down to me.

His black hoodie, with a flannel and gray joggers have been his go to look here and I have to admit, it's a really good look on him.

"Hey," he greets me with a smile.

"Hey, how was your hike?" I ask as he grabs the side of the hammock.

"It was great. I listened to two episodes of the podcast you sent me. I actually think I even learned a thing or two."

"I'm glad."

"Scooch." Nate stops the hammock from moving and attempts to get on with me. Although, it turns out that hammocks aren't exactly user friendly, and trying to get on while someone else is already on it, is actually a fucking disaster.

Nate's trying to steadily get on the hammock so he doesn't flip this thing with both of us in it, but in his effort, he falls flat on top of me. His chest practically lands on my face and his waist lines up directly on top of mine, almost in a straddle. Instinctively, I reach my hand between us to try and maneuver myself over to give him more room, but all I end up doing is grazing the outside of his joggers with the back of my hand and very obviously touching his stupidly large penis.

"Oh my God, I'm sorry," I say, pulling my hand back as he finally gets himself shifted beside me.

My hands cover my face as we lie there, but Nate isn't fazed. He laughs at me and then wiggles his arm under my neck to get himself more comfortable while we both lay here.

"Don't sweat it, Smalls. How was your day?"

"Well," I begin. "Your sisters are a trip. I had fun though. And I'm happy you had a good day too."

"It was a good day. I feel good. Those podcasts got me thinking a lot. I don't know, it just might be time for me to make some real changes."

The beginning of a smirk looked like it was tipping the corners of his mouth as I glanced up.

"Like what?" I ask quietly, looking out over the lake.

"I've been ashamed of everything I've been dealing with for months. I didn't tell anyone until the night I told you, and by that time I was easily a few months in. I didn't want to be judged.

But I was losing myself for a while. Mentally, I just wasn't there. My body, my routines, everything was functioning on autopilot, but I wasn't really there for it. I don't know if this makes any fucking sense, but I'm just trying to get it out, to tell someone. And one thing I'm constantly noticing is that talking to you makes me feel better. I've just felt broken for the longest time."

Nate exhales a deep breath.

"Things that are broken can be mended," I say to him quietly, and feel his lips against the top of my head. A familiar gesture that brings me so much comfort.

"I need to find my purpose. I've accomplished so many things already and I'm grateful for all of it, and you'd think that might make all of this better, and easier to deal with, but it really only added pressure. I need to find my purpose *outside* of football. I need to find my why. It can't be only football."

"Well, how can I help?"

"You're already helping." His eyes close as we lie here, while the sun is nearly setting.

"By making you take a road trip to relax?"

Nate smiles while his eyes are still closed and then shakes his head back and forth.

His blue eyes open and connect with mine, sending my pulse into a frenzy. "By existing."

I can practically hear my heartbeat with the way it's pounding. Nate's still been acting like my best friend, but on steroids lately. Everything is escalated. I'm suddenly realizing how present he has been in my life and how well he knows every little thing about me. I'm noticing how close we are, and how well we interact.

Sometimes the things he does and says make me long for just a little more. He buys me keychains with my name any time he sees them, because one day I made a comment about being on a field trip as a kid where they didn't have my name and I was devastated. He knows my coffee order, for hot and cold because they aren't the same. He just knows me, and he gets me, and that kind of bond is really hard to find.

I think, on some level, I can agree that Nate's feelings for me have changed, but what I'm more focused on is how that makes me feel.

CHAPTER NINETEEN

NATE

Today, everything feels right. Everything feels good.

Who knows how many miles I walked on the hike, but it brought me some clarity that I didn't expect. Football has been my life. The only thing that's ever really mattered. I've worked my ass off for years to achieve my goals. Most of them I've already achieved. So what am I doing? What's my purpose at this stage in the game?

When I was listening to a podcast Mia suggested, one of the hosts said something that stuck with me. He said, ask yourself what makes you come alive. Find out what drives you. Find what makes you happy and run with that. Once you figure out what gives you purpose, you'll find happiness and fulfillment.

My answer to all of those questions isn't a thing.

It's a person.

I haven't taken the time to slow down in years. I've been chasing one professional goal after the next and living life in the fast lane. I've loved it, but I don't want it anymore.

I want a house on a piece of land. I want quiet Friday nights in. I want slow mornings and a woman I can't get enough of. I want all of that and more—with Mia.

"You probably want to change," I say, pointing to the flannel shirt hanging on the chair.

"I'll be warm enough in this," Mia argues, tugging at the sweater she has on.

"You don't want the smell of a bonfire on that for days. Wear the flannel, Mia." I turn and walk out of the room, not giving her the opportunity to fight back.

As I'm tossing another few logs into the fire, Mia starts walking down the steps towards me. She's wearing my flannel over a pair of leggings and some slippers she slid her feet into.

"Is this just for us?" she asks, noticing only two chairs pulled around the flames.

"That a problem?"

She hesitates briefly. "No, no problem."

I hand her a blanket before taking a seat across from her. The flames rise up quickly, then fall back to a steady pace. All I hear is the faint sound of music across the lake and the crackling of this fire between us.

Her fingers are gently tapping on the nearly empty bottle in her hand.

"The sky is so gorgeous out here. I'm mad at myself for not taking advantage of it when I lived here. Now all I get are high rises and street lights. The stars, the moon… this is so peaceful. I would love to eventually live in a place where I can see the sky like this all the time."

"Well, for now, we always have the field," I say, tipping my beer towards her.

"To the field." She raises her bottle in a toast and we both laugh.

We've spent the last hour going on and on about music, and normally I'd love it, but it's not the conversation I want to have with her tonight. The vision for what I want is so goddamn clear, I just need to see if she sees it too.

"So, you and Hughes." Her eyes dart to mine, her heavy eyelashes that shadow her cheeks in the light fly up before she shifts her gaze.

"There is no me and Hughes, Nate."

"No? You said there was a date on the horizon."

Mia pulls her knees up to her chest, holding them close. She sighs and I instantly have the urge to apologize for asking.

But I don't.

"If we're stepping into talking about relationships, I'd love to know what's going on with you?" I should have seen this question coming. Mia's smart. She isn't going to let me just run the show here.

"Literally nothing. Not since Laura. Now, back to my question."

"And you haven't been with anyone since her?"

My lips twitched with amusement at her question.

"Nope."

She lets out an exasperated sigh. "To answer your question, I told him I would text him when I got back into town. We haven't set anything up yet."

Figuring out how to navigate being best friends but wanting more is fucking difficult. Every instinct in me wants to just twist a handful of her hair into my fist and kiss her until we're both gasping for breath. But I can't, not yet. Not until I know for sure it's what she wants me to do.

"Why do you care if I go on a date with Connor?"

"I always care about who you're with, Mi. I want you to be happy and safe." Leaning forward, I adjust my flannel as I watch her. My eyes trained on her facial expressions, hoping to get a read on her.

"I know that much. But you've never cared this much before, where you're asking questions like you have been." Her chestnut colored hair starts blowing in the slight breeze. She pulls it out of her face and I see nothing but questions in her eyes. Everything I've done and said over the last few days has her head spinning —I can see it.

"You're right," I retreat. Slouching a little in the chair as the flames flicker in front of me.

"Why?" It's a whisper. But I hear it. Part of me thinks she knows the answer, but just wants to hear me say it.

A tinge of pain rips through my chest before I reply, bracing myself for what could possibly come after tonight if I lay it all out there.

It's close to midnight. We need to go to sleep, but everything I want to say is on the tip of my tongue. I buried my feelings for years. Unknowingly for the most part, but when I look back, it's always been her. Any time my mind has searched for peace, it's gone to Mia. You don't just risk all of that unless you're sure. I need to be sure.

"Come on, Smalls…" I plead, seeing if she can meet me halfway in this conversation because now my nerves are kicking in.

Glancing towards Mia, I see her fidgeting with the sleeves of the flannel. Her body keeps repositioning in that chair and she's barely made eye contact with me in the last few moments. Everything is right there, just begging to spill out of my mouth, but doubt creeps in. My throat feels thick and now I can't stop fidgeting either. I've never had a hard time telling a woman I'm interested, but with Mia it's so much more than just being interested in her. I'm invested. I'm committed. I'm so fucking consumed by everything about her.

That's all that I can get out before a rumble of thunder sounds in the distance, causing both of us to glance towards the sky.

"We should head in." Her voice is soft and slightly shaking.

Both of us stand, and I grab the blanket from her chair, wrapping it around her body tightly.

"I'll clean up, you go inside."

Mia only nods and follows my directions while I put out the fire and straighten out the chairs. Lining them up against the cabin as they were previously positioned before heading inside.

The shower in the bathroom is running as I step into the bedroom. My body collapses on the chair in the corner of the room, head falling back and eyes closing in thought. I was so close tonight. So close to spitting it out. I've never had trouble opening up to Mia and this shouldn't be any different. I know I said I couldn't control who she dates, and fuck, I can't... but I can try to show her why she should go on a date with me instead. I've had a lot of fucking time to think about it, and what I've concluded is that Mia knows me as her best friend and nothing more, so I just have to show her I can be more than that. She knows I'll be there for her through anything. But she doesn't know Boyfriend Nate. She doesn't know how good this can be, but I do. So I have to find a way to help her see it too.

"You can have the bed tonight since I so selfishly hogged it last night." As if on cue, Mia is back to her normal self as she steps out of the bathroom, wearing nothing but a flimsy white towel wrapped around her body. There are still water droplets on her shoulders and I'm doing my best to stay focused on her face when every instinct wants my eyes to work up and down her barely dressed body.

"I think we can manage sharing a bed, Mi. I'm going to take a shower." I walk by her, inhaling her lavender scent and my fingers feather along the back of her arm just above her elbow as I walk by. The goosebumps that flare up could be from just stepping out of a warm shower into the cooler bedroom or they could be from my touch.

"Okay, yeah, it should be fine." She perks up, almost sounding shrill in her response.

THE END ZONE

Letting the warm water flow down my back as I stand with my head under the shower and my hands against the wall, I feel my cock twitch as a brief thought of Mia crosses my mind knowing that her naked body was just in this shower. Knowing that her barely dressed skin is just on the other side of this door and my mind wanders.

We're at Summerfest a few years ago. She's wearing a yellow sundress and white sneakers. Her long brown hair is blowing in her face and she keeps complaining about it getting stuck in her lip gloss, but refuses to put it up. I lift her up on my shoulders so she can get a better view when our favorite band comes on stage. She smells like lavender and honey. My hands grip her smooth, toned legs to keep her balanced as she sits on my shoulders swaying back and forth, dancing to the music. If I just rotate her around, my face is right—

Fuck.

Without realizing it, I'm stroking myself hard, with thoughts about Mia. Very, very inappropriate thoughts of my best friend are clouding my mind. The groans that are involuntarily leaving my chest can't be contained and I'm certain she can hear me, but just the thought of her is too good.

With one hand gripping the side of the wall, I jerk myself harder, faster, barely able to keep up with the thoughts that are racing through my mind. Seconds later, I come so fucking hard I swear I'm about to pass out on this shower floor as Mia's name leaves my lips. I've thought of Mia before, but never in a way that made me desperate to touch her. Desperate for it to be her lips around my cock, sucking me off, making me come as I grip her hair around my wrist.

CHAPTER TWENTY
MIA

"*Mia.*" I hear a deep growl of my name as I'm sitting on the edge of the bed, still in my towel, nearly panting myself. From the other side of this door for the last fifteen minutes, I've heard shallow grunts and moans, the frequency of them brought me to sitting right here.

What the fuck is happening tonight?

There's a dull throb between my legs. I'd like to say it's sudden, but I've felt it for hours. Maybe I'm just lonely and horny, and the extra attention from Nate is playing tricks on my mind. After all, it's been practically a year at this point since I've had sex and I can't give myself an orgasm no matter how hard I try. And Nate's over here saying things and acting certain ways and it's affecting me in a way it shouldn't. But hearing my name come from his lips while he's in the shower? That sends a whole new level of tension through me.

The bathroom door opens and my eyes immediately shoot up. Nate shakes his hair as he's walking out in nothing but a towel, and there's the throb again. A little pulse between my legs reminding me that even though he's my best friend, he's still devastatingly handsome. His chest is firm and tan with each muscle outlined down to the V-shape at his waist. His towel looks like it's barely hanging on, and my memory is fully intact as I recall what's beneath.

"You aren't dressed." His voice is low, almost ragged.

"I got sidetracked scrolling my phone. Have a good shower?" The lie is a waste as his eyes drift to the dresser where my phone sits plugged into the charger on the other side of the room.

"Very." He doesn't try to hide the smirk that casts over his face. Does he not care that I just heard him moan my name? He wasn't quiet, he has to know I heard him.

As he looks back to me, my heart pounds in response. I'm pressing my thighs together so tightly to stop the ache. This is all too much. Too many things I'm feeling that I shouldn't be. My mind and body are just very confused and I need to get it back on the right track. I stand on slightly wobbly legs and reach for my clothes to change, heading to the bathroom. He starts to move the towel off of his body before I have the door completely closed and I stand there, frozen, with my heart secretly wondering what this would be like.

"Come on in, the water is fine," Nate jokes once I come back into the bedroom. He's bare chested but I can see his shorts as the comforter is resting near his knees.

"Cute PJs, Mi."

"Well it was either these pancake and waffle shorts and this tank top or stealing one of your t-shirts."

"I'd be fine with that." He shrugs and begins to pull the comforter up over us as I get in next to him. Nate teeters back and forth between normal, playful conversation and then the serious, more desirable tone, and I'm just not sure who to expect when he opens his mouth at this point.

Turning on my side, I can feel his breath behind me. I know

he's awake due to the deep sighs that keep coming from his side of the bed. It's almost one in the morning, but I have no idea how I'll get any sleep tonight. I'm too wound up. I can feel it everywhere. Everything is tingling. I don't want it to, but I don't know how to stop the burning.

Nate opened a new door for us when we talked about sex, and then again tonight with how he's acting. A door I thought was closed back in college. He probably doesn't even remember the night we almost kissed. Sometimes I wish I could have it back, that I could redo it and let him kiss me.

I've always found Nate attractive, that's never been the issue. The thing always standing in my way of doing anything is the fact that he's everything to me. Every happy memory I have in the last few years, Nate is at the root of those. He's been there for me through every single hard time too. Part of me is surprised that he's even having these feelings. He knows how important our friendship is to me, I know he wouldn't risk that unless he was serious.

Two fifteen. My arm slings across my forehead and I whip the covers off of my body. When I glance over, Nate's facing the other way but his body is moving up and down slowly. Maybe he was finally able to fall asleep, but I sure as hell can't.

I need relief.

I need to at least fucking try.

My suitcase is on the floor right next to me so I grab the sweater that my vibrator is under and pull it out of my bag, tucking it under my arm before I tiptoe out of the bedroom to the living room and close the door behind me. It's far enough away that Nate shouldn't wake up.

"Okay," I whisper. A mini pep talk seems reasonable at two thirty in the morning before I'm about to use a vibrator with my best friend in the next room. God, what the hell is happening? He's the whole reason I'm even going to this extreme level right now.

I slip out of my shorts as I lay back on the couch, my head resting on the arm facing away from the bedroom door. I don't have much faith in this, but it's my last-ditch effort to be able to get some sleep.

The second I turn it on, it hums for a second with a low buzzing before I turn it off. Fuck. No, I can't use this. He'll hear it. It's loud. I groan out in frustration with my underwear sporting a wet spot right in the center.

"Son of a bitch," I whisper in misery. The ache is still there, even more prominent than before at this point. Leaning my head all the way back I take a deep breath and exhale. Desperate for some relief, I slowly inch my hand down my body and just under the waistband of my underwear. I haven't done this in so long, and who the hell knows if it's going to work but if I don't try to have an orgasm right now, I think I might die.

My mind starts to piece together memories of men I've been with. Celebrities or someone I find attractive. Someone who I'd fold for if they were standing in front of me at this moment. I slip one finger down my center and actually feel how wet I am. I fight my mind to not think of the man who made me this way. A soft whimper flows from my lips once I press on my clit, and I hear a groan behind me. I shoot up off the couch, standing in the middle of the living room wearing only a tank top and a pair of underwear, desire running through my veins. Nate's standing in the doorway of the bedroom, rubbing himself from the outside of his shorts.

"Nate! You scared me. I thought you were asleep," I say with this fire only growing stronger inside my belly.

"I wasn't." He saunters towards me.

"Come to bed, Mia." Oh, fuck. He rarely uses my full name. How long was he standing there? Did he catch my disappointing vibrator moment?

"Yeah, you're right. I should get some sleep." My hands reach for my shorts to pull them on, but Nate's body gets closer to me. He stares at me with intensity. Something I'm not used to and sure as hell am not able to resist in my current state. He looks down at my shorts and the discarded vibrator. His nostrils flare and he takes a deep breath before he picks them both up and walks back to the bedroom. I take a deep breath and follow him.

I slip into bed realizing I'm still just in my underwear and tank top, but before I can move to reach for something, I notice Nate standing at the edge of the bed.

"I had a release. It's only fair you should too," he says.

The tension I'm feeling between us right now is palpable. My hands are shaking and clammy, my brain says go to bed, get away from this situation, but every other instinct in me tells me to stay in the moment.

"I don't think I can…" I whisper. Appalled I'm even admitting this to him. "I've never actually been able to do this myself, it's fine. I'm going to get some sleep." I begin to move and pull at the comforter, but Nate pulls it back so it's sitting just at my waist.

"Want my help?" Surely, I just heard him wrong. Did he just offer to help me have an orgasm?

"Uhhh." I have absolutely no words because how do I say yes, but no, but yes without sounding like an idiot.

"I won't touch you, not until you tell me that's what you want. But I'll talk you through it. You need a release, so let me use my words to give you one. I can tell you exactly how you should be played with. Use your fingers, this toy if you want, but I promise I can make you come with just my words."

I'm dreaming. I'm in some *Stranger Things*, upside down world bullshit, because there is no way he just said he'd make me come with his words. How can I be okay with this? How can he?

Even though the room is dark, there's a light from the window casting a small shadow where he's standing. And the shorts he's wearing do nothing to hide the outlined bulge I can see so clearly. I quickly picture the length, the size, and it feels wrong looking at my best friend and wanting him to talk me through an orgasm. But after the last few days, I've lost all sense of reason. I never expected this from him. The way he's talking and moving his body. The stares and the touching. Is this how he is when he's romantic with women? If so, I understand why so many fall at his feet.

"Nate, I can't do this with you."

"Sure, you can. You know what I look like, use me." My eyes shift again back to his shorts. *Ah, so he does know I saw it.* Except I want nothing more than to not picture him, yet here he is giving me full consent to do just that.

"Come on, Mi. Listen to my words. Let me help you get your release. You want that, right? Let me talk you through it."

I nod hesitantly at his question.

He stares at me as he paces the edge of the bed, a sly grin forming on his features.

"The best part is the beginning. I love to see my girl aching for my touch. But where will I touch her first?" *Fucking hell, is this really happening? Is he really about to tell me how he'd please a woman?* "I might drag my fingers across her inner thighs…"

The ache is only getting stronger with every word he speaks, and I can't resist the temptation to try. I hesitantly glide my hand down near the waistband of my underwear, sliding just underneath it. I can't believe I'm doing this, but I'm actually aching for this man right now.

"That's it. Spread your legs apart. Will I have to hold them down or will she keep them spread for me?" His tongue swipes over his bottom lip slowly. I'm letting my body just react at this point, there's no use fighting it.

This is happening.

"I'd bring my lips to her hip bones. Planting small kisses all the way down until I'm right there." His last words are spread out, he's speaking slowly and there's a huskiness to his voice that's sending chills across my body.

"Hovering just above the spot she wants the most attention. I'd have her throbbing for even the slightest touch." Oh God, I can feel the sweat on my lower back.

"Slide your fingers through your pussy, Mia. Tease yourself. Does it ache?"

I can't look him in the eye. I don't know what's gotten into us on this trip, but there's no going back from what we're doing right now. My head nods up and down in quick motions before I give in and just lean back against the headboard, closing my eyes.

"Eyes on me." His tone is sharp.

Reluctantly, my eyes open and I bring them back to his.

God, I'm so turned on right now—and by my best friend, of all people. All reason has vanished and I can't focus on anything aside from his voice and the way our eyes have interlocked in such an intense gaze. We're experiencing each other in different ways tonight and I'm mesmerized by the way my best friend's lips move every time he talks and the way the blue of his eyes become a deep sapphire.

"I bet you're soaked. How wet are you, Smalls? Dripping?" Afraid to make any movements, I sit there breathing heavily as a sly smirk crosses his face.

"I can tell. Keep going. Slide one finger in and then another. Give your cunt exactly what it wants. Play with it. Faster, Mia." Nate's arms are planted on the end of the bed, staring at me the whole time with an intensity so fierce, so consuming, I can't look away.

"Now, once I know she can't handle the ache any longer, I'd have her sit on my face. I'd need to taste her. I'd need her riding my face, getting as messy as she pleases."

I swallow hard, rocking myself against my hand, picturing what I shouldn't be, but can't escape from.

"I wouldn't forget about her breasts either. I'd make sure to play with them too. Gently squeezing as she rides me. Use your other hand and play with your nipple. Does that feel good?" His voice is low, almost a mumble. The silence in here makes my cries and whimpers sound so much louder, but I do as he says, bringing my hand up my shirt, pinching my nipple.

"Scream if you need to. I'd want to hear my girl scream." My chest is pounding, and I can barely breathe.

"Fuck, Mia. You look so hot like this. I bet you taste so fucking sweet too."

Oh my God, this feels good.

"Now, stop."

"W–what?" I breathe out. I'm so close. Fuck, I'm actually so close and he says stop?

"The buildup..." He walks closer to my side of the bed from where he was standing by the edge. His mouth comes dangerously close to my neck as he breathes words into my ear. "The buildup is what makes you come. Hard. You were close, weren't you?"

My head nods up and down ferociously.

"Good." His lips lift to the left in a grin.

"You can start again in a minute," he says, reaching on the nightstand and grabbing the vibrator.

My eyes go wide at him as I watch him power it on.

"Put this vibrator right on your clit and let me see you ride your hand until you fucking come for me."

I'm never going to be able to see Nate in the same light after this. My heart pounds as I rock against my hand, trying to keep my eyes on Nate while also desperately trying to think of someone, anyone, other than my best friend.

"Does that feel good? Let yourself go. It'll feel even better," he whispers, this time directly into my ear, sending my body into shock as I feel his warm breath against my skin.

"Oh God," I cry out, my body shaking frantically as I come hard. Harder than I think I've ever been able to and he didn't even touch me.

He didn't even touch me and I saw fucking stars.

Fuck, I want this feeling again. It was pure ecstasy. His words. His voice. It's a side of Nate I never expected to experience, but I just did. I should be freaking out. I'm sure I will in the morning. But right now, all I feel is so satisfied.

"One day, that'll be my name you're screaming," he says in my ear before walking away.

He steps away from the bed and comes back with a towel and hands it to me before he reaches for my shorts and also hands me those. I slide them on before getting up to use the bathroom and by the time I get back, Nate's already passed out on his side of the bed as if what we just did wasn't crossing a huge line in our friendship.

CHAPTER TWENTY-ONE

NATE

The events of last night were the last thing I ever expected. Mia thought I was asleep, but as soon as the door clicked shut, I rolled over and realized that she left the room. I laid there for a moment, contemplating giving her space, if that's what she was looking for. But when I heard a humming noise, I knew what was happening on the other side of that door and considering I'd bet I was the reason, I wasn't missing it.

Seeing Mia in that state was a fucking marvel. She looked like a goddess on that bed, spread out and touching herself, using my words to make herself come. I'm still fucking stiff just from being in the same room as her last night while she did that.

I barely slept last night, but it was worth it. It was the small sign I needed that there's potential here. Maybe she thinks this isn't so far-fetched after all.

"I'm helping your mom and sisters set up for their party tonight." Mia's dainty fingers grip the zipper of her jacket as she pulls it up. There's no discussion of last night, and honestly, I don't expect there to be. She needs time to process it all and I'm not going to force anything.

"Sounds good. I'm going fishing with my dad."

Mia offers me a smile before she walks out, and I grab my boots from near the front door and head out the back.

"Hey, pops." My dad reaches his arm out for a hug as I approach him. He's bundled up from head to toe in a sweater, boots, long pants and a baseball hat, even though it's really not that cold out this morning. He's always hated the cold, but any time I've mentioned moving somewhere else now that all of us kids are done with school, he always shoots me down. "Your mother loves it here," is his response every time.

"Think we'll catch any walleye?" I ask, casting a line.

"Prime time for em' right now. So, we'll see." My dad opens a small cooler he brought, grabbing a bag of sliced apples and a water bottle. How times have changed since he and I used to go fishing when I was a kid.

"Apples and water huh? Where's the beer and beef jerky?"

"Your mom packed me this." He gives me a look and takes a bite of an apple slice.

"When do you think you'll be back on the field?"

We're both sitting back, relaxed on the boat while our lines bob in the water waiting for a bite.

"I don't know. I would like to say in time for the Chicago game, but I can't be sure. Once I'm back, it's up to Coach Aarons when he wants to play me."

"Can I ask what happened? Or what's been going on? Your mom and I have been wanting to give you space, of course, but we also would like to understand." I've never had to question my family's love and support. I know I'm lucky. I'm reminded of it any time I see Mia interact with her family. You'd think based on her circumstances she'd be jaded. That she wouldn't be the light that she is, but she's actual sunshine.

"My mind hasn't been right in months. Something's just been wrong, been off. I thought I could play through it, hide it, but things have only gotten worse. It's like a monster that just keeps building and building. The pressure felt like it was slowly killing me from the inside out. All the voices—internally and out in the public—just telling me I'm not good enough, I'm losing it, it all just feeds into the anxieties. I can't help but feel like I'm letting the team down by taking a leave of absence, but you saw that play. I can't be out on the field and risk that happening again."

"It takes a man to admit his demons, Nate. I'm proud of you. I won't pretend to understand what you're facing. I've always thought that the spotlight and pressure of the game was a lot, but I know my son. And the people who know you, love you. We're rooting for you, we're here for whatever you need. Take it one day at a time."

"Thanks, dad."

"We're happy you've come for longer than just the party. I know your mother is happy to have you home."

I'm actually happy to have had this extra time home too.

"Yeah, it was Mia's idea, actually. But I'm glad I took her up on it."

He laughs a little and looks over at me, smiling and shaking his head.

"What?"

"That girl. She's going to be the one to settle you down, you watch."

"I don't know, pops. We'll see if she'll have me."

My line starts to pull just a little as we sit there in conversation. I glance over at it, just watching, waiting for the right moment to get up and start reeling it in.

"Might take her a minute to realize it, but souls that are meant to be together will always find their way to one another."

I glance back at him as I'm reeling in my line. Whatever yanked on it a minute ago is long gone, because I pulled it up to half-eaten bait and nothing hooked.

"Life of a fisherman," my dad jokes as I cast it back out again.

"Almost ready?" I call out to Mia from the living room. Tonight's party for my parents isn't anything fancy, thankfully.

"Yes," she replies. "I'm ready."

Mia steps through the door frame into the living room and it's the moment you hear about in songs and movies. The moment where angels sing and there's a halo floating above her head. She's wearing a long blue skirt with some flower pattern on it, but there's a slit that goes all the way up to her thigh. The white sweater she has on hangs off one shoulder and her long brown hair is curled and flowing down one side of her body. Her dark eyelashes flutter as she smiles walking towards me. She's not even showing that much skin, and I'm about to lose my mind.

I want to stay stuck in this moment for a little longer just to stare at her. In a split second, I see everything I want in life. A future, a house, a family. And I see it all with Mia the moment she stepped out of that bedroom to come to this party with me. I force myself not to say anything. Nothing I even say will come close to how stunning she looks. There aren't enough words in the English language to explain how Mia just made me feel when I saw her.

She adjusts the collar of her sweater just near her collarbone and walks up to me, grabbing my forearm and pulling at my sleeves.

"They aren't even," she says softly, taking her fingers and gently unrolling the sleeves, only to pull at my shirt and roll them up again. Is this actually making me hard? Sleeve action? Jesus.

Once she has them to her liking, I subtly adjust myself. I went for navy blue pants and a white button up, and I guess without realizing it, Mia and I have color coordinated for tonight.

"Your mom and aunts did such a cute job decorating everything. One of them asked if she could put up a sign that said 'same penis for thirty years.'"

"Jesus. They probably had way too much fun with it." I laugh. My mom and her sisters are inappropriate as hell in their fifties, I can only imagine how they were growing up.

As we walk into the reception hall, everything looks great as expected. A slideshow of pictures plays on the big screen at the forefront of the party and there are tables set up with chairs and different wedding photos from when they got married. Mia goes off and mingles on her own and my eyes follow her for just a second. She's so good at this. Being around people. Even though she doesn't know everyone here, she just slides right into conversation and everyone is always just taken with her.

My dad gets up to do a toast before we eat, one that inevitably brings my mom to tears. He shares about their last thirty years, the laughs, the highs and the lows. I told them I'd give a speech, but now I'm faltering… I don't even know what to say. I made a few notes but don't even feel like that'll do them justice.

"Nate? Honey, did you want to say something before we eat?" My aunt comes to my side and without me actually answering, she hands me a microphone. Fuck. I'm not good at talking about feelings. I have no idea how I'm going to do this.

"Uh, hey everyone. Mom, dad, congratulations on thirty years. I love you both." I freeze for a moment, my eyes scanning the room as I'm panicking over what to say next. These are my parents, how the hell am I having such a hard time talking about them? They have the purest love. The best relationship. I switch hands because the hand that was holding the mic is all clammy. Before the pause gets too long and awkward, I find Mia standing at the center of the room. She smiles and gives me a reassuring nod. She's sandwiched between Grandpa Harry and Uncle Frank and suddenly I don't feel so anxious anymore.

I look to my parents. "My mom and dad have a marriage I

can only hope to have one day." And then I look back at Mia. "A marriage based on love. Based on commitment. Filled with laughter. They choose each other, every day. The good days and the bad days… especially the bad days. My parents are best friends who are also soul mates. They make each other laugh, they support each other through the hard times. Thirty years is a long time to be with someone. But when it's the right person, your person… thirty years probably feels like thirty seconds and no time will ever be long enough. So, cheers, mom and dad. And I think I speak for everyone in this room when I say we're wishing you a hundred more." I raise my glass to my parents on my right, but my eyes don't move from Mia.

My mom gets up and hugs me while my dad shakes my hand and from then on, I barely see the two of them the rest of the night. They still act like they're in their twenties, dancing and having the time of their life with one another. I've spent a lot of tonight catching up with family members that I haven't seen in a while and filling them in on the current state of my life, except, of course, leaving out specific details. Most of them saw the game, or at least heard about it. Everyone's given me words of encouragement, which I'm thankful for.

"Ahem, I love this song so you're going to have to dance with me." Mia's hand is already pulling my forearm out to the center of the dance floor. We've never actually done this. Slow danced. I've never held her like this, with my hand resting on the small of her back, so close to her perfect round ass. I could inch my hand down and grab a hold of it, claiming her as mine. She's leaning into me, letting herself nearly melt into my body and I'm accepting it. I pull her closer as we stand there, swaying to the music. Her hands are gripping behind my neck and I can feel the hairs standing as her fingers lightly graze the skin near the collar on my shirt.

"They sang this at Summerfest that year we went," I whisper

low into Mia's ear. The summer I was just fantasizing about last night.

"I know. I think that's when it became my favorite. I loved seeing it live." She inhales a deep breath, and I just let myself react. I don't hold back because fuck, at this point I don't think I can any more. Between the road trip here, last night and now tonight… I'm just at my breaking point.

I pull her body closer to mine, filling any distance that's between us on this dance floor. Looking down at her, I see her close her eyes for a moment and she blows out a slow, steady breath through barely puckered lips.

The song by REO Speedwagon continues to play in the background. The lyrics sink into me as I'm standing there holding my best friend knowing that I can't handle being just her best friend anymore.

There's more here. I feel it. And I actually think she feels it too.

CHAPTER TWENTY-TWO

MIA

I hear Nate clear his throat only to realize the music has stopped playing, but I was just so lost in the moment of standing there with him, I hadn't actually registered it.

"Well, let me go, caveman." I shake my head and try to laugh it off. Pulling myself from his embrace as if I wasn't just relishing in it.

I've spent the majority of the evening spreading my attention between Nate's sisters, parents, and extended family. He comes from so much love, so much support. I'm honestly jealous. I don't have even a shred of this. I have no contact with my mother. My father is a constant work in progress. And my sister probably hates the fact that she even has a sister at all. And I wouldn't even know my extended family if I was standing next to one of them on an elevator either. So that just leaves me. It's why I lean into my friends so much, especially with Nate.

It's so clear to me that he's everything to his family. It makes me wonder if he even knows how much they all love and admire him. Grandpa Harry went on and on, almost getting emotional talking to me, about how proud of Nate he is. It's really heartwarming, to be honest, hearing how much the people in this room respect the man he's become. His sisters, whether they would say it to his face or not, consider him their hero. And Helen and Bruce, his parents, are just incredible. They raised Nate well and take a lot of pride in that. Also, they'll make the best grandparents one day. With Bruce's random storytelling and the way that Helen can make anything into something fun… they'll be amazing.

The way Nate made me feel last night was unlike anything I've ever experienced. I felt desired, I felt wanted, I felt… sexy. And the man didn't even lay a single finger on me, yet I came so hard I didn't know when it would stop.

There's a definite chill in the air as I walk out of the venue. I've had so much fun tonight, but could go for some hot chocolate, cozy socks, and a movie, if I'm being honest. Nate's been spending time with his family most of the evening, which I'm happy about. He seems like he's doing well, like this trip has actually been good for him.

"Do you want to camp out with us, Mia?" Gretchen's blonde hair swings in her high ponytail as she walks towards me.

I hesitantly shake my head. "I don't think I'm the camping type. Lions, tigers and bears… oh my!"

"Well, send Nate out in the tent then, that way you'll get the bed to yourself. He can sleep outside." She elbows me before walking away to catch up with her sister.

"I'm not camping outside." Nate's deep voice causes my head to turn and sends a jolt of excitement between my legs. *God dammit.*

He's leaning against the brick wall of this building, a few more buttons undone on his dress shirt, giving his chest some room to breathe with both arms crossed in front of him. His forearms flex as my eyes meet them, and I can't tell if that's something he did on purpose or not, but it sends an involuntary shiver down my back.

"How did I completely miss you standing there?"

"Not sure, Smalls. I'm kind of hard to miss." He pushes himself off the wall and begins to walk with me back towards the cabin.

"I'm planning for a hot chocolate and movie night with cozy socks and blankets. Nothing too exciting. So if you want to go camping or hang out with your sisters, you should." My hand comes up to my mouth to cover a yawn and Nate just shakes his head no at my suggestion. "Okay, well I have my reasons why I'm not sleeping outside, what about you? Didn't you grow up doing this?"

"Your reasons are my reasons," he says.

"Ah, so you also think you could be eaten by mountain lions in the middle of the night and no one would hear your screams?"

His hand runs through his hair as he laughs. "Did you say mountain lions? I could have sworn it was lions and tigers and bears less than two minutes ago." He cocks an eyebrow at me.

"I'm a very independent, self-sufficient woman until sleeping outside is brought into the equation and then I'm a twenty-six-year-old baby."

"And that's why we're sleeping in the cabin, I'm not letting you out of my sight tonight."

It's hardly what he says, but the way he says it. And the way my stomach drops. Nate's always been over protective of me, but he's never phrased it in that way. The possessiveness is new. It's intense, but makes me feel... good?

The moment we get into the cabin, Nate heads into the bedroom to change and I take the opportunity to text the girls. I haven't talked with Abby and Summer in a few days and I just need to word vomit all over them right now.

> Nate just told me he's not letting me out of his sight tonight when I said I was afraid to sleep with the lions and tigers and bears. And mountain lions.

THE END ZONE

ABBY

... I'm going to need more context?

SUMMER

Your text makes no sense, but oddly enough I think I know what you mean. Translation: he's being hot and you're confused?

> He pulled me off the bar the other night.

SUMMER

You were on a bar? Were you cleaning it? Helping someone else down from it?

> I was doing karaoke.

SUMMER

Ohhhh okay, that makes more sense.

ABBY

Why'd he pull you off of the bar?

> He told me not to bend over and give people a show, even though I had a flannel around my waist and you couldn't see anything. But the point is... he was acting overly protective. Like more than normal. Things have... I don't know, shifted. And every time he looks at me lately, I swear he's about to kiss me and there may or may not be, but mostly is, a small part of me that is curious if he will.

SUMMER

Wow. He got jealous? And has been giving you lusty looks? It's almost like someone already warned you about this.

> Yes, all hail Summer Kincaid. Genius and relationship expert.

ABBY

Has he tried anything?

> I don't know how to answer that. But, I guess I'll just say he hasn't touched me.

ABBY

I am so lost.

SUMMER

Just kiss him already.

Tossing my phone, I throw myself back on the couch as I hear the bedroom door open.

Nate walks in the doorway of the bedroom and stops, leaning himself against the door frame. He traded his white button up for a flannel jacket and sweatpants and my God, he looks like a hot fucking lumberjack and it's just adding to the swirling confusion.

"You look very Wisconsin." I cross my arms over my chest, smiling at him. Trying not to completely drool over the sight of my best friend right now.

"And you look overdressed for a movie night. Wear this." His voice is commanding as he holds up his sweater. It's one of the old vintage team sweaters they had available a few years ago. He bought me my own, but I always end up wearing his. Something about a man's sweatshirt just feels cozier than one in my own size.

"I love these throwback sweaters."

"I know," he quips quickly as he walks the sweater over to me.

I grab the sweater from his hands and walk into the bedroom to change into it along with a pair of leggings.

"*Transformers* or *Saving Private Ryan*?" Nate yells from the living room.

"Those cannot be the only two options," I say, narrowing my eyes at the television. I walk over and sit next to Nate on the couch as he taps through different movie options on the guide.

"What's the one movie where the guy's daughter gets kidnapped? Fuck. It's so good, I can't remember the name. We watched it back in college. Do you know what I'm talking about?"

"Yeah, but I can't remember the name either."

Nate pulls out his phone and brings up his photos app as I'm sitting next to him. He scrolls through and you'd think I'd be looking at the pictures on his phone as he scrolls, but I can't. I'm too focused on his hands. I pay extra attention to the veins protruding every time he flexes or repositions his hand. I watch his thumb scroll and he's moving so fast, I don't even know how his brain is registering anything he's seeing.

"Damn it, where is it?" he mutters.

"What are you looking for?"

"We watched this movie in your dorm. I remember taking a picture that had the actors name in it."

"Well, you're scrolling so fast."—I swallow a lump in my throat—"you probably already flew right past it."

"I know what I'm looking for, I didn't pass it." Son of a bitch, his smirk is ridiculously handsome right now.

He switches from his thumb to his index finger and slows down just a little before he glances at me. "Better?"

Nate glides his finger against the screen of his phone and all I'm thinking about is the way his fingers might feel gliding through me like that. He didn't even touch me last night and he sent me into an oblivion. I can only imagine what his hands would do.

"Liam Neeson!" he shouts as his finger stops on a picture of me, standing in front of the television in my dorm room and the credits are rolling in the background where the main character's name is showing.

"That's hardly a picture of the guy's name, I mean it's there, sure. But that's clearly me looking like an idiot." Shaking my head, I lean in to look closer. "Why'd you take this? I know it wasn't for the guy's name. You can barely see it without zooming in.

"Look at what you're wearing."

I'm in one of Nate's jerseys, but that's nothing new. I wear them all the time.

"That was the first time you wore my jersey to a game."

"You—wait, how do you know it was the first time?"

Nate puts his phone down and turns to face me, blue eyes sparkling like the damn Titanic necklace.

"I remember telling you that, aside from my family, no girl had ever worn my jersey. Then you showed up to the game wearing it, and it made me happy. So I snapped the picture when we were back at your dorm. You've worn my name and number on your back ever since." He shrugs like it's no big deal, but this a huge, gigantic, massive, enormous deal to me.

"I can't believe you remember that."

He shifts himself back towards the television. "Don't look so surprised, Smalls. Everything with you is a core memory."

My head falls back against the couch where Nate's arm is resting as I think about the words he said. Not only the words just now, but the words he's been saying. The things he's even been saying without actually saying them. His body language. His actions. And now, I'm rethinking everything.

CHAPTER TWENTY-THREE

NATE

I remember more than I'd probably ever admit to Mia. How she looked the night I almost kissed her, how she smelled. The way her chest moved up and down so rapidly as I stood next to her in that hallway. The way her nail polish was chipped, and how her hair fell in her face. Fuck, there are so many memories, so many moments with Mia. Looking back, I can't believe I ever agreed to just be her friend when I was so obviously crazy about her from the start.

Her head is resting on my shoulder as she's drifting to sleep on this couch while *Taken* plays on the television. Her hot chocolate is still practically full sitting on the coffee table in front of us. A small moan comes from her lips as she closes her eyes and this time, they stay closed. Her dark eyelashes fan her perfect olive skin. She nestles herself in closer to me and I'm stuck between carrying her into bed or just saying fuck it and find a way to fall asleep on this couch in this position. Her closeness to me is everything right now. Feeling her body next to mine is a comfort and a peace that I've desperately needed for so long.

Knowing that we are heading back on the road tomorrow, I

take my chances and scoop her into my arms as I stand from the couch. She doesn't open her eyes, but she makes a few small sounds as I pull her close to my chest, walking her into the bedroom. When I lie her down she curls up into a ball on one side of the bed and I lower my body into the other side, pulling the comforter up over both of us. Mia scoots herself closer to my side of the bed and I turn on my side, adjusting my body just behind hers.

Even in all her clothes, I'm still turned on and can feel my cock reacting to the closeness of her ass up against me. It's a subtle, barely-there kind of touch, but if she scoots back any further, she'll be right up against me and I honestly don't know if I'll be able to handle that. As I'm lying here trying to focus on falling asleep and not my insanely gorgeous best friend next to me, she turns her body to lie flat on her back. The sweater of mine rides up on her hip, exposing a small portion of her hip bone.

Fuck. New weakness unlocked. Mia's fucking hip bones.

Again, a light moan escapes Mia's lips, except this time it's followed by a shallow whimper and her body moving just slightly closer to mine again. Is she awake? Is she dreaming? She's tossing and turning her body between her back and her side, moving her hips back and forth every few seconds. How am I supposed to fall asleep when this is happening next to me? She's practically on top of me with the way she's continuously getting closer. My dick is basically standing at attention for her at this point and I can't tell him otherwise. When she moves to her back again, I slowly move myself to try and get up from the bed. Once I stand up, before I can take a single step I hear Mia's voice.

"Stay," she whispers.

Her hand outstretched on the mattress, eyes fluttering over to me. My night vision is perfect right now and I can see her arms pulling the sweater over her head. She's left in a tank top and leggings as she's lying there, asking me to stay in bed when I don't know how much self-control I have left.

Her eyes roam over my bare chest, I can see the way her lips are parting and her legs are still moving under the comforter every few seconds, like she's clenching her thighs together.

"Stay," she says again, and fuck, I cave.

Once I lie back down, Mia brings her body close to me again and I wrap my arms around her as we lie there. Her back is flush against my chest when she tilts her head and whispers,

"I want you to touch me."

Oh, fuck.

"Are you sure, Mi?"

She nods her head against my chest and pushes her ass back into me, no doubt feeling how hard I am right now.

I take my hand and run it lightly over her hip, letting my fingers feather her skin as we lie close together. She slowly rolls to her back, arching her neck as a small sound leaves her lips, letting me know she likes this, she's okay with it, and even better, letting me know she wants it.

My fingers trail along the waistband of her leggings before she moves her hips up slightly, urging me to go lower.

I bring my forehead down against her head, breathing her in and exhaling out against her ear.

"Fuck," I whisper. "Do you need me between your legs?"

"Please," she begs and it's the most satisfying 'please' I've ever heard.

I pull the waistband of her leggings down and she shimmies out of them completely, leaving her in just her underwear and a tank top. My fingers graze the outside of her underwear and it's clear she's already wet. My thumb presses lightly against her through the fabric and she moans as her body twitches at just that simple touch.

I just want to feel her. I already know Mia's going to fucking ruin me, but tonight is about her. She needs this and I'll happily give her anything she wants.

"You're wet, Mia." I whisper again, causing more whimpers as she thrusts her hips up towards my hand as I tease her from the outside of her underwear, running my fingers back and forth.

But teasing her is also killing me. Taking my fingers, I move her underwear to the side and slide a finger down her center nice and slow. I inhale a deep breath, because feeling Mia this wet is unbelievable and I'm going to lose my mind over here. A low growl comes from my chest as she swirls her hips around on the bed, begging for more.

"Nate," she whimpers as my thumb finds her clit and presses gently, before moving in circles. A series of moans and whimpers come from Mia. She's not quiet in the bedroom and I find that sexy as hell. I pick up the pace with my thumb just slightly, and slowly push one finger into her. Goddammit, she's tight. I push another finger in and thrust harder, hearing her cry out in pleasure again, only fueling me on.

The need to taste her is consuming every piece of my mind, but I continue to let my hand do the work. I prop myself up on my other hand, leaning over her and pressing my cock right against her thigh. Seeing her underneath me like this is a sight I never thought I'd get to experience. She is so fucking beautiful I can't stand it.

"Fuck, you're beautiful." It spills out of my mouth as I move my hip against her leg.

Mia's hand reaches for my sweatpants and I feel her hand on my dick a second later. Even through all the material, just having her touch me like this, I'm about to explode with my hand inside of her.

I keep circling my thumb against her clit as she writhes under me, one hand cupping my cock and the other gripping at the bedsheets.

Her hips buck more rapidly at the motion of my fingers, but I slow my thrusts just a little.

"Not so fast, Mi. We aren't done yet."

My hand presses into her inner thigh, squeezing and spreading her legs even further apart. "I want you to open wider for me." Her legs spread, letting me see just how fucking perfect she is.

"Fuck. Look at you, Mia. Spread open like this. Such a good girl."

My fingers continue to pump through Mia's pussy as she makes whimper after whimper and moves her hips up and down. My thumb presses more aggressively now on her swollen clit. She's dripping onto my hand, and I know she's close. Seeing Mia in a state like this is fucking incredible. She's comfortable. She's trusting and confident. A woman's sounds have never turned me on the way that Mia's sounds do.

"Oh, oh, God. I'm—" Mia's words are drowned out by her screams as her hips move vigorously back and forth and her back arches. I continue flicking her clit and don't pull my hand away, not until I know she's able to ride the whole orgasm until the end. Mia pants underneath me as her knuckles go white from gripping the bed sheets with so much force.

Once her body begins to slow down and rest, I pull my hand out from her underwear. I can feel the mess she made all over my hand and fuck, I love it.

"Messy girl," I say, as I lean back on my heels, watching her chest continue to pulse up and down.

My tongue pulls out and swipes over my lips before I take two fingers and bring them up to my mouth and suck.

Just as I thought. Sweetest fucking thing I've ever tasted.

When I get back to the bed after cleaning up, I hand Mia a small towel as she's lying on her back. Her chest is still pounding up and down and her eyes are wide and focused on the ceiling fan spinning above her.

"Are you okay?" I really fucking hope she isn't instantly regretting it, because I'd do it every day if she let me.

"Yes," she answers. It's short and whispered, but I do catch the smallest hint of a smile when she eventually curls herself up on her side and her eyes begin to flutter shut again. I run my hand along her arm as she lays there, going back and forth.

"Good night, Smalls," I whisper just as she closes her eyes.

Sleep eluded me last night, but I should have expected that. After everything that happened between us, I couldn't stop thinking about it. Thinking about how perfect this would be, and how fucking stupid I've been the last few years never letting my feelings for her come to the surface. All it took was seeing my friend try to date her, to pull my head out of my ass.

Since taking a break from football, life has felt peaceful, like I'm not running on empty and overextending myself, but my tank is actually staying full. My mind hasn't been racing. My heart hasn't been pounding with anxiety. The separation from my usual day to day has been good to give me some perspective. I know I'll need to still work on being able to manage it when I'm back in my normal element, but the one thing I have now that I didn't have before is understanding.

The way I've looked at my life, at my job on the field has been do or die.

Either be the best, or you're the worst.

I can't keep living that way. There are so many amazing things about my life that have nothing to do with the football field. Learning how to focus on those things when the football side gets tough is what I need to work on. Becoming the best version of myself—of just Nate—is where my focus needs to be. Especially if I think I deserve a shot with Mia.

I stretch out my arms in front of me as I walk out of the bedroom into the kitchen. We're about to head back on the road and as expected, Mia already has everything packed up and ready to be loaded. I was able to throw my things into my suitcase quickly this morning. She's zooming around the kitchen, wiping down the counters and putting the coffee mugs away. It's clear she's avoiding eye contact with me after last night. Hell, she has nothing to be embarrassed or feel awkward about though.

"Are you hungry? I grabbed these from the cabinet." Mia rips open a granola bar and holds it out to me. Her eyes still don't meet mine, so I lean down to get the bags from the floor.

"My hands are full," I say as I'm carrying both our suitcases.

My mouth opens wide for her to put it right in and I take a giant bite. That gets her to look at me. She stares for a brief second and the way her mouth moves lets me know she's biting back a smile.

"You're a caveman." Her eyes roll with amusement as I turn to walk towards the truck.

"That's the last of it, though. Ready to get on the road?" I ask from the truck.

Mia gives me a playful salute as she walks past me to the passenger door. My hand reaches out in front of hers, opening the door and allowing her to climb in. She settles herself into the seat and before she can reach for the seatbelt, my hand already has a hold of it, pulling it over her body and clicking it safely in place. She pulls her lips in, eyeing me with a curious stare as she just watched me buckle her into my truck. I close the door and get myself in.

"Drops of Jupiter" plays in the background as we drive onto the interstate and away from the peaceful bubble we've been in all week.

A few hours in and Mia's fast asleep with her body huddled

underneath a blanket that has a bunch of cats all over it. I joked with her when she got it that it was childish, but she says it's the coziest one she has. Her long eyelashes fan out over her cheekbones. Her full, round lips are slightly parted and I keep stealing glances at her every chance I get as I'm driving.

With the traffic starting to pick up now that we're in the early morning rush, I'm expecting our pace to slow down. Mia stirs next to me and gives me a sleepy smile when her eyes officially open. The music continues to play, it's another old song that Mia and I used to listen to in her dorm room. Her fingers start tapping on her phone and at first, I assume she's tapping to the beat until she sighs and tosses her head back against the headrest.

"Well, someone bought the building," she quips. Her laugh fills the cab of the truck, but I know it's not a funny ha-ha laugh, it's more of an amused and slightly upset laugh.

"Yeah? How do you know?"

She places her phone in the center console on the charger and sticks her arm out the window, letting it get caught in the cool breeze as we drive.

"Before anything happened with my dad, I asked Quinn to let me know if someone else put in an offer. I'm not sure if that's even something she can do, but it doesn't matter anyway because I have an email from her saying the property is no longer available, but she has others she can show me if I'm still interested." Her eyes close half way through that sentence as she lets the warm sun hit her face. Bringing out the tiny freckles that she has on her nose.

"Are you still interested in finding a place now or not?"

Usually, I'd be pushing the speed limit trying to get us back quickly, but right now, all I want is to take my time and savor the alone time I've had with Mia.

"Yes and no. Of course I want my own place, but I'm not going to look at anything right now. Maybe after the new year."

I nod my head at her answer.

"Hey," I say. "Want to do a singalong?"

Mia smiles and it turns into a laugh as she grabs her phone and scrolls through to find something. A familiar tune starts to play through the speakers and at this moment, everything feels so right.

CHAPTER TWENTY-FOUR

MIA

Every time I look at Nate, the memories of the two nights he made me have life-altering orgasms come rushing back to me. I think it's safe to say that I've let my mild attraction and lady bits call the shots this week, finally. After years of wondering what Nate would be like, I feel like I kind of have somewhat of an answer. My mind wondered what his hands felt like, and man oh man, they did not disappoint. The power within those fingers already has me clenching and wanting more as I watch him grip the steering wheel while we drive.

His gray and white flannel is wrapping around his broad shoulders, hugging tightly. I have this lingering feeling that he could probably flex and bust out of it like the Hulk and I'd have no other choice but to just climb him like a tree.

I gave into almost every instinct with him last night. Exploring that side of Nate and I isn't something I ever thought I'd risk, but I couldn't resist him. The way things have felt between us over the last few weeks has been noticeably different. My body has been reacting to him in ways I never expected, and any restraint I thought I had is merely hanging by a thread at this point. He's said things and done things that have made me question everything I thought I was always so sure of.

"What do you think about grabbing something to eat and stopping for the night?" Nate's attention flashes to me. It's just before eight, I'm surprised he wants to stop so early, considering last time it wasn't until closer to midnight. But maybe he's tired, after all he's been driving all day.

"Whatever you want to do is fine with me."

He pulls off at a populated exit somewhere in Tennessee. There's an old run-down bar on the left, next to a hotel and I notice Nate pulling into the bar parking lot.

"A bar, Nate?" My head tilts in his direction with slightly judging eyes.

His hand runs through his hair before he starts to pull the flannel off, leaving him in an old band t-shirt and I'm instantly brought back to being in college with him. The tousled look of his hair, the old shirt, dark denim and the bluest eyes I've ever seen. "Their website said they have karaoke."

My lips part slowly, looking at the neon sign that's lit up with "Boots & Chaps" except one of the O's is out so it looks more like Bots and Chaps from afar.

"You're taking me to do karaoke?"

"Is that okay? If you don't want to, we don't have to. I just figured since I wouldn't do one with you last weekend... I kind of owe you." His crystal eyes line up with mine and there's an unsettling feeling in my stomach. But not a feeling of concern or worry, just adoration. Last night was an entirely new experience between Nate and I, and while I would love to say that can't ever happen again, there are body parts that are already craving a repeat.

"No, I love it. I'm just surprised. You haven't done karaoke with me in years, except in the car. You may have lost your touch," I tease.

He shakes his head, laughing as we both hop out of the truck.

Nate's shirt brings me back to the night we first met. An old band t-shirt, except now he fills them out even more. The outlines of his muscular shoulders strain against the fabric. His jeans hug his thighs as he moves in such sure strides. His hands are big and overpowering. Nate's never lacked confidence, that's one thing I know for certain.

As we walk through the crowded bar, he leads us to the end where we can order a drink. Both of us chose beer before taking a seat, looking out at the crowd of people gathering in front of a small makeshift stage while a few women are up there singing Shania.

Nate's hand reaches for the seat of my stool and in one swift movement, he pulls my chair closer to his.

"Take your pick, it's up to you… although I'd appreciate it if you picked one I know," Nate says, handing me a small book with songs to choose from. I sift through the sticky pages, already sure of what I want, but I need to check if they have it. Once I find the song, I turn it over on the bar top behind us.

"Are you really not going to let me see before we get up there, Smalls? Do you just want me to embarrass myself in front of these people?" His hand reaches for the book but I stop it by placing my hand on top. His hand is warm to the touch and the veins are bulging as he flexes.

"The women in this bar won't care what you're singing, Nate. They'll all be too distracted by your face." He pulls back slightly, staring at me with a blush on his cheeks. I'm not sure why I went that route for a response… but it just felt right in the moment.

"That something you know from experience?" His reddened cheeks nearly hidden behind his hand as he pulls at his jaw with a smirk.

"You two ready?" A man with a black cowboy hat interrupts, handing us microphones.

"We sure are," Nate proclaims, rising from the chair and offering his hand to me as I hop off of the bar stool.

I'm feeling a lot of nostalgia tonight, with Nate's outfit and the impromptu karaoke. Nate and I haven't actually done karaoke together in years, unless you count our ridiculous car duets, but it's just something that's fun, something that brings me back to being a twenty-year-old.

The music starts and as soon as the first note hits, Nate's head falls back and he starts laughing and pulls me into a hug. We sway for just a second before it's my turn to start. We switch off verses just like the first night we met, only letting our voices collide during the chorus. We don't look out into the bar patrons the entire time. It's four minutes of us singing to each other, laughing through notes, fumbling over misremembered words and using extreme hand and arm motions as we belt out about a small town girl and a city boy.

We don't feel like just best friends tonight. We haven't for a few weeks, if I'm going to be honest. We feel like more and I'm not sure what to think of it. I've never shied away from my love for Nate. I dote on him every chance that I get. But it's never been in a romantic way, at least not really.

I remember the night he almost kissed me. I wanted him to, at least part of me did, but I was trying to think about it logically, being responsible. I pulled away in fear of ruining our friendship, but I'd be lying if I said curiosity didn't almost win. Since then, we've always kept each other safely planted in the friend zone. We work there. I never had any intention of taking things out of that zone, but lately it seems like that's exactly what Nate's trying to do. For years, I've wondered if he'd try again, but it seemed that my window of opportunity closed when I turned him down and I accepted that.

I've watched Nate date around for years. Gorgeous girl after gorgeous girl, and yet I still never felt like any of them were good enough for him. I confided in Abby last year, telling her that I sometimes wish I would've been more spontaneous with Nate when we were younger. But I always just felt like I missed my chance. Maybe this is him giving me a second one.

"We both could use some fine-tuning on that song," I say, taking the final sip of my beer before placing it back on the counter.

It's probably about time we find a hotel for the night. We have another long day on the road. Nate's finally been back in touch with the team, or at least his coach, since everything happened, and he seems eager to get back. It's hard to keep a competitive spirit away from competition for too long, but if you ask me, I'd say a few weeks away from it has done Nate some good.

"I'm ready to pass out. Let's walk to the hotel down the road," he says, before he stretches and pays the tab and we head out of the bar over to the hotel.

This hotel is so damn cute. It's very western and I guess that makes sense considering we're in Tennessee, but I love it. This whole town seems fun. The street we're staying on has bars and restaurants all lined up along it. I'd bet this would be a fun place to come for a weekend. The front desk sign says 'y'all come back now' and it made me snicker.

"Yes, we have a room available on the second floor." I hear the receptionist say. I walk over to the desk where Nate is standing, resting my elbows on the cold counter.

"Great, we'll take it." Nate looks at me after I just spoke for the both of us.

"Okay, it's a king with a pullout couch. Here's your key card. Have a nice night." She hands Nate the card, giving me a questioning look.

"I can ask for two beds, Mi," he tells me in a hushed voice.

"We made it work at the cabin, we can do it again for another night."

After we get into the room and Nate does his little security check, I shower and change before he does the same. The fluorescent lights in the bathroom are blinding as I turn on the water to brush my teeth. Thankfully there's a smaller, dimmer light that I can turn on instead.

Nate's standing next to me, drying his hair with a towel as I've got toothpaste running down my chin, trying to hurry up. He only has on a white t-shirt and a pair of athletic shorts, one hand is leaning on the bathroom counter, causing the muscles to flex in his arm every time he puts more pressure on it. My eyes continuously dart to where he's standing and every time I look at him, he's staring back at me.

Wiping my mouth with the towel, I place my toothbrush back in my travel holder.

"Turn," he tells me. Gripping my hips lightly with his fingers. He positions me to face him.

Seriously! Why am I throbbing again? You just had an orgasm last night, don't get greedy.

Nate takes the pad of his thumb and swipes at the corner of my mouth, dragging just slightly when he hits my bottom lip.

"Toothpaste," he says, huskiness lingering within his tone. He stares at his thumb for the briefest second, a small sliver of white residue on it and then, out of nowhere Nate slips the pad of his thumb in his mouth and sucks.

Oh, hell.

Fucking vagina, please stop betraying me.

CHAPTER TWENTY-FIVE

NATE

Everything about tonight felt natural and real and just fucking incredible. After the last couple of days, and everything that Mia's done for me lately just in general, I wanted to do something for her tonight. Something that I knew would make her smile. There wasn't too much off the interstate, but I did come across this hole-in-the-wall, kind of honky-tonk little bar just inside Tennessee. Their website said they had karaoke and I knew that'd be something Mia would enjoy.

Mia's wet hair is dripping in this bathroom next to me as she's aggressively brushing her teeth. You'd think she just ate an entire bucket of caramel corn with how vigorously she's scrubbing. Her little pajama set tonight is fucking cute as hell. It's actually something that matches which is never the case with Mia, as far as I've known. It's a silky light blue with stripes and she looks so sexy in it. The shorts show just enough with leaving a little room for imagination and the shirt has buttons down the center that are just begging to be ripped open.

"Turn," I say, noticing a spot of toothpaste in the corner of her mouth. My hands grip around her waist, turning her to face me. The contact feels so good. Touching Mia sends all of the blood to my dick immediately and a quick memory of her coming apart from my touch passes through.

My thumb drags at the corner of her mouth, getting the toothpaste and then I take an extra swipe and pull my thumb down slightly brushing near her bottom lip. Her chest is moving up and down as I stand there in front of her.

"Toothpaste," I say, bringing my thumb into my mouth. The toothpaste is minty, but it's Mia's bottom lip that I'm dying to taste. Dying to have between my teeth.

We're standing here, in this small, humid bathroom, feeling the air crackle between us.

"Nate," she whispers, slowly leaning her head back and closing her eyes as I place a hand on her stomach and walk us backwards, towards the wall.

She breathes out and I can feel my pulse jumping. I know how important a moment like this is to her. I have never had a clearer vision than I do right now. I have wanted Mia, on some level, for years. And I never let myself act on it. If our road trip has taught me anything when it comes to her, it's that she also thought this wasn't in the cards anymore, but maybe she's opening herself up to it. Showing her how good we could be together is all I can think of.

Mia's back gently hits the wall, and my hands instinctively spread out on either side of her head. I can smell her shampoo as I take a deep breath and she reaches her hand out and lightly slides it up under my shirt. Her delicate fingers graze over my lower abdomen and up my side. A growl leaves my chest.

Mia, please fucking tell me you want this. Tell me you want me to fucking ruin you because it's all I can think about.

I watch her eyes move up my body, like she's not sure if what she's doing is right, but fuck, it's so right, she has no idea how right this feels. Once her eyes meet mine her mouth opens, just the smallest amount and she sucks in a breath of air. Her body is trembling beneath me and I lean my forehead down against hers.

"Mia." My chest feels tight as I speak.

Her hand starts to gather the bottom of my t-shirt into her fist and I feel the slightest yank before she lets go. She pulls her hand back down, but keeps her body up against the wall. The light keeps flickering and there's still a humid feeling lingering in this small bathroom as we stand here in silence.

I step back, pulling myself away from her slightly so I can look her in the eyes. I see the desire. I see the spark, the fire, and the sheer curiosity floating around in her giant brown eyes. She wants this, but she isn't sure about what comes next. I know her so well; I can see it all playing out in her mind as we stare at each other.

She exhales a slow shaky breath before breaking eye contact and slightly turning her head to the side. Mia's long hair is leaving a small wet patch on the shoulder of her pajama shirt as she stands there. Her chest is moving up and down in deep breaths. The need to hold her, touch her, fucking kiss her is enough to make my skin feel like it's on fire.

I run my hand through my hair at the same time her big brown eyes look back to me with a yearning stare before she quickly shakes her head back and forth, darting around me and out the bathroom door.

"I'm so sorry," she says quietly as I turn around, seeing her sitting on the bed.

"You're sorry for what?"

"We're best—"

"Say we're *just best friends*, Mia. I dare you."

"But Nate, we are best friends. And I've been making us cross the line and I'm just sorry. I–I think I'm just lonely and I'm misdirecting those feelings. I shouldn't have put you in that situation the other night either, I'm really sorry for that."

Ouch.

I scoff as I shake my head. She can't tell me she isn't feeling what I'm feeling, or at least even a small percentage of what I feel. These aren't misdirected feelings. I know my best friend. She wants this, but she's afraid.

"Stop apologizing, Mia." Both of my hands go up in front of my chest. "I'm a grown man. If I don't want to do something, I sure as hell don't have to. You don't need to apologize for anything. Everything that has happened, I've wanted to happen."

"Since when?" The tone of her question has an edge to it. A challenge, almost. Like she's testing me. Is this a new realization or something I've wanted all along?

"I think I've always wanted you." My voice carries across the room, grabbing her attention. Her head turns back to me as I'm standing in the doorway of the bedroom and bathroom of this hotel room.

"Back in college, you needed a friend and I wanted to be that for you. So I channeled all of my adoration and desire for you into that, into our friendship. I never tried anything again. I told myself I wouldn't. Not until I knew without a shadow of a doubt that you wanted it too." Mia sits against the headboard, lips slightly parted, staring at me as I spew out a bunch of things I hadn't intended on saying.

"So, tell me. Tell me when you want me. I'll be here. I've been here all along."

Our eyes lock in this confusing, tell-all kind of gaze, as if she's searching for something.

Mia doesn't take risks. She doesn't do things outside of her comfort zone. She's calculated and assesses everything. She makes choices with her head, not her heart, and she weighs out all potential outcomes before she makes any decisions. She isn't a fly by the seat of her pants kind of woman. It's something I've admired about her, just her ability to resist the urge to jump into things and instead takes her time. I'm usually an act now, think later kind of guy. We've always balanced each other out in that respect. But right now, I hate the fact that she's a thinker. Because instead of going with the way her body is reacting to me, to us, she's sitting on this bed overthinking and overanalyzing every single detail of the last few weeks. It's hard to tell if she wants to give in or if she wants nothing more than to get back home and never speak to me again.

"You remember the frat party?" Her expression softens. The tension that was so visibly making her body stiff has melted away with that question.

I get into the bed next to Mia, turn off the bedside light on the nightstand and lay on my back.

"If you think I forgot about that, you're dead wrong," I whisper in the dark. "It was the night of the Homecoming game. You didn't want to go to the after party, but I promised we wouldn't stay long. Your shoes were dirty. They were once white converse, but they were fucking trashed. The NWU sweater almost hit your knees. Underneath, I know you had my jersey on, though. The sleeves on the sweater were rolled up, exposing the blue scrunchie around your wrist. You smelled like hot chocolate. Your lips were full and pouty and I wanted to taste them. God, I wanted to touch you. I wanted to push you against the wall in that hallway and kiss you until we both had no other choice but to come up for air. I wanted to kiss you, Mia. But you pulled away."

I feel her shift in the bed and when I glance over, she's also lying flat on her back staring at the ceiling. There isn't even the smallest glimmer of light coming from anywhere in this hotel room, it's pitch black but my eyes adjust to make out her figure next to me. Both of my hands are resting on either side of my body as I take big deep breaths.

"I would've bet money you didn't remember that night," her soft voice whispers.

"Blocked a little from my memory maybe to protect my precious ego." I lightly laugh. "But not completely forgotten."

Her laugh fills the air around us as her hand lands next to mine between us on the bed. I feel the tip of her pinky graze the top of mine before she lets her finger rest just between mine, interlocking them just slightly as we both drift off.

"Are you kidding me? Well, I'm not in town right now... I should be back tonight, so I can call you then, okay?"

I hear Mia's voice as I'm stirring awake and see her standing over her bag, tossing items in with the phone between her shoulder and ear. Slowly sitting up, I glance at the time. Felt good to get some decent sleep, but now we need to get back on the road.

"Everything okay?" I ask as she rushes past me, grabbing her toiletries from the bathroom.

"Yep. All good." The smile she just gave me was completely forced. I'm actually offended that she thinks I would buy that shit.

The way she's flying around the room, tossing things in her bag, tells me she just wants to get on the road.

The GPS reads six hours left until we're back in Florida. Mia's been quiet most of the ride, texting on her phone and dozing off every now and then. I can't help but be a nervous fucking wreck about my confession last night. That wasn't in the plan, hell none of this was in the plan. I had no intention of rediscovering my feelings for her, but everything changed when I had the real thought that someday another guy could come in and replace me. We'd always be friends, sure, but the reality of it is, if she were to meet someone else and end up marrying them, there goes our impromptu dinners, or daily FaceTime calls. No more Monday morning workouts or late nights at the abandoned lot. The thought of another man doing those things with her makes me fucking crazy. Crazy enough to spill all of my thoughts and feelings all over her last night.

"Is everything okay, Mi? That phone call this morning

seemed to upset you." Gripping the steering wheel, I brace myself for her reply.

"Yeah." She sighs. "It was Hannah. I think she's about to be evicted." Her laugh is sarcastic and forced. And it kills me that she's carrying everyone else's weight around with her.

"What? Why?"

"Funny story... Well, actually, it's not. But Hannah has been seeing someone, which is news to me, but he apparently stole money from her and then left her." Mia presses her thumbs into the bridge of her nose before continuing. "She really knows how to pick them."

Having someone just up and leave is a big fear of Mia's, that much I know. While she doesn't talk about her mom a ton, I know the gist of what happened.

"So she needs to borrow money?" I ask.

"Well, sadly for her I'm fresh out after paying for everything my dad needed. So if she wants my help, she'll have to accept it in the form of a guest bedroom. I don't have extra money to just throw at her problems right now, but I guess she can stay with me if she needs to. She's going to hate that idea though." The dinging sound of a text message comes through and Mia glances at her phone with the shake of her head.

"Ha. See." She holds up the message on her phone, showing me where her sister says 'pass' when Mia offers to have her stay with her.

"You'd think she would just accept the help. I told her she can stay with me for a while to find another cheaper place and get back on her feet."

"Some people are just too stubborn to accept help, Mi. You're doing more than enough for your dad and your sister, it's on her if she doesn't want to accept your help. You did your part, you offered her a solution."

Her head nods at me as she turns to face the window. The sound of the drops hitting the windshield is the only thing I hear for the next hour, and once we're within Florida state lines, Mia's attention is back on her phone, scrolling through emails and getting herself ready to dive back into reality tomorrow.

Back to normal.

Back to probably planning her date with Hughes.

CHAPTER TWENTY-SIX

MIA

God, I almost kissed him. I almost pulled his mouth against mine in that dingy hotel bathroom all because my body parts were in agony remembering the way it felt being in his arms the night before. Every time Nate has looked at me over the course of the last week, it's felt like I've been back in college. We've always been flirty with one another—that's not new. But it felt deeper, more real and more intense. Plus, the fact that he showed me just how good he is with his hands is doing all sorts of things to me mentally and emotionally.

I can't believe he remembered everything about the night in college so vividly. I know people have been telling me for a while that there's more to my friendship with Nate, and while I never completely ruled it out, I also never fed into it. I realize that back in college he had feelings for me—hell, he flat out admitted all of that. But hearing from him that the feelings are still there, that he still wants me in the same way he did years ago… I didn't expect it. Maybe that makes me naïve to sit here and say I had no idea my best friend feels that way, but I didn't. I think we can always speculate all we want, but until someone says something, it's all just assumptions and guessing. But now, there's no more guessing, no more speculating or assuming... Nate said to tell him when I'm ready. So now what the fuck do I do?

I think for a long time I hoped he'd try again. Part of me hoped that maybe I'd get a chance to redo what I passed up on the first time, if for nothing but simply out of curiosity. I'd seen him with other women and always wondered how they felt being on the receiving end of such devotion, such intimate stares and touches.

I never wanted to admit it. I never thought I'd be in the situation again. Sure, at times I wished I would've just given in that night and not been so in my head about the aftermath. But if I would've given in back then, would we still have the friendship we have now? Would Nate still be my best friend or would he be just a distant memory of someone I once knew?

Lately, everything feels like it's straight out of a movie. Some romcom, where the best friends realize they have feelings for each other while sitting outside next to a bonfire.

I have a lot of uncertain people in my life, but Nate's never been one of them. He's been my safe place, my solace, the steady and reliable man in my life that I've so desperately needed since I was fifteen. But it's a bold-faced lie to sit here and say that I've never thought of us being more than friends. Our friendship has always taken precedence over anything else.

I'm supposed to meet Summer and Abby for brunch, but called to have them just come over instead. I don't feel like putting on real clothes and the chances of me crying right now feel dangerously high. I don't know what's going on with me, but everything feels like too much. I'm not a crier generally, but in the last few weeks I've been more emotional. Between things with my dad, my sister and the lost dream of that studio, I just feel so defeated. And now, add the confusion with Nate on top of it, I don't know what to do.

"Mia." I hear my name as I'm lying on the floor in my living room. This feels over dramatic, but the hard floor under this area rug feels good on my back and staring up at the moving fan, following a single blade around and around is distracting me from my actual thoughts and feelings.

"Down here," I say, raising an arm in the air.

"Oh, God. She's broken."

Summer comes and sits next to me, while I catch Abby grabbing paper plates from the pantry.

"Something clearly happened, what's going on?" Summer's blue eyes remind me of Nate's as I'm looking at her right now. Except his eyes have so much more sapphire to them.

"I'm coming, I'm coming." Abby scurries to the living room floor and sits on the other side of me, bringing coffee and bagels and setting them down. I pull myself up and lean against the couch as both of them stare at me intently.

"I almost kissed him," I confess. "I wanted to. God, I wanted to. But in an instant, years of friendship flew through my mind and I panicked. Because once we kiss, that crosses another line —a more intimate one."

"What do you mean by another line? What else happened?" Summer takes a bite of her bagel, but watches me as she chews.

"Something happened. Well, two things. God, it was good. No, it was unbelievable. One night, I heard him in the shower… he said my name." Summer and Abby exchange looks as I continue. "And it felt so good. For a moment, I remembered what it felt like to be wanted by Nate Campbell and that just ignited something inside me."

"Well, I think you knew that his feelings were there…" Summer trails off.

"I just… I didn't believe it because his actions have always been the same. Until that night—that night, the actions were very different. After that, I started to consider it as a real possibility."

Being the object of Nate's affection is both exciting and intimidating. Over the last few weeks I've experienced a side to

Nate that I've never seen—never thought I'd see—and while it was confusing in a lot of ways, it was also captivating and made me feel desired in a way I've never felt.

"He didn't touch me. Not a single finger. And it was the hardest I've ever come from an orgasm. Until of course, the next time, when he *did* touch me and I swear my soul left my body." I place both hands on my cheeks, moving them to my eyes and running them down my face. "It was what he said, his words. The way he would talk to a woman that he's intimate with… it's a side of Nate that I never knew existed, but now that I do… I can't look at him the same. I don't know how to." Reaching for the coffee on my right, I take a quick sip.

"Oh my gosh, I'm sweating just picturing it. Sorry, I shouldn't be picturing it, but Nate is hot." Summer's comment makes me laugh.

"But it wasn't even just that. Nate and I have this… understanding, this connection, we've just always been each other's person and I'm just torn, I think. We had the best time on the road trip. Honestly, it was so much fun. I watched Nate's worries just fall off him. I know that sounds cliché and weird, but I swear his happiness depended on this time away." As I'm sitting here on the floor, sulking over my incredibly dramatic feelings—between the two girls who told me this was bound to happen—a wave of awareness washes over me.

I've been afraid of commitment my whole life. I've been terrified that letting someone into my personal space, or into my heart, is too risky and will only lead to me being let down and heartbroken like my dad was. I've gone through boyfriends and shitty dates for years. Never deeming any of them worthy enough for the long haul because I just didn't trust it. Didn't trust them. But I know Nate's heart. I know that when he says he'd never let anything happen to me, I believe him.

I've been so afraid this whole time of losing him as a friend if we ever crossed that line, but I never even considered how it might feel having him in my life as both. I've always just assumed if we did take the leap, it would mean losing him as my best friend… but maybe that doesn't have to be true.

Bringing my knees up to my chest, I look back and forth between Abby and Summer as we sit there in my living room.

An ache forms in my chest as I sit there, eyes welling up. "I think…um, I think I…"

Abby's hand lands on my knee as she nods her head at me. "We know," she whispers.

Summer reaches over and hugs me and I just sit there in the realization of what I just came to terms with.

———

> Hey, Connor. I'm back in town.

I'm not someone who can just leave a person hanging. Talking to Connor is the first matter of business on my agenda this morning. Yesterday, Abby and Summer let me have my lightbulb moment while we were sitting in my living room, stuffing our faces with carbs and re-watching *One Tree Hill*.

CONNOR
> That's great! Hope you had a good trip. I'm in town until tomorrow then we have a road stretch. Are you free tonight?

> I'd love to just stop by and talk if you're home?

CONNOR
> I'm home. I'll be here all day.

As I'm riding the elevator up to Connor's, all I'm thinking is I hope Nate doesn't happen to catch me coming or going.

Last night, I talked to Nate for maybe three minutes. It was the fastest conversation we've ever had. It felt like both of us honestly just wanted to get off the phone. He's going to meet with his agent about something this morning, but he was pretty tight-lipped on the details.

"Come on in!" I hear from the other side of the door as I knock.

I see Connor standing in his dining room, wearing a Tampa Angels t-shirt and black joggers. His dirty blonde hair is just messy enough to look hot, without looking unkempt and while I can look at him and acknowledge he's attractive, I'm not looking at him the same way I did when we first met.

"How was Wisconsin?" Connor walks over and reaches out to hug me, something we hadn't done before but I accept it.

"Very... eye opening," I answer, honestly.

Connor leans himself against the kitchen counter as I stand there, placing my bag on the chair next to me.

"Connor... I wanted to just talk before we go any further or go on any dates." I'm struggling to make eye contact with him. He's so sweet and seems like such a good man, so I hate what I have to say for his sake. "You're a really nice guy. You're sweet and you're funny. You've been such a gentleman every time we've seen each other... and"—I sigh—"you're a good man, you may even be the better one—"

"But I'm not Nate," Connor interrupts.

I hang my head, shaking it back and forth before looking back up at him.

"No... and I'm sorry. Fuck, I'm so sorry. I know I told you we were just friends, and we were—we *are*. This past week things have just gotten really confusing for me and I just... I need to sort them out."

Connor walks closer to me, reaching his arms out and wrapping me in a hug.

"Hey, I get it."

"You're not mad at me?"

"Nah, that'd be a dick move to be mad about that." He smiles and it somehow feels like he's giving me permission to smile back.

"I'm glad that you told me now. Campbell's a good guy. I'm sure he knows how lucky he is to have someone like you." He pulls back. "But if you have any single friends, send them my way." Connor winks as I collect my bag.

"Thanks, Connor."

He smiles as I leave and I feel… so much clarity.

CHAPTER TWENTY-SEVEN

NATE

It's a beast.

Anxiety, that is.

It's there when I go to bed and it's there when I wake up, hell it's there in the middle of the night jolting me out of my sleep in a panic.

Except today, I woke up with less. And the day before it was the same. A little less each morning.

Anxiety is constantly feeling like something isn't right. And when you can't figure out what it is, your mind starts to convince yourself that it's you.

If someone told me a few months ago that I'd be starting my mornings with podcasts and journals instead of sports highlights and funny memes, I'd have laughed in their face. A podcast? Sitting and listening to other people babble on about things? Never anticipated I'd be a subscriber to this podcast, but ever since Mia introduced me to this one by Dan Hart, I can't start the day without it.

It's like everything he says are things I've felt. He played football in college—never made it to the NFL, but it doesn't matter. The feelings are the same, the pressure, the anxiety of it all. Playing any high intensity competitive sport can bring even the toughest men to their knees. Just because I'm in the NFL doesn't mean I'm immune to the feeling of being anxious. I'm no longer too proud to admit that I'm struggling with it. Every day I'm making the conscious choice to work through it and overcome it. It's part of the reason I've barely talked to Mia since we've been back. It's been almost a week. Aside from everything else I learned about myself during this hiatus, I really learned that if I want to be exactly who Mia needs, I can't give her a half-ass version of myself. I need to be worthy of it. Cockiness tells me I already am, but until my mind feels more like myself, the humble part of me knows I still have work to do.

"Are you all set to go in a few days? Demi has been on my ass wanting an interview with you. You don't have to do it though, it's completely up to you. If you aren't ready just say the word. It's still widely known that you've simply taken time for yourself. Nothing more, nothing less."

There were fifteen voicemails on my phone when I finally got home and decided to listen to them. Some from my agent, others from my publicist, a few from friends and family, and then one very simple and to the point voicemail from Demi Sanchez. She's a sports reporter and someone who I've spoken to a handful of times in interviews on the field. They've always been quick recaps of the game, how I've felt after a big win or a tough loss. She's feisty and challenging. Liam loves to rile her up. Watching them interact is a constant show. For every time he hits on her, she has three ego shots just ready to fire back.

"I respect Demi. If anyone is going to properly handle an interview with me, it'll be her," I reply to my publicist's question confidently.

"She seems to feel strongly about mental health, so I think that's why she's gunning so hard for this interview." The tone of Bex's voice comes off sounding annoyed. I know she's been handling a lot of things for me while I took time off.

"Thanks for handling all of this, Bex. And just always handling my shit," I say, not remembering the last time I actually thanked her for everything she takes care of for me.

"Oh. Yeah, that's what I'm here for. It's my job."

"Yeah, I know… but thank you."

I couldn't do half of what I do without the team of people who help me. Taking time away would have been a fucking nightmare without Bex and Phil. They were always just a text away, they didn't share anything about where I went or who I was with, even though both of them knew.

"Are you doing okay?" she asks just before we end the call.

"I'm better." It's honest. "Hey, Bex?"

"Yeah?"

"Can you help me with one more thing?"

Visiting with Hannah Clark hasn't ever been on the list of things I want to be doing. She's rude and selfish and as far as I'm concerned, some kind of dark sorcery witch.

I turn off my truck after finding a parking spot and head up to her apartment. The building is cold and smells almost like a hospital. My knuckles tap on the outside of her door a few times before I finally hear her flick the lock. When she opens the door, her arm has a bandage around her forearm, it looks like gauze as if she had it done at the emergency room or something.

When she sees it's me, she quickly moves her arm behind her back, trying to hide what I've already seen. My eyes dart up to hers as she stands there. Tired, sad eyes stare back at me.

"Hannah, did something happen?" I ask, gesturing to her arm.

"I burned my arm taking pizza out of the oven." I've been lying to people for the last few months. I know what a lie looks like. And Hannah Clark just lied to my face.

"Is my sister here?" She looks around me and her body language somehow tells me she hopes she is.

"Just me today."

"Oh." Her body sulks back slightly as we stand in the doorway.

In typical Hannah fashion, she doesn't invite me in, doesn't ask anything about how I'm doing or what I'm even doing standing at her apartment. She just stands there. Almost looking like a damn zombie. I'm actually surprised there isn't any snarky comment coming out of her mouth.

"I wanted to talk to you. Mia doesn't know I'm here."

"Okay, talk then." She waves her hand in the air at me.

"I will only make this offer one time, Hannah. And I'm making it because your sister is my best friend and I love her. She didn't tell me much, but I know you're in some shit right now. Mia offered for you to stay with her until you can get back on your feet, which if you ask me, is a really fucking generous offer and she didn't have to do that. She's worried about you. Even if she didn't flat out tell me, I can see it on her, I can hear it in her voice. Your sister is a helper. It's engrained in her human body to just fucking help people, even if it means hurting herself. I made a commitment to no longer sit back and let her suffer as she flails around trying to pour into everyone else's cup while hers is bone dry."

"What are you getting at, golden boy?" God, she's infuriating.

"You can either take this check from me, catch yourself up on rent, utilities, whatever the hell you need… or you can call your sister, accept her offer and make amends with her. Get over whatever bullshit reason you have for disliking her and be a good sister. I hope you'll choose the latter, because it'd mean a lot to her." I sigh, realizing I have so much I want to say to Hannah as I stand here knowing everything I know. "You have no idea the things she's had to endure, face, give up for you.

She'll never tell you about her hardships, because to Mia, she's just doing what a big sister is supposed to do. She deserves for you to at least treat her with respect. You don't want a relationship with her? It's your fucking loss, Hannah. But have some goddamn respect for the woman who practically raised you."

"Wow." Hannah's arms cross over her chest and I swear this might be the first time I've seen Wednesday Addams crack a smile.

"You like, *love her, love her*, don't you?"

I pause before replying. Because, yes. I do. And I don't know why it's taken me so fucking long to show her.

"Yeah. I do. I've loved your sister for years. I was just a fucking idiot and I never showed it. No one ever shows it. No one ever thinks of Mia. We all like to believe she's strong and tough because she carries all the burdens of everyone so well, and she is those things, but she also needs to know it's okay to put it all down. She deserves to be shown love."

Hannah's head nods up and down and as expected she extends her hand and takes the check from my grasp.

"Thanks, Campbell." She waves the check at me and closes the door.

―――――

"Did you sleep with the realtor of this place? She wouldn't shut up about you. If you did, just tell me now so I can get ahead of it." Bex says as she hands me the keys outside of the building I leased.

"I definitely did not sleep with her. She's just an enthusiastic fan. Thanks for grabbing these." I wiggle the key into the lock and open the door. I have a list of things I need to get done quickly.

"Meg will be here soon, she's the interior designer you had me call."

"Great, thank you so much. I'm going to do some demo today. I already asked about making some changes, the landlord didn't care one way or another, so I'm taking out the desk here, and the bars along those mirrors. I'm keeping the mirrors on that whole wall, so we'll need to gently take the bars down. Liam's going to meet me here and help after practice."

"Okay, I'm going to head back to the office. Check with Phil on that other property you mentioned in your email, I haven't heard back from him yet." Bex waves as she exits and I strip free from my flannel shirt and get to work hammering away at this old desk.

"Hey, I brought reinforcements," Liam says as he walks in the door barely thirty minutes later with Abby following behind him.

"Reinforcements would have been Ford or Chase," I joke, pulling Abby into a hug.

"Well, I have the Pinterest board you need, but I'm happy to leave and go back to my *New Girl* re-watch, if you don't want my help." Her shoulders shrug and I just squeeze tighter.

"I'm kidding, please stay." Batting my eyes at her, she pulls up her phone and starts scrolling.

"How was your trip?" Liam slings the sledge hammer and material goes flying.

"Really fucking good. I have a plan for everything right now. My anxiety, the team, Mia… I finally feel focused and sure and I haven't felt like this in such a long time. The hit that Barns threw at me was the wake-up call I needed to just take a fucking beat."

"We sure have missed you, man. Chase and Ford are tired of my shit, I can tell." He laughs and I would bet thousands that he's right about that.

"Next week I'll be back. I have to meet with Coach Aarons first and go over some things."

"And what's the plan with all of this?" He motions his hand around us as we stand in front of a pile of debris.

"This," I say with a deep exhale. "This is all for Mia."

Liam smiles with a nod, slapping his hand on my shoulder as he picks up the hammer to start knocking away at the rest of the desk in front of him.

"You know, I'm proud of you." Abby's voice takes me away from measuring the now clean area for a new desk.

"Well, that's all I've ever wanted. To make little Hunt proud."

"Come on, I'm serious." She nudges me with her shoulder and I decide to give her my full attention.

"It's brave to admit when things aren't right. When something feels off and you don't even understand it, but you know deep down you need to heal. I feel pretty stupid saying this, but I guess I just never associated athletes with mental health struggles. I know anyone can experience them, but I don't know... you just never hear about it within professional athletes, at least not much. After everything happened with you, I researched. Well, Mia and I researched. Well, let me rephrase, she assigned me something specific to look up. She actually assigned us all minor tasks." She laughs, but my facial expression is pure confusion.

"What do you mean she assigned you minor tasks?"

"All of us, except Chase, for obvious reasons. She wanted as much information on anxiety as possible, specifically in athletes. She found podcasts and articles, but she also wanted to know more about how they overcome it, how they handle it on a daily basis, triggers even. Believe it or not, I actually think it helped Ford and Liam learn a little bit more about themselves too."

"Hang on," I say, wiping my forehead with a towel. "Mia asked you guys to look up ways to help me with my anxiety?"

"She wanted all of us to be safe places for you. She said you needed more people than just her in your corner. She wanted to learn how to help you. I have the most random text messages from her at all hours of the night to prove it."

"Abby's right," Liam chimes in as he walks back to the front of the building. He's been such a help today taking all of the old shit out of this place. Tomorrow, I can come in with fresh paint and some new flooring and then we can get the new furniture added.

"Which is usually the case with this one." He fluffs her hair as he walks closer to me and extends his hand out to shake mine. "Can you go get your girl now?"

It's no secret that Mia's been wanting to help me through everything. I never expected her to rope in the rest of the group, or for them to actually be willing participants.

Once I walk out of the building and close the door behind me, I feel the cooler air against my face. The time change is about to happen within the next week since I can already see the effect as the sun is hanging lower this evening against the water across the way.

For the first time in a really long fucking time, I'm seeing clearly. Things aren't blurred. Voices aren't in my head telling me I can't or I shouldn't. What I should have done was tell Mia every single thing I've been feeling the moment I started feeling them. Because now, it's just going to come out like word vomit the second I see her. The moments shared with Mia in the last few weeks were some of the realest feelings I've ever felt for someone. My adrenaline starts pumping and I take off running.

"Excuse me!" I shout, jogging through the crowds downtown, weaving in and out of people.

"Shit, sorry," I say, bumping into someone on the sidewalk. Everyone has somewhere to be tonight, apparently, and I do too.

I turn, jogging backwards as I wave my hand to the poor guy I almost just tackled. "I have to go see my best friend!"

CHAPTER TWENTY-EIGHT
MIA

I've planned my evening around the food I'll be eating tonight and that seems very on brand for me. I'm watching reruns of *Friends* and I just loaded a banana bread into the oven. If my timing is right, it'll be done right around the time that the episode comes on when Ross and Rachel kiss in Central Perk so I can eat my feelings.

The baseball game was on earlier, so I caught an inning or two while I was prepping it. I saw Connor make a really good play at shortstop and when they flashed to his face, he sported a giant smile. That guy doesn't need me. He'll be just fine.

Now I just need to figure out how to handle these feelings for Nate. The way I feel about him is clear, but also confusing. I know that I have feelings for him, but the fear of messing up what we have as friends is still very present.

"Mia!" Loud banging comes from my door, and I hear Nate's voice right away.

Wow, universe... Okay, I need a million dollars—where's that when I think of it?

"Mia, it's me!" he shouts again as I'm getting up from the

couch. My hair looks like a giant bird's nest on my head, I'm wearing the same leggings I wore yesterday and the oversized t-shirt probably makes me look so sloppy. I'm just going to ignore the fact that I look like I live under a bridge right now.

"Coming!" I say as I open the door, and Nate comes flying in. His cedar scent overtakes me as he rushes past the entrance.

"You can't go on a date with Hughes," he commands. "Please don't go on a date with him," he begs.

The words spill out of his mouth and I stand there frozen as Nate starts pacing in my living room before I can even get the front door closed.

"I can't ignore everything that happened between us, everything I felt. I know you felt it too. I know there's something here. You're nervous and that's okay, but please give this a chance. Give us a chance. I've buried everything I felt for years with you, Mia. Please. If I need to do it again, I will. But I really don't fucking want to."

My hands feel clammy, the air in here feels thick, but seeing him come barging through my door has my heart hammering in my ears.

Nate stands there in my living room with dark jeans and an old band t-shirt under a flannel. His clean-shaven face makes him look a little younger, but in my mind, I'm instantly transported back in time. I'm looking at the man I met all those years ago. The sweet, music loving, goofy, Nate Campbell… and all I want to do is kiss him.

He walks towards me as I stand in the foyer of my apartment, and I'm still stunned by everything he just said but also aching at the thought of him walking away without me telling him everything I feel too.

"I'm not going out with Connor," I whisper, heart racing and my head spinning.

Nate stops in front of me before he brings the most beautiful blue eyes to mine, staring so far into me, I swear he can see right into my soul.

His hand reaches out and cups my cheek. I let my head tilt into the warmth of his palm as he backs me up against the wall. God, this feels so good. His embrace like this feels so right.

There's the smallest speck of hesitation as he tilts his head, looking over my face as we stand there.

"You're not?" A glimmer of hope flashes in his eyes.

Shaking my head, my lips tremble through a smile as I look up to him, and a sigh of what I can only assume is relief leaves his chest. Everything in me wants him to kiss me, and I can feel the tension between us as he stands there probably contemplating the same things I am. His forehead comes down closer to mine before I hear him speak.

"*Fuck it*," he mutters under his breath, just before his lips meet mine.

It's fireworks and explosions. It's a Hallmark holiday movie and a passionate romance novel. It's playful, yet possessive. It's everything.

The kiss is hungry, but perfect. Like we've waited years for this moment and it's finally here and neither of us can actually believe it's happening. His hand travels into my hair and to the back of my neck, gripping in place and his body presses mine against the wall as our kiss deepens. His lips are persuasive and I follow his lead as his tongue strokes my own in a rhythm so perfectly tailored to the two of us. Nate's lips feel like velvet moving seamlessly against mine. Our lips slowly part while we each stand there in my dimly lit foyer. I look up at him, pressing my lips together at the memory of his tongue just seconds ago, feeling heat rising in every crevice of my body as he's still firmly pressed against me.

"Fuck," he breathes out, trailing his fingers along my jaw.

I'll never experience another kiss like that in my lifetime. I already know it. That was absolute magic.

Nate leans forward, burying his face into my neck and plants small kisses just below my ear. "God, you're amazing," he whispers before pulling back again and my body arches at his touch, at his words.

I bring my hands down from around his neck and rest them on his chest as he stands in front of me. The fabric of his flannel feels soft under my palms, but below that his muscles are firm as I gently lean into him.

"I've waited for you, Mia. God, I've wanted you so much longer than I ever let myself admit." My heart turns over every single time his gaze meets mine. "I was a goddamn fool for not saying something sooner."

The way Nate speaks to me, and simply just his presence alone, soothes me in a way that I've never felt. My feelings for him are intensifying even in just this brief moment. Every time he talks, I swear they're growing stronger.

"I'm so scared of losing you," I whisper, almost wanting to take it back immediately, in fear of ruining the moment. But the feeling is true, it's valid. I can't imagine my life without him.

"You won't." He runs a hand down my arm and stops when he gets to my hand, gripping it in his own.

"We wouldn't have made it in college," he says, squeezing my hand. "I've thought about it and I don't think we would have. I wasn't good enough for you back then. Hell, I hope I'm good enough for you now. But I'm going to try like my life depends on it to be the man you need. You won't lose me, Smalls. I promise. This is it for me, you're it."

"I'm just… surprised is all. I'm nothing like the women you typically go for." I shrug as he pulls my body closer to his, my head resting on his chest before he looks down at me. His hands come up to my cheeks, cupping them in his warm embrace.

"None of those women were you." His steel blue eyes focus on mine.

"What?"

"They were not you."

The gentle sound of Nate's voice as he's speaking is bringing a wave of realization over me. He's looking at me with such sincerity and so much hope.

"It's always been you, Mia. I tried to trick myself into thinking I could be with someone else, that I could want someone else." His head shakes back and forth with a nearly sarcastic scoff. "But the truth is, I've just always been avoiding the fact that I didn't actually want any of them. Because I want you."

"I want you," he repeats.

And every wall I had up, every reason or excuse why this wouldn't work, every single thing I tried to convince myself of comes crumbling down.

Because in this moment, I know I want him too.

I'm leading with my heart for once in my damn life. I'm choosing my happiness. I'm choosing Nate.

I lift onto my tippy toes, pulling his face down to mine and wrapping my arms around his neck as I fuse my mouth with his. Nate picks me up and brings our bodies to the couch. My legs straddle over his as we sit there and my body naturally grinds against his. He groans as I pull my mouth away from him.

"Sorry," I say, covering my lips with my fingers just as the timer for the banana bread goes off. I reluctantly hop off him to go grab it. If I wasn't afraid that leaving it in there wouldn't start a fire, I'd just ignore it.

"Extra walnuts and chocolate chips?" he asks.

I laugh. "Like there's any other way to make it?" When I take the loaf out, I place it on the hot plate on the counter before turning off the oven and going back into the living room.

"Is it stupid and immature to say I really just want to sit and make out with you for hours?" I ask, standing in front of him.

I'm not good at this part, but I do know that Nate's lips are literally my favorite thing I've ever tasted.

"Mia, you can do whatever you want with me." He smirks and crooks his middle fingers at me from the couch and I don't even hide my smile as I lean forward and let my lips collide with his for the rest of the night.

Did I wake up this morning and immediately replay the events of last night?

You bet your ass I did.

I kissed my best friend. And I liked it. And I want to keep doing it.

> LIAM
>
> Boat leaves in 30. If you're not at the dock,
> guess you're swimming.

Today is technically the last day before Nate is supposed to return to the facility and check in with the team. It was Liam's idea to take the boat and jet ski out on the water today, and it's rare that any of us pass up an invite.

"Hi," Nate says as he grabs my hand and kisses it before he helps me onto the boat. I blush at his simple gesture as I take a seat next to Chase and Kristen. I'm actually shocked to see Kristen on this boat, but I know Chase, and he wants to do whatever he can to make this whole situation work—for the sake of the baby. Summer, Abby and Ford hop onto the boat just as Liam is untying the rope.

Liam cruises us out to Bottle Island as Nate follows closely behind on the jet ski. I watch as his hair blows in the wind while he whips it around and speeds up close to us. I try to bite back a smile as I watch him, but it's no use. He looks hot on that thing.

There's a strip of island that sits out here and everyone pulls their boats right up onto it. I guess from a bird's eye view it looks like it's in the shape of a beer bottle, hence the name. The water is pretty shallow and you can usually see to the bottom which is nice, considering if I can't see the bottom, I'm not going in. The guys all get up and head to the bow of the boat. A term I've learned coming out here with all of these seasoned professionals.

Abby, Summer and I all jump out and head up to the island to set up a sheet to sit down on the sand.

"Kristen," I call out. "Do you want to sit with us?"

"Really, Mia?" Summer gives me a disgusted look.

"What? She's by herself… and if she and Chase are trying to make this work, shouldn't we try to be friends with her?"

"No," Summer says with a flat and annoyed tone as she moves her towel further away. Abby just rolls her eyes and moves her bag to make room for Kristen who is walking towards us.

"Thanks," she says while placing her bag down, and I smile at her.

"So, how's the baby, Kristen?" I ask, trying to make small talk.

"Ugh. Never sleeps. Thankfully, Diane is over this week so hopefully she can do the middle of the night wake ups." Kristen pulls out her phone and opens the camera, checking her appearance. I want to ask more, but I'm getting the impression that Kristen doesn't want to chat so I just leave it at that. I lean over to look at Summer and she gives me a 'see, she sucks' look.

Nate walks over and tosses me his hat before he runs back over to the boat. I place the hat backwards on my head as I lean on my elbows, waiting to see what they're all congregating about.

Nate looks so happy. I know the true test will be seeing how he is on the field, but I swear he looks lighter. He looks relaxed and rejuvenated. His eyes don't look sad or broken anymore. He stands tall and confident, instead of hesitant.

The guys pull out a football from the boat and Liam tosses it to Ford who makes a dash down the sand. I guess Chase and Nate are on a team because they both seem to be trying to defend Ford.

"Oh my God." Summer comes and sits between Abby and I. "Are we living in a *Top Gun* beach scene right now or what?"

I look back to the guys, running all over this beach. They're all sweaty and their tanned skin glistens in the sunlight. I swallow and clear my throat, trying not to stare too long. Nate's brown hair hangs in his face, the sun always makes it look lighter, almost like a dirty blonde. He swipes it back with his hand before he bursts out a fit of laughter at something Liam says. His crystal blue eyes stand out even more against his tanned face. And I probably shouldn't let my eyes linger on his stomach, but it's hard not to.

"Come here, Clarky!" Liam shouts, and I stand, walking over to him. Liam tosses me the football and I jog to try and make the catch, but I very clearly miss.

"Here, let me show you. Campbell! Throw the ball to Mia, I'm going to help her catch it." I really hope Liam doesn't use this move on women, because it's the oldest, most tired trick in the book. He positions my body just in front of him, wrapping his arms around mine. Nate's eyes are like daggers on Liam and I can see Liam from the corner of my eye smirking.

"Let's see what he does," Liam whispers in my ear, causing my head to turn up in his direction. But before I can ask anything, Nate's already standing in front of me.

"You're the quarterback," he growls to Liam, moving his arm off of mine and shoving the ball into his chest. I watch Liam's mouth open in laughter as he falters back a few steps and jogs backwards, winking at me. Nate's standing to the side of me like a bodyguard.

"I really don't need help catching a football. I know how. I prefer to just sit there and watch."

"I know you do." Nate leans close to me, his hand resting on the small of my back. "Now, go sit back down and watch me." He smirks and my stomach drops to my knees.

CHAPTER TWENTY-NINE

NATE

"Let's keep our hands to ourselves, yeah?" I give Liam a stern look as we walk back to the boat.

"He does that for your reaction, you know that, right?" Chase laughs as he pats my shoulder, pulling a beer out of the cooler.

"Yeah, well, I told her everything," I say, standing in front of Ford, Chase and Liam. All three of them stare at me blankly, waiting for me to elaborate.

"About fucking time," Ford says, blowing out a sigh.

"Told her what exactly?"

"Big daddy has been a little out of the loop with all the sleepless nights and hot mom sex. You might need to fill him in," Liam chimes in, but Chase interrupts him.

"There's no hot mom sex happening. She just had a baby. It's completely up to her when we have sex. She's overwhelmed. Which is the reason I wanted to take her out here today. I know her hormones are all over the place and she's the sole food source of a needy infant, she needed a break. I'm there to support her. Don't downgrade her to just a hot mom, you fucking idiot." Chase flicks the bottle cap into the open cooler and takes a long swig.

"So, things are going well with her then?" I ask, knowing just a few months ago things were rocky at best. But to be fair, I've been so caught up with my own problems, I've barely paid attention to anyone else's.

"It's day to day, but today, things are good. So, that's what we're flying with."

"And you and Clark?" Liam asks just as the girls walk up to the boat. Mia's in a white swimsuit with strings everywhere. I want nothing more than to take all the strings and untie them with my teeth.

I pull Mia to my side, planting a kiss on her cheek as she leans into me.

Summer's jaw hangs as she sees my hands roam over Mia's hips and the smile on Mia's face.

"Oh my God. Wait. So what does this mean?" Summer shouts, and Chase holds his hands up to her, motioning for her to calm down.

I look down at Mia and we smile at each other. She reaches for the sunscreen and squirts a tiny bit on her fingers before she rubs it into her cheeks and over her nose and forehead.

"It um... it means we are trying this? Right? A test run?" she says hesitantly.

I pull back in amusement at her word choice. "Oh yeah? Just a trial for you?" I quip, grabbing the key for the jet ski and hopping on. "I'm fully invested. I don't need a trial period, sign me up right now, Clark." My eyes trail over her slender body as she stands there with one hand on her hip.

"Well—" she begins, but I have a better idea. Something that will put any questions or 'trial runs' to rest.

"Come on, Smalls. Get on." I hold my hand out for her to grab.

"Want to have some fun with me? Let's get started on this trial run of yours."

She scoffs and looks back at Abby and Summer before

rubbing the remaining sunscreen over her thighs and reaching for my hand.

Mia swings her legs over each side and grabs the lifejacket from Abby's outstretched arm.

"Careful," Abby says as I start to back up.

"Oh, don't worry. I'll take real good care of her." I smirk, and feel Mia's arms squeeze around my middle a little tighter at that comment.

There's a hidden canal down back towards the shore. It's quiet and shallow and usually doesn't get many visitors. It's a shame because it's really a beautiful spot. Trees hang over and the water is calm and still.

"I've always wondered what this canal looked like. We pass it all the time," Mia says once I slow to an idle speed.

"I love it. You can just cruise down without a bunch of speedboats creating wake." I turn off the jet ski and let us just drift a little bit.

Mia takes the lifejacket off and hangs it on the handlebar and then slides herself into the shallow water. It's only about waist deep on her and it's one of the clearer spots. I watch her run her fingers through her hair, pulling it back and fastening it with a scrunchie into a bun.

"You're beautiful," I say as I stare at her. Words I've always wanted to just blurt out when I've thought them, but always held back.

She blushes and walks to the back of the jet ski. She's within arm's reach, so I pick her up effortlessly and sit her right on my lap. Good thing I sprung for the three person jet ski, we've got plenty of room here.

She sucks in a small breath once her body clashes with mine. Her legs spread out in front of me, straddling over the seat. I bring my lips down to her neck and Mia tilts her head back, giving me more access.

"A trial run, huh?" I whisper as my fingers graze the inside of her thighs. I watch her body clench against the seat and she moves back and forth just slightly, creating friction between her legs as she sits there.

"We never talked about what we're telling anyone, so I, uh… just guessed."

"Well, let me take any of the guessing out of it." My finger glides against the outside of her bathing suit bottom and I bring my lips centimeters away from hers. "I've watched you date lesser men for years. Men who didn't deserve even a fraction of your time. Knowing they were touching you, tasting you, fucking you…" From the outside of her swimsuit, I add pressure against her clit with my thumb and she jerks back with a whimper.

"We're together, Mia. I'm yours. And I'm not going to wait another fucking second without taking what's always been mine."

My thumb presses firmly against the fabric on her clit at the same moment I bring my mouth down to hers. She reacts instantly as her hands pull on my neck, dragging me closer to her. I slip my fingers underneath the fabric, already feeling how turned on she is. She thrusts her body down into my hand.

"Please, Nate," she begs against my lips, rocking her pussy against my hand. I press my thumb into her clit, moving in circles and she moves herself faster and harder, trying to create more friction and pressure.

The lanyard around my neck grazes the outside of her swimsuit against her nipple as she pulls me closer to her. The white fabric does a shit job at concealing anything, it's obvious how turned on she is just by how firm her nipples are. Each time I lean forward and thrust my hand further into her swimsuit, the lanyard lightly swipes across her chest, and every time, she moans at the touch.

"Let's give you exactly what you need." I lie her back on the seat of this jet ski, glancing around confirming there isn't a soul in sight.

"Is someone coming?" she asks frantically.

"No. I'd never let anyone else see my girl like this."

There's a good chance I'm going to absolutely blow my fucking load in a split second the moment I get a taste of her, but it's too tempting and she wants it too badly to deny it.

I inhale a deep breath as Mia leans back with her legs spread. My knees hit the floor board of the jet ski and I bring my teeth up to the string that keeps one side tied, pulling it to give me better access to the spot I want. Mia's hands reach into my hair and she does the smallest tug, but it may as well be a full yank. It sets off an animalistic need for her. A possessiveness. A caveman-like urge to absolutely devour her.

I look up at her with a devilish grin. Taking my fingers and pulling down the rest of her swimsuit, she's practically dripping and my dick is begging for a release.

"You're fucking gorgeous like this; do you know that? Spread wide open for me." I kiss the inside of her thigh, then move to the next one as Mia's head falls back. My tongue runs over my lips as I hover over her pussy before I swipe just the tip of my tongue all the way through. Stopping at her clit and pressing my tongue into her over and over. Mia's cries could probably be heard by someone even if they were a hundred yards away, but I like it like that.

"Be as loud as you want, baby," I say, licking my lips before going back for seconds. Sucking on her swollen clit becomes my focus and I thrust two fingers into her pussy as she writhes underneath me.

She likes this. She likes when I'm pushing harder.

Pulling my lips away for a moment, I breathe right over her. "Squeeze my fingers, Mia. That's my girl." I can feel her muscles contracting around my fingers as she fucks my hand.

When I bring my mouth back down against her clit, I run my

tongue over her again and again. My teeth hit her clit and it does something to her.

"Oh my God, I'm—" With my face between her legs and fingers deep inside her, I can feel the release building up. Her hands are pushing my head down into her, begging for more contact and at that moment, the hottest fucking thing happens just before she completely loses herself in my hand. I can feel every bit of it. Every pulsing, throbbing, piece of her falling apart is in the palm of my hand and I'm a fucking goner.

"Oh my God. I've–I've never done that before," she pants as she's riding out her orgasm.

I felt the squirt as soon as she reacted to my teeth against her clit. It streams near my chin as I continue to suck and taste every inch of what she had to give me.

When I pull back, she leans herself forward on an elbow.

"That felt so fucking good," she says with a sated smile on her face. "I've never come like that. I don't even know how it happened." She blushes as she sits up.

"Well, I did say a while ago I had a magic tongue and knew how to use it." My wink only earns an eye roll and a lousy effort at a punch to my bicep. A gesture I'd normally interfere with, taking her wrist in mine, but I'm too lost in the thought of being with Mia like this.

"Should we head back?" I ask, as she slips back into her bathing suit while I'm holding her lifejacket, waiting to secure it back onto her body.

She nods her head, shyly allowing me to clip the jacket in place before I start the jet ski and ride back to the boat.

"Shh, shh, it's okay, baby girl," Chase whispers as he pats his daughter's back.

"They're bringing the last bit of equipment over later. Your sister was such a help with this," I say, wiping down the newly installed counter.

Chase stopped by the building to see the progress. I'm really fucking proud of how this turned out and I can't wait to show Mia.

"It looks good. Mia's going to lose her mind." He laughs as he hums a song and walks around, bouncing her on his chest.

"I'm meeting with Coach at four, so I'm going to get going. Thanks for all of your help with this, man. And just in general. I know you've been dealing with your own shit, so I appreciate you always showing up for mine."

"We all struggle with something, the first part of working on it is admitting that it exists." Chase shakes my hand as we leave.

The day I went for a hike by myself in Wisconsin, I brought a notepad with me. I wrote down a list of things that I wanted to accomplish that had nothing to do with football. The last few weeks have been amazing. And not just because of everything that happened with Mia, although that's definitely one of the highlights.

Spending time away from my stressors opened my eyes to a lot more around me. Football is one of the greatest loves of my life—it's my passion and my job, but it's not my purpose. It's not my endgame or my reason for existing. Sure, I love the high of getting into the end zone every weekend, and I know I'll miss that when all of this is over. But the real goal is living a life outside of the football field that I'm proud of. Making a difference to people for more than just what I do every Sunday.

Athletes don't talk about their mental health. At least not nearly as much as we should. And yet, over thirty percent of us experience mental health struggles. We think we're supposed to be tougher than our problems, that we're supposed to suck it up and do our job. We live a life that most people would do anything to have, but it doesn't make us immune from struggles. I want to help end the stigma surrounding athletes and mental health. I want to be part of the solution, instead of just another statistic in the column.

I'm walking back into this facility today with a clear vision and a hunger to take charge of the things that have been weighing me down, and flipping them into something good, something worth talking about. I've always known that I wanted to make a difference for people, to give back and use the platform that I have to inflict change. But the vision for it wasn't clear until these last few weeks.

The Christmas tree is already up in the entrance of the facility as I walk in. The receptionist at the front waves me in and I offer her a smile. It's nearly Thanksgiving, but it already smells like Christmas in here, like someone actually just has a pine scented air freshener plugged in around every corner.

When I turn down the hall to where the coach's office is located, I feel a small wave of nerves wash over me, but nothing extreme. It feels bearable. Like I'm just excited to be back within these walls.

As I walk down the hall, it feels like I'm coming back to school after being home for Christmas break. Everything feels new, fresh and like the possibilities are endless. Taking a break to look at things from a different perspective really helped me see the bigger picture here.

I've realized there are so many things I want to do with my life and my time here, aside from being on the football field. I want to finish this season as best as I can, however that looks. I don't expect to start on Sunday. I'll be okay if I don't. But I'm ready to be around the guys again, back in that environment. There are plenty of things to discuss before I step foot back on the field, but just being back here brings me some comfort. Something I didn't actually feel a month ago, just solidifying the fact that the break was needed and it helped.

"Coach," I say, tapping on his door as I push it open.

He walks up to me, wrapping me in a bear hug before letting

go and taking a seat on the other side of his desk. His bright red windbreaker stands out against my black and white flannel.

"How are you feeling?" His eyes are pleading for the truth and this time I give it to him.

"I spent the majority of the last few weeks letting myself wander, letting my body and my mind just relax. I've listened to podcasts and done a lot of self-reflecting. I've honestly just been trying to survey my life. Which sounds so fucking weird to say, but something I learned during my time away is that I need to be better about communicating. I've never been good at it, but I never considered it an issue. Until all of this. Not telling you that I was struggling put the team at risk. I'm just so fucking sorry for everything."

"Listen, I know this game puts a lot of pressure on all of you. It's mentally, emotionally and physically a tough game, a tough career path. You don't owe me an apology, Campbell."

"I do though, Coach," I say. He pulls his glasses from his face, placing them on the desk in front of him. "I knew there was a problem and I didn't speak up. You gave me every opportunity to ask for help and I was too ashamed to admit I needed it. It felt weak."

Shaking his head back and forth, he looks at me. "You have to be ready to talk about it. I could have asked a dozen more times before you finally said something. You weren't ready."

"I am now. I've spent time trying to relearn some things about myself in my time off. Trying to understand my purpose in all of this. I can admit I still need help fully understanding and managing all of it, but at least I feel like I have a better self-awareness now. I needed the time away." I sigh. "And now, I need you to tell me how I can contact the team therapist."

His lips press together in a firm line as he nods his head and extends his hand out to shake mine. "Anything you need, son."

CHAPTER THIRTY

MIA

When I heard knocking at my door at six thirty in the morning, I had half a mind to grab a baseball bat.

"Hannah, is everything okay?"

My sister's eyes are red and puffy, her hair looks like she hasn't showered in days and there's a bandage on her forearm that looks like it needs to be changed.

"Can I stay here?" she squeaks out in a broken voice, holding her arms against her chest. There's a small suitcase to her left, but it's barely the size of a carry on. There's no way that all of her belongings fit in there.

"Of course." I usher her inside and peek my head out down the hall. It's still dark and everything is quiet. "Are you okay? What happened?"

Her eyes well up with tears as she stands in my kitchen leaning against the counter. I flip on the dining room light and start a pot of coffee before grabbing her some clothes and a towel from the bathroom. She doesn't answer me, but I don't take it personally.

"Go ahead," I softly say, gesturing towards the guest bedroom and bathroom. I watch as her frail body moves slowly through the living room over to the bedroom. The white shirt she's wearing is covered in wrinkles and could definitely use a wash. It almost looks like she's been wearing it for days.

> Hannah just showed up at my door.
> Something's wrong.

It's early in the morning, but something urges me to reach out to him. His reply comes not even a minute later.

> NATE
> I'm on my way.

Nate's at my door before Hannah even resurfaces from the bathroom. He comes in, kisses me sweetly and takes a seat at the table.

"Did she say what happened?" he asks, rubbing his eyes. It's clear my text woke him up.

"No. She barely said anything." I keep my voice at a whisper. "But, Nate. She has a bandage on her arm and if my true crime addiction has taught me anything, I'm afraid she's hiding something." My heart is racing at all of the different scenarios that are flashing through my mind.

Before Nate can answer, the sound of the bathroom door causes both of us to look in her direction. She's at least showered and has put on clean clothes. She still looks run down and tired, but she makes her way over to the table and sits down across from Nate. She stares at him for a moment, like she's not sure if he was here the whole time or just showed up.

"Do you want to talk about anything, Hannah?" he asks.

She shakes her head back and forth before taking a sip of her coffee.

"Not yet," she says into the cup, closing her eyes and blowing into the steam. "But… I'm sorry, Mia. For the way I've treated you, the things I've said, just all of it… I should have been a better sister." Her fingers grip the sides of the coffee cup as she takes another long sip.

"Why'd you shut me out, Han?" It doesn't feel like the best time to ask her, but curiosity takes over. Hannah's quiet for a moment, her eyes boring into mine before she answers.

"How were you fine after mom left?" she whispers. Her dark brown eyes narrow. "Dad crumbled. I got lost in the shuffle and you just seemed… fine. I guess I resented you for not being angry at her. At both of them. How'd you do it? Move past it like everything was fine."

"You don't think I was mad? Hannah, I was devastated. I was angry and upset, but I had you to think of. I couldn't let our lives fall apart because of how dad handled it. Do you think I wanted to go straight to a job at the grocery store after school every single night? Everything around you fell apart, Han. I had to step up for you."

Hannah stands from her seat, shuffling over to where I'm seated and leans down. For the first time in who knows how long, my little sister hugs me. It sends a wave of emotions through me as I sit there and hold her. My eyes lock with Nate's as his lips are set in a firm line and he gives me a reassuring nod. I still don't have answers as to what caused her to show up at my door this morning, but right now, she's safe and she's hugging me, and I'm counting this as a win.

It's quarter after twelve and I don't have much to show for my day so far. I have a client later this afternoon, but aside from that I've just been trying to be around in case Hannah needs me or finally wants to talk. She finally agreed to go get some rest and she's still actually asleep now.

My thoughts of what happened are narrowed down to a few. The most obvious feels like something happened with her shitty boyfriend and that angers me enough to consider accepting jail time. But then within the anger there's also regret and guilt. Should I have tried to find another way to help her? Did her moving down here just destine her for this kind of life? Problem solving mode is activated, but it's put on a brief hold when Nate's FaceTime comes through. He's back with the team, gearing up for an interview he has later in the week, but today he said he's meeting with the team therapist for the first time.

"Hey, Smalls." His face comes into view on my screen and my heart just bursts at the sight of his smile.

"Hey, how was it?" I ask.

"First time, so it was okay. I was nervous, but she's nice… and seems to know what she's talking about." His tongue darts out over his lips as he watches me through the screen. I don't know if there will ever be a time that I'm used to the way Nate looks at me.

"How's your sister?"

Sighing, I pick up the phone from the dresser. "She's actually been asleep since you left."

His lips curl into a smirk as I watch him get into his truck and start it. "Oh, well that's good. I'm on my way over."

"Okay, I have to leave in about an hour though," I reply.

"It takes approximately seven seconds to kiss you." He grins into the screen.

"Seven seconds, huh?" My lips curve at the way his blue eyes light up.

"Unless there are other ways you want to spend the time." He smirks and it causes my cheeks to heat.

"I'll see you soon," we both say in unison before the call ends.

The moment Nate walks in his hands are on me. I guess in some ways we're making up for lost time, but it still feels so new to me to be held like this.

"Your love language is definitely physical touch," I say as his hands run down my back, cupping my ass.

"*You* are my love language."

My eyes narrow at him slightly as we stand in the doorway of my bedroom. "How do you do that?" I ask.

"Do what?" The Henley he's wearing has the top button undone, and I can't stop staring at the way the blue shirt looks against his eyes.

"Take an otherwise ordinary moment, a simple sentence, and make it... so... meaningful, so perfect?"

He chuckles as he walks us backwards into my bedroom, closing the door and flicking the lock behind him.

"I guess because to me, even really ordinary moments with you are a dream, Smalls. I still can't believe I get to be with you." His grip around my waist tightens as he slides two fingers into either side of my leggings slowly moving them down just the smallest amount on my hips.

My teeth bite down into my bottom lip as he lays me down on my bed. His tall frame standing over me with the sunlight from the window casting a perfect spotlight on him.

"You should, uh, take those off," I say, wagging my finger at his jeans.

His eyebrows shoot up as he sarcastically points down to his jeans. "These?" he asks.

My head bobs up and down as I lean on my elbows against my bed.

"You want it... you can come get it." He pulls his belt through the loops and tosses it on the floor.

I inch myself closer to the edge of the bed where he's standing and reach my hands up to the button and zipper. My heart is screaming in my chest, considering I have a very vivid memory of what I'm about to be face to face with.

Once I pull his jeans down around his thighs, the thickness

stands out behind his boxers. Nate pulls his shirt off and I'm left staring at every woman's fantasy.

"It's just unfair," I whine, my tongue involuntarily running between my lips. "You looking like this."

"On your knees." Nate's voice when he's turned on sounds like a different person. It's still him, but he's so much more commanding. Like if I don't follow his order, he'll punish me and I have a love hate relationship with how that makes me feel.

"Well it's a hard wood floor, so…" I snark back, liking the way it feels to taunt him.

A smirk that mimics the devil himself spreads across Nate's face.

"Since you want to have such a fucking attitude lately, let's put that mouth to better use, Smalls. Get. On. Your. Knees."

I think I'll just see myself out at this point. I'm about to fall over and roll out the door and down the stairs for my best friend right now.

Nate pulls his boxers down enough to free his cock and I can't tear my eyes away from it. Seeing it through the phone screen didn't do it justice.

"Don't look so surprised, this isn't new for you," he says looking down at me. "Think I didn't know you got a show on the FaceTime call?" He strokes himself as he stands there, staring at me.

"Suck," he growls, and my hand pushes his out of the way, feeling the size and strength of him before I bring my mouth down around him.

I feel him hitting the back of my throat every time he moves, but he's not being forceful. Nate's actually holding himself back, he's gentle while still displaying dominance as I kneel in front of him. His hand is in my hair, gripping as I run my tongue along the base to the tip and back down my throat.

"Look how fucking well you take me." His words only fuel me to keep going. My hand reaches underneath, cupping his balls as he pushes himself further and I can already taste some of the pre cum every time he hits the back of my throat.

"Fucking hell, this is so good." He breathes in as his nostrils flare and low moans leave his chest. He hasn't removed his hand from my hair the entire time and while he's not pulling it, he's gripping it in a way that sends shivers down my spine, directly to my fucking vagina.

I pull away from him briefly to catch my breath. Licking my lips, I taste him on me and I press my thumb into the corner of my mouth. I suck on it as he watches.

"Are you wet for me?" he asks while his hand strokes his cock. I simply nod my head up and down at his question.

"Take these off." His head falls back with another moan as I slip out of my leggings. "I need to taste you."

Nate turns, lying himself on the bed, his cock still intimidatingly tempting as he strokes himself.

"Up here," he demands, pointing to his face as I was about to lie down next to him.

"Are you sure?"

"No, I'm not sure," he says, giving me a frustrated stare. "Of course, I'm fucking sure, Mia. I've thought about nothing else for the last month other than your legs wrapped around my head. Now, hold onto the headboard."

I move my body up against his chin and the second I feel the smallest bit of his stubble against my clit, I cry out.

"Sit," Nate demands again, pulling my hips and planting me directly on top of his tongue as it moves through me immediately. Nate moans the second we make contact and my entire soul feels like it leaves my body as he pulls his tongue through me and I rock back and forth against his face.

"Nate, oh my—" My thoughts and words are jumbled by his ability to put me into a complete trance. What's the record for fastest orgasm because I think I'm about to break it? An orgasm from Nate Campbell is truly unmatched. With every motion I can feel it building and building before I'm making a mess all over his face and trying to pull myself away, but his hands grip my thighs, keeping me in place as his tongue continues to work through me.

"Oh, my God. It's too much, Nate. I can't—" My whole body falls back as he finally loosens his grip against my thighs and I pant like a damn dog trying to catch my breath as I move lower.

Nate reaches his hand up into my tank top and seamlessly unhooks my bra from the back.

"Wow, not your first time, huh?" I tease.

He tugs at the hem of my shirt, helping me pull it up over my head as my bra falls off with it.

"You are without a doubt the most stunning woman I've ever seen, Mia Clark." Nate's shirtless chest leans into me as he kisses the swell of my breast, causing my head to fall back with lust. His fingers pinch my nipple as I sit in his lap, still feeling his length against me.

I reach my hand down and wrap my fingers around him, causing him to hiss in pleasure at the touch.

"Tell me what you want," he whispers into my mouth.

My eyes lock with his as my fingers feather over the tip of him, feeling how firm he still is.

"Ruin me," I beg.

CHAPTER THIRTY-ONE

NATE

"Ruin me." Her voice is laced with desire.

I smirk at her request as she pulls herself up closer to me.

"You want to ride me, Smalls?" Her head nods up and down quickly as I watch her hair fall into her face.

"In the nightstand," she moans and I reach over, finding a condom in the drawer and slide it on. Her breasts rise and fall with each deep breath she takes and it's as if my mouth has no other choice but to pull her nipple between my teeth. She whimpers at the gentle nibble and then slides herself down, taking my entire length in one sitting.

"Fuck, Mia," I mumble against her chest, feeling how fucking tight she is. She cries out as my hands roam her thighs, squeezing into her skin.

"Oh my gosh," she says, steadying herself as she takes all of me.

I whisper against her ear, "You can take it. My cock was made for you, Mia. It's the perfect fit."

She begins to rock her hips back and forth, moving herself up and down in the most incredible way. The way her eyes close and her head falls back, her chipped fingernails digging into my shoulders as she braces herself every time she comes back down.

"Oh fuck, Nate," she cries. "I'm trying not to be too loud, but it's so good."

I need more control. The desire to drive into her is too strong to pass up. I wrap my arms around her, flipping our bodies so she's lying on her back. A squeal leaves her pouty lips as she lays there beneath me. My eyes scan over her body, a fucking breathtaking sight, as I lean over her.

"You're a dream," I say, pressing my forehead against hers just before thrusting into her. Her pussy feels so good squeezing me like she is. I can't believe we haven't been doing this the whole time, we've been sexually depriving ourselves because this… this is fucking heavenly.

"Nate, push harder." Her words are a plea and I happily oblige to her request.

We move in such a rhythm, like this is something we've been perfecting for years.

"Yes, like that," she pants. "Oh my gosh. Yes."

Our bodies are clashing as our lips collide and sweat beads form on my chest. Taking Mia's leg in my hand, I lift it onto my shoulder, giving better access as I thrust into her over and over. Her screams are sure to wake a hibernating bear, but neither of us give a shit at this point.

"Scream, Mia. Let everyone in this building hear you."

When I pull Mia's hair, even just slightly, she cries out again.

"You like when I pull your hair, Smalls?"

She only whimpers. Her sounds encourage me to keep going, keep pushing. And then I feel her body start to shake beneath me as she yells a stream of curse words, letting another orgasm rip through her body.

"That's my girl," I praise.

Feeling her clench around me only pulls my own orgasm out of me moments later. The way Mia's body feels against mine is everything I imagined. She fits like a damn glove and I'm already addicted to this feeling.

"Fuck," I pant against her skin. "I knew being with you would blow my mind. But that was explosive, Mia."

Her hands run through her hair as she pulls herself up, biting her bottom lip. I kiss the curve of her shoulder before she glances beside us at the clock on her nightstand.

"Is it terrible if I say I need to get going?"

"Wow, just took what you need and now you're ditching me?" I joke, and she rolls her eyes at me.

"Yeah, exactly. Thanks for the best sex of my life, see you later." She salutes and I pull her by the waist back to me, kissing her forcefully as she laughs.

"When you get home, I want to take you on a date," I say, watching her get up.

She walks into the bathroom and then back to the room and slips into her clothing that we discarded earlier. She slides her legs, one by one, back into her leggings and she does this little hop as she pulls them up over her ass and thighs. I could watch her forever.

"A date, huh?" She smirks as her tank top comes over her head. I stand, tossing the condom in the trash before cleaning up and fastening my jeans. When I pull my shirt back over my head, she's staring at me with a small blush to her cheeks.

"Yeah, a date. I'll be back at seven to get you." She comes over and kisses my cheek as she reaches for her shoes, lacing them up.

"Where are we going?"

"A surprise." I shrug as she pulls her hair back into a low bun, grabs her phone from the nightstand and unlocks her bedroom door.

Hannah is one heavy sleeper, either that or she heard us and is now scarred for life.

"I'll hang until Hannah wakes up, so she isn't alone."

Mia eyes me, questioning my sudden concern for her sister, who up until recently, I was convinced was plotting my demise.

"You hate Hannah."

"No. Hate is a strong word. I think, if anything, I'm deathly afraid of her." I laugh pulling Mia into a hug before she leaves her apartment.

Once Mia leaves, I unload her dishwasher and warm up a cup of coffee. In my flannel pocket, I reach for the Post-it notes I brought with me as part of the surprise for our date tonight. Since Hannah is still asleep, I begin writing on each one with a sharpie.

I hear a noise from behind me and turn to see a sleepy Hannah walking out with one of my sweatshirts on and a pair of shorts with crew socks on her feet.

"Here." She offers me a piece of paper and when I look at it, it's the check I previously gave her.

"Thank you for offering it… but I don't want your money." She attempts a smile, but it's easy to see how hard that is for her at the moment. I've never given much thought to Hannah's life, but seeing her in this state, and knowing how it's killing Mia, suddenly there's an urge to want to get to know her better.

"What changed your mind?" I ask as I get up and pour her a cup of coffee.

"Is she here?"

I shake my head at her. "With a client. She'll be back in a few hours though."

Hannah nods as she takes a seat at the kitchen table with me.

"I guess what you said just made me think. I wanted to take that check and cash it, honestly. But I needed to get out of that situation I was in. Letting Brad think I had no money was better than letting him take what you gave me."

"Brad is your boyfriend?" I ask, raising a brow.

"No. Brad's my… situation. *Was* my situation. He stole from me. And then when I tried to confront him about it, that didn't go so well." Hannah raises her arm, the one with the bandage on it and I can feel the rage simmering under my skin.

"He hit you?"

She shakes her head back and forth. "He didn't hit me. Just grabbed my arm tight enough to leave a bruise. I only covered it so people wouldn't ask questions, but I guess that backfired."

Shaking my head back and forth, my fingers pinch the bridge of my nose. "You're not going back there. Do you hear me?"

She nods her head up and down before she stands up. "Oh, by the way"—she stops halfway down the hall and turns back—"sounds like you gave my sister the ride of her life this morning. Good. She needs to loosen up a little." Hannah cracks a smile and I think it's the first time I've ever seen one. "You're not so bad, golden boy."

"Neither are you, Wednesday."

"Meg, this is perfect. You nailed everything, thank you so much. I owe you." My eyes can't even focus on everything I'm seeing. It's all overwhelming, but in the best fucking way. Meg is the interior designer who basically took one look at Mia's Pinterest board and said copy-paste.

The colors are bright and airy, the equipment is all brand new and spread out. Nothing is cluttered together. The mirrors on the wall were able to be salvaged so all we had to do was give them a good cleaning. Four televisions are installed above the windows in front of cardio machines and rowing machines. There's a small refrigerator next to the front desk with water, energy drinks and caffeinated drinks. The only room we didn't touch is the one in the back. It's Mia's office and I wanted her to be able to hand pick everything in there. It's where she'll spend most of her time planning, and I know that she'll have a specific vision for that.

"Her taste is very chic. This was a fun project, thank you for bringing me on board for it."

"Anything you want. Please. If you want two tickets for the game Sunday, they're yours," I offer, eagerly.

"You know what? That would be great, thank you."

I shake her hand as she leaves and I take one last look around before closing the door behind me. It's almost seven and I told Mia I'd be there by then. I did see a missed call from her and a couple of texts, but I want to respond to her in person. I take the five-minute walk to Mia's and cut it in half, practically running the whole way there, dying to see her.

When I knock on her door and she answers, the sight of her would send any man straight into an early grave. Her long brown hair is in big loose curls and the navy blue dress she has on sends all the blood to my dick the second I see her.

"On second thought, let's just stay here," I say, all but drooling as I walk in and she kisses my cheek.

She doesn't reply to my comment, she simply stares at me, eyes glossy like she wants to cry, or maybe has been.

"The Post-it notes," she whispers. "You wrote down everything you love about me and plastered them all over my apartment?" She takes my hands into hers.

"I wanted you to see something amazing about yourself everywhere you looked, Mia. You're inspiring." I lift my hand to caress her cheek.

"When I walked in here an hour ago, I didn't even know what to make of it at first. I think I cried before I even read them all." Her laughter bellows from her chest and all I want to do for the rest of my life is be the reason behind it.

"I went through a lot of fucking Post-its." I chuckle. "Don't bother looking for any within a five-mile radius, they're sold out now."

She brings her forehead to my chest with another laugh, shaking her head.

"You're really... good, Nate. Just down to your core. You're good."

Shrugging, I put my hands in my pockets as she turns to put her shoes on.

"I have one more thing before dinner that I want to show you," I say. A nervous feeling is inching up my throat. Mia has always told me she didn't want my help when it came to buying a building. She's always told me that she wanted to do things on her own. But knowing how much she loved the building and how torn she was about not getting it because she helped her dad, I instantly knew that I didn't care if she got mad at me for it. Because I know that she deserves this.

"Something that'll top hundreds of Post-it notes? We'll see about that," she says as she steps out in front of me.

CHAPTER THIRTY-TWO

MIA

Okay, Post-it notes all over my apartment is easily the most romantic thing a man has ever done for me. As if Nate needed to do more things that would make me fall for him even harder. I walked into a true smorgasbord of words, quotes, song lyrics and simple drawings that took me by complete surprise. He did leave one in my closet that was more of a question. *"Can we buy you a pair of cowgirl boots so the image of you in them isn't tied to my sister?"* I laughed out loud when I read that one.

Earlier today, I had the best sex I've ever had. Hands down. It was the most passionate and fulfilling. I never knew it could be like that. Where it feels amazing physically, but also emotionally. Like everything about the moments we shared were connected on a deeper level. It was an intimacy I never thought I'd experience.

"Can you believe Thanksgiving is this Thursday? I'm so glad you guys don't play again. I'm excited to have dinner with everyone."

Nate grabs my hand as we walk down the sidewalk and it's the first time we're doing this. The first time we're in public and he's searching for my hand. His fingers grip mine, interlocking our hands. The warmth I feel from his touch moves all the way through my body.

"I'm looking forward to just spending the day with you," he says, giving my hand a squeeze.

As we're walking, I notice that we're just near the corner of Main and Marshall. The lights are on in the building I had wanted to rent and it's hard not to look into the windows to see what the new owners are doing with it.

"Oh, wow. Whoever bought this did a quick turn around," I say as Nate stops us in front of the giant window.

"I can't believe they're making it a gym. See, I told you it was the perfect spot for it." I shake my head, turning, but Nate's hand lands on my stomach, stopping me in place.

"Look at it again," he says.

I turn my head, looking into the window. "Why? It just upsets me. I mean look, they did exactly what I would do with the mirrors and the weight racks. I love the fridge up at the front too, such a cute touch. There's even a new desk," I scoff, shaking my head in annoyance how it's almost like someone just went into my brain and took every idea I had in addition to taking the building from me.

"Let's go in," Nate says. "We have time."

"Fine. I'd love to meet the new owner. They clearly have great taste." I storm in ahead of Nate as he opens the door for me. But no one greets us. No one is here working out. There isn't a single person in this building except for the two of us.

"Great ownership. They leave the door unlocked and the lights on and then just leave. Plus, where's the sign for this place? What's it called?"

Nate's cheeks turn red as he shakes his head at me. His hands reach out to mine, holding them in front of us as we stand next to the front desk here. Soft music plays over the speakers and just another kick in the gut, it's something I'd play in here too.

Nate's long sleeves are pulled up just a little, showcasing his forearms as I stare down at our hands together. The way he's holding my hand gives me a feeling that I can't explain, but it's just this sense of awareness, this realization that I don't want to hold anyone else's hand. Ever.

"It's yours," he says, in a low, smooth voice. My eyes slowly rise to meet his, confusion and shock swirling in my mind.

"Wh–what?" I step back, briefly and he brings his index finger to my chin and holds it in place.

"It's yours. This building. Everything in it. Yours."

Heat rises and seeps out of every inch of my skin as I take a full two steps back, completely out of his embrace and just stare at him. There's no way I just heard him right. This is *mine*?

"Are you mad? Please don't be mad." Nate takes a step forward. His boots shuffle across the new flooring.

"Mad?" I ask through a shaky breath.

I know I told him I didn't want his help, that I didn't want his charity. I didn't want to feel like I owed him something, but this has to be one of, if not the most romantic thing anyone's ever done for me.

"No, God. No, I'm not mad… I just… I didn't want to feel indebted to you, like I owed you."

"What? I'd never—" His brows crease in concern, but I take his hand in mine again.

"I know," I say, reassuring him. "The idea of having a friend buy you a literal building is intimidating, though. I think even you can admit that." My eyebrows cock up at him.

But Nate shakes his back and forth, his lips turn down before he speaks.

"Maybe for just a friend, but Mia, you're so much more than that. You always have been."

My eyes begin to well up with tears as he pulls me into a hug. The lights in the room are dim and the music is changing between alternative rock and 2000's hip hop, causing me to let out a laugh when the song changes from Foo Fighters to "Hot in Here" by Nelly.

"I can't believe you did this. Thank you," I say.

He tilts my chin up to him, planting a soft kiss on my lips. When I look around, everything is as I would've wanted it. The new desk is perfect, the paint on the walls, the inspiring quotes on the wall. Even down to the little calendar on the desk that has a quote of the day.

"I had help. A lot of it," he says as he takes me by the hand down the hall to where the office is and stops us in front of the door.

"The only space I didn't touch is this. I figured you can spend time here, envision how you want it, where you want things. I wasn't sure if you were set on a name yet either, so I left that paperwork up front for you to decide. Right now, it's just under your name. Once you decide, we'll get a sign made. A really fucking big one. But behind this door is the office and I know you'll spend the most time in here, so I wanted to make sure you have the final say on what goes in this room. But, can I suggest we get a lock for this door?" He smirks and twists the handle opening up the small room with fresh paint and new floors. The only thing in this room is a Post-it note on the far wall.

"It'll only ever be you."

It's written in Nate's chicken scratch handwriting and I pull the paper off the wall, turning back towards him as he stands in the doorway. Leaning against the frame, dark blue Henley with the sleeves pulled up and denim jeans, he smiles at me. His blue eyes are on fire tonight as I stare across the room at him. When Nate pulls himself away from the door, he meets me in the center of the room.

His hands cup my cheeks and slowly make their way to the sides of my neck, just below my ears. "I didn't want the world to see who I'd become. But I've never had to pretend around you.

There are so many parts of me that I was ashamed of, so many cracks within the man I was. But you filled those cracks. Every single one, Mia. You filled them with understanding, with laughter and compassion, with love. All of it was slowly killing me, I was breaking down, I could feel it. But as always, my best friend was the anchor that held me in place. You kept me from falling too far off course." His eyes close as he leans his head down to mine and whispers. "Eres mi sol, mi luna y todas mis estrellas."

You are my sun, my moon and all my stars.

"I love you. I've loved you since before I really even knew what that word meant. I just knew it was you. It was always supposed to be you."

There's a pull in my chest, a yank so strong and so full of force that I can't ignore it. The words I've been holding onto spill from my lips.

"You got the Spanish right." I quietly laugh as he smiles down at me. "Being with you used to scare me, Nate. I used to think that being anything more than your best friend meant losing that part of you, of us. But one thing I've learned is that just because you're scared of the risk doesn't mean you shouldn't take it. And if you love someone, you tell them. Even if it scares the hell out of you, you say it. Because if you don't, you'll never know if you just missed out on the best part of your life. And I love you, Nate. In a really big and stupid way that makes me pretend to care about your golf obsession, and give you the last pink Starburst, in a hopelessly romantic kind of way that scares the ever loving crap out of me. But I know if I don't just let myself feel the feelings and say them, I'll regret it."

Nate's lips curve into a smile just before he leans his head down and kisses me.

I've realized that oftentimes, if you want big rewards, you need to take big risks. You'll probably never be completely ready, there might always be the small one percent that has you holding back, but if you don't take the chance on the things you want, you'll never know.

———

"Ready to get back?" I ask Nate as he walks around his apartment this morning with me on FaceTime.

"Yeah, actually. Oddly enough, I think I need it." His laugh is deep and rich. "I had my meeting with Coach Aarons, met with the team briefly already and I saw the team therapist the other day. Only thing left really is to get on the field and see what happens."

Placing the phone down against my lamp, I walk into my closet and grab my jersey that bears the name Campbell with number 23 on the back.

"Seeing you in that today, knowing that you're really mine, makes the sight so much sweeter." His eyes full of desire as he stares at me pulling it over my head.

"Well, I've always been your biggest fan."

"Yeah, but now I get to give you orgasms, so I'm really winning." A devilish look washes over his eyes as I shake my head at him.

"Time to go, Campbell. Go have fun." I nod and he blows a kiss through the phone before we disconnect.

CHAPTER THIRTY-THREE

NATE

"Back in the black and red, baby!" Liam sees me walking into the locker room before I've barely got both feet through the door.

Coach Aarons walks over, giving me a handshake as I place my bag on the bench near my locker. His grip is firm on my hand and he gives me a steadfast look and nods his head before he simply walks away.

All I can think about right now is the sixty minutes of game time that I need to be ready for. I've done more work on my mental state in the last three weeks than I think I've done in my whole goddamn lifetime. Dana, the team therapist, encouraged me to let myself feel all the things today. When I shared that I felt ready, but still had some nerves about coming back, she assured me that those were normal feelings. I felt like I let the guys down in my last game. I wasn't honest with them about what I was going through and ultimately it ended up catching up with me.

"A lot of athletes, especially at your level, experience this type of pressure and anxiety, Nate. You aren't in the minority, even if you may feel that way. Unfortunately, most never talk

about it. Men suffer in silence a lot more often than we all think because their fear of being viewed as weak is stronger than their desire to heal. You being here is a great step into overcoming what you're dealing with. You should be proud of yourself."

Dana's words during our first meeting were spot on. For the longest time, the thought of telling anyone I was struggling wasn't even an option. When I told Mia, it was merely by mistake, I had no intention, it just trickled out of me one night and from then on, it snowballed.

A three-week hiatus and one therapy session aren't the answer to my problems, but it's a damn good start. I haven't felt this good in a while. While the nerves are still coursing through me, I've developed ways to help level them out.

"You enjoy competition, a challenge. So instead of looking at what you're dealing with as a threat, flip the narrative. Work through this as something to manage and overcome, not something that's bound to destroy you."

I replay her words as I'm suiting up in the locker room. While I look around, everything is the same. Not that I anticipated for the guys to change, but for a while, I just stopped paying attention to things around me. I was so in my head that Liam's pregame speech would go in one ear and out the other, Chase's prayer would fall on deaf ears and Graham's country music serenade would be completely overshadowed by the screaming voices in my head.

Not today though.

I hear it all. I soak it all in.

Because for the first time in a long time, I realize exactly what I have.

"Heading out for warm-ups?" Chase comes up next to me as he's taping his hands. I nod my head in his direction and stuff a sharpie into my chest as I turn and walk out behind him.

Liam is already out here, slinging passes to Ford and the

other receivers on our team. Chase starts stretching next to the other defensive players and I walk over the sidelines.

"Nate! Nate! Over here!" At least a dozen kids stand against the railings as I jog over to them, grabbing the sharpie out of my chest protector.

"Glad you're back!" one kid shouts. He's probably around twelve, if I had to guess. He's wearing my jersey and has a small boy under his arm, pulling him close.

"Thanks, man," I say, and I point to the smaller kid next to him also wearing my jersey with eye black under his eyes and a Tampa Knights hat on his head. His glasses nearly fall off his face when he lunges towards me as I reach my hand out to give him a high five.

This is the part that matters.

I sign the kid's hat among a plethora of other items that a bunch of people hand to me and take pictures with any of the kids who ask me. Once I'm done and about to head onto the field to get in at least a few warm-up reps, I glance into the stands quickly. Noticing a small brunette with a red jersey and a high ponytail staring at me. Mia's smile beams down towards me and I blow a kiss in her direction before I walk backwards onto the field. Her hands go up into a heart shape and I mimic the gesture, not giving a fuck if anyone sees. Because I'm in love with my best friend and I don't care who knows it.

"Look at her," Liam says as we walk back into the tunnel after a few throws. He tilts his head over at Demi Sanchez standing on the sidelines. "When's your interview with her?"

"Next week."

"Need me there? You know, for moral support or anything?"

I tilt my head down, raising an eyebrow at him. "Demi can't stand you, champ. Just leave her alone."

"She loves me, what are you talking about?"

"Uh huh. She's also married, which should be your first

reason to leave her the hell alone," I say, pushing the door open as we enter the locker room.

"Not married. Engaged. There's a difference." Liam's gloved hand points to me as we part ways and he takes a seat on the chair next to his locker.

When I agreed to do an interview discussing my absence and the reason behind it, Bex said that a few reporters had approached her. I didn't want to do a story with someone who just wanted to spin it and ask me questions that didn't really matter. Demi Sanchez is smart. And she's feisty. She always asks questions that really tell a story and make a difference, so I knew if I actually planned on publicly talking about it, I'd be doing it with her.

"Let's go do our job and come out with the win," Liam says.

The guys lost two of the three games I was absent for and while I know it isn't my fault, I still kick myself for not being able to be here for them.

Running out onto the field, there's a very noticeable difference in how I feel today versus how I felt my last game. I'm still quieting the voices and the insecurities, but instead of balling them up and shoving them into a corner in my mind, trying to ignore that they even exist, I'm talking back to them. I'm reassuring myself that I do belong on this field and my will to overcome this is stronger than anything or anyone that tells me I can't.

"Campbell to the twenty, to the fifteen, five, four, three, two… touchdown Tampa Bay! Welcome back, Nate Campbell!" the announcer's voice yells through the stadium.

I've heard him call out my plays for years over the speakers, the same high energy, excited voice tracking all of my home games for the last six years. The screams from the crowd erupt around me and I jog over to the sidelines right as Ford and Liam come up slapping the sides of my helmet.

"Didn't miss a beat," Ford says as he takes off his helmet.

I'm playing more than I expected to, but I can tell Coach is still treading lightly on putting me in for too many plays. I get the impression he doesn't want to overwhelm me and hell, right now I'll take what I can get.

"Get in there, Campbell." I hear as I'm already standing when I see Liam on the field pointing at me and motioning for me to get in the huddle.

Liam snaps the ball and fakes like he's handing it to me. I sell it well against the defensive line, making more than half of them falter left to follow me. When in reality, Liam throws the ball down the field to a wide open receiver and another six points ends up on the board for us.

It's a well fought game, one where I felt really fucking good during every quarter. I was happy to be on the field today, happy to be suited up on one of the best teams, with the best people surrounding me. Our team wins 27-17, and even though I didn't play half as many snaps as I normally would, I'm calling it a personal win too.

"Happy Friendsgiving!" Mia shouts as we walk through the doors of Ford and Abby's house. The whole house smells amazing as we make our way from the foyer into the kitchen where everyone is sitting and munching on the buffet of appetizers Abby has laid out.

I set the green bean casserole down on the counter, taking another look under the foil just to check my craftsmanship one final time. *Fucking perfection.* It's pretty hard to screw up a casserole, though.

"Hi, sweet baby," Mia says as she reaches towards Chase

while he's holding his baby girl against his chest. He hands her to Mia and she walks into the living room with Summer and Abby as I take a seat next to Chase at the bar. Ford walks in with four beer bottles and places them down in front of us.

"Is Kristen coming?" Liam asks Chase once he pops the top from his beer bottle.

"Kristen left," Chase answers with absolutely no emotion behind his words. As if he still can't believe it. Before any of us can respond to him, a loud thud causes all of us to turn our heads.

"She what?" Summer's standing in the archway of the kitchen and dining room as an empty bottle falls from her hands.

"I think she wants daddy," Abby interrupts as she walks in with a screaming baby in her arms. Chase gets up and takes her from Abby. He pats her back and whispers in her ear as he walks into another room, Summer on his heels with steam practically shooting from her ears.

My eyes go wide as Mia walks in, and puts her arms around my waist from behind. My hand instinctively reaches behind us both and rubs the small of her back.

"So, did Nate rope all of you into helping him with that building?" Mia asks, a desperate attempt to change the subject of Kristen up and leaving her two-month old baby.

"I have no idea what you're talking about." Abby crosses her arms over her chest as Ford kisses her cheek.

"I slaved in there, Clarky."

"Well, thank you, Liam," she jokes, reaching a hand to pat him on the shoulder.

Thanksgiving is always one of my favorite holidays. There's no pressure, you just come in, wear your stretchy pants, eat a shit ton of food and watch football all day. A damn dream if you ask me.

The girls set the table while Ford carves the turkey and I check on the rest of the food, making sure everything is ready to go before we sit down. I have so much to be thankful for, but the most prevalent thing is the people in this room. Specifically, the tiny brunette who I used to pretend was just my friend. As we take a seat next to one another, Mia's hand lands on my thigh and I look over at her, smiling. I mouth "I love you" just before everyone digs in and at this moment, everything feels right. Everything feels perfect. And I know all the struggles and insecurities I've faced and still the ones yet to come, won't be nearly as tough with Mia by my side.

"Hi, Nate." Demi gives me a hug as I step in front of the cameras with her. There's a chair for her and one for me in a darkened room with spotlights pointing at the chairs in the center.

We sit down across from one another and I bring my left ankle over my knee, trying to get myself comfortable. I met with the team therapist again earlier today. So, it's big day for talking about feelings.

Bex was able to get most of the dialogue that Demi wanted to discuss ahead of time, just to make sure there wouldn't be anything too far into left field that we'd have to diffuse later. Even though I don't expect anything shady from Demi.

She tells me the cameras are going to start rolling and I reach for the water bottle beside me, taking a quick sip and wipe my hands on my jeans.

"Nate, this is the first time you're sitting down with someone since you've been back on the Knights after your absence. Can you walk us through what happened that day against Philadelphia?"

I nod my head after a deep breath and begin to break down everything that happened that day. How I felt leading up to the game, the moments before the hit, all of it.

"I told my best friend that something was going on. I

couldn't explain it, but something wasn't right and I needed to step away from all of it to try to get a hold of it. So I left."

"You were gone for three weeks?" Demi's eyes stay focused on me the entire time.

Nodding my head, I answer. "I went back home. I spent time with my family, with my best friend. I spent time with myself. I had a hard time even communicating what I was going through because I didn't understand it. It was like I lost touch of things. The time away helped me re-center myself, I almost relearned how to be just me. Not the football player. But just Nate."

Demi nods along with me, almost looking sorry for me.

"I hated leaving the guys like that, but honestly I was more of a liability to them than an asset, and I couldn't put them at risk because of my mental state. I'm a work in progress. I didn't find the magic button or anything like that, I'm still working on myself every day. But I have a better vision now, a purpose and I plan on doing some good with what I've learned."

Demi sits up straighter in the chair and I watch her fingers twist her engagement ring on her hand. "I've also struggled with anxiety, as I know a lot of people do. Of course, the levels are much different for someone in your position. But can you describe the way it felt for you? I'm sure there are so many athletes who probably feel similarly."

"Suffocating. Blurred. Downright debilitating." My throat clears before I continue. "I felt weak and I felt anger and frustration that I couldn't get a hold of things. I didn't know what was happening to me and I tried like hell to hide it, to ignore all of it. I was ashamed. Until that game when I knew I couldn't hide it anymore."

"I know the team is happy to have you back. We all are. Talking about this takes courage, and I know we're all proud of you for starting this conversation around the league. What kind of advice do you have for anyone who is also having this experience?"

I pause briefly, as a million things come to my mind, but one stands out above the rest.

"Find someone you trust and tell them. Talk about it. Don't suffer in silence because you're too ashamed to say you need help. Start somewhere. There's help out there, you just have to admit you want it. We have to talk about it. I know in this sport we want to be seen as tough competitors, but we still have the same struggles as anyone else."

"You're right. Thank you, Nate," Demi says in a sweet voice, and the lights dim as the cameras click off and she lets out a deep sigh.

"Thank you for letting me interview you about this. I think what you have to say is really important and I'm glad you spoke up."

I wrap Demi into a hug before she turns to another member of the crew.

As I turn, Mia's waiting in the back behind the cameras for me. Her brown hair in a French braid with a pair of bright pink leggings and a black crew neck sweater hanging over her.

"Proud of you," she whispers as I sling my arm over her shoulder and walk us out.

My healing journey wouldn't have even begun without the belief that Mia instills in me. Even on the days I feel like shit she builds me up. She'll admit when things are tough, but always helps me see the silver lining. She's a helper to her core, the kind of person I want my kids to look up to. She's my eternal sunshine and I'm so glad that we found our way out of the friend zone, because this right here is exactly what I want.

My purpose.

My future.

The place I'm constantly running towards is her. My end zone is Mia.

EPILOGUE

NATE

THREE YEARS LATER

"Babe, can you grab the diaper bag, please?" Mia tosses me a package of wet wipes as she moves around the kitchen island, cleaning up the mess from breakfast. The sun is streaming through the front windows of the home we built together in the last year.

Placing the wet wipes along with the extra clothes into the bag, I zip it up and sling it over my shoulder.

"Got it. I'm going to put this in the truck, I'll be right back," I say, walking towards the front door.

When I step outside, it's quiet. It's always quiet here. There's open land all around me and a swing set out back. Planters in front of the white house with black shutters and a doormat in front of the door that says 'wipe your paws.' I bought this land before Mia and I were even engaged. I knew it was where I wanted to build a house and make a home, make a life... with her. It's where we used to spend so many nights talking about everything and nothing, and now, we still spend our nights out in this field, but instead of it being an abandoned lot, it has four walls and is filled with love and laughter. It's where we're raising our family.

"Do we want to make a bet on whether or not we think Kristen will show up?" I ask when I step back inside.

Mia rolls her eyes as a loud huff leaves her chest. "Well, she's oh for two, so I'm going to guess she also won't be attending her child's third birthday. God, it really bothers me. I know we've talked about it, but I'll just never understand it. I mean, I look at our boys and I just melt into a puddle, there's nothing I wouldn't do for them." And that right there is one of the many reasons I know I married the right woman.

"And that's why you are mom of the year… of the century." My hands latch onto her waist, as we stand in the kitchen. Did I ever dream I'd be married to Mia? I think in some life, some version of my dreams, I wanted it… but I just never knew it was actually possible. She still gives me a hard time about not saying anything sooner, but I give it right back to her. We both had some feelings that we didn't think the other reciprocated and we were also both terrified as fuck to lose the other, but sometimes things are just too loud to ignore.

She leans up on her toes, kissing my cheek before walking into the other room where a light cry has started to only get louder.

"Someone is up," I say.

Mia grabs the baby monitor, waving it around. "Looks like they both are."

I follow Mia towards the bedroom where our sons sleep, the room that Mia so carefully and thoughtfully decorated. It's full of spaceships and stars, the moon and this pretty amazing picture of the night sky that I had framed for her. It's the sky above the home we share. This place means something to Mia and I. It's more than just a piece of land, a house we filled with furniture… it's our home, our beginning, the place where our children will be raised. It's where I asked Mia to be mine forever. It's where I promised to love her for the rest of my life. We've shared countless milkshakes out in this field. Late night talks when we were just friends trying to figure out life.

Life is good out here. As of last year, the *Your Mind Matters Foundation* is in full swing. We've helped so many young athletes work through their mental health struggles. Providing them a safe and supportive community of current and former athletes to lean on for guidance. We have psychologists on staff, as well as other players from the NFL, MLB, NHL and NBA—local and out of state—who have come to speak and provide mentorship. They've opened up about their experiences and it's only helped others understand their own struggles and ways to cope.

I still see Dana once a week and she volunteers her time with the Foundation often. I'm so fucking proud of it. I wanted to leave something meaningful behind as my legacy after football and I feel like this Foundation is it.

Mia just opened another studio less than five minutes away from here. She's been killing it downtown and needed to expand. She hired her sister to help at the downtown studio and they've been working on their relationship a lot. I wasn't wrong about Hannah, she truly is terrifying, and I stand by the fact that I think she's Wednesday Addams come to life, but she's also really fucking good with my kids and is making a really strong effort to help her sister. Returning all the years of support that Mia provided her.

"Oliver is going to want you, that little momma's boy…so I'll grab Luke." I smirk walking up the stairs behind Mia. "Can't blame him though." I pinch Mia's thigh as we walk up and she turns around to swat my arm, but I grab her wrist just before she has the chance to.

"You know, Mr. Campbell, when you're old and gray and have lost all of your quick reflexes, you won't catch me," she teases.

"I'm always going to catch you, Smalls."

After we get the twins from their room and have them dressed and ready to go, we head over to Chase's apartment. I can't believe he is about to have a three-year-old. Hell, I can't believe I'm about to have one-year-old twins.

"Where are my boys?" Summer runs over when we walk into Chase's apartment and reaches for the car seats I just set down near my feet.

"Take your pick," I state. "Although Luke's probably due for a blowout, he chugged a bottle before we got here." My comment doesn't deter Summer though, she reaches in and picks up Luke while Abby grabs Oliver and they walk away to the other side of the room with Mia.

"How's dad life going?" Liam reaches his hand out to me, shaking it firmly.

"Little sleep. But fuck, give me ten more. I love my little guys. Plus, seeing Mia be a mom is so goddamn sexy." It's impossible to tear my eyes from her. I know how Ford feels. I get it. The desire to just be around one person all the time. It's addicting. Liam nods, and we both look over at Chase who looks like he's had about ten years added to his life since the last time I saw him.

I know all of this bullshit with Kristen still bothers him. He's been a single dad now for three years and no matter how much we all offer to help and tell him that he's doing a fucking rockstar job, I know he feels like he's not doing enough. He's trying to fill both shoes and I just feel for him.

"Happy three years of being the best damn dad," I say, slapping his back. Now that I know how hard it is being a parent, I respect the hell out of him, especially doing it on his own.

"I can't fucking believe Kristen... I sent her a text, like I have the last two years giving her all the details and she never replied and hasn't shown up... probably won't show up." Chase hangs his head just as the sweetest soon to be three-year-old starts calling for him and he walks away.

"Hey babe, I'm going to sit outside with the girls. Diane is playing with the boys in the little ball pit over there." Mia points to the living room and I watch my boys laugh as Chase and Abby's mom plays peek-a-boo with them. Mia's lips softly graze mine as she leans into me and my arms wrap her up in a hug, deepening the kiss just for a moment. When she pulls away, it only leaves me wanting more, like always. I'm breathless every time I kiss Mia.

She saved me. There's really no other way to say it. I was a wrecking ball, a bull in a china shop... whatever kind of metaphor you want to use for complete chaos. Even before she was mine, she was always my safe space, my comfort, the sun in all my darkness. Every amazing thing I have in this life is because I met a girl one night at a party and she became my best friend for years, until finally she became mine.

MIA

"Can we just please take a moment to appreciate the hotness happening around us?" Summer says, staring through the window.

I'm sitting on the patio with Summer and Abby, we're sweating our asses off, but I haven't been alone with my girlfriends in way too long so we'll take what we can get. Even if it'll only end up being fifteen minutes before someone needs one of us. I look through the sliding glass door to a sight that sends heat through my body. Nate is playing with Luke on the floor,

Chase has one toddler hanging off of his back, while Ford has Oliver pulling at his hair. Seeing Nate as a dad has made me fall in love with him all over again.

I used to look at him and just see my best friend who slept around and never wanted to take relationships seriously, to falling in love during one random road trip and realizing I couldn't bear the thought of him with someone else. Somewhere along the way, I realized part of me was always in love with him. There was a part of me that wanted him to choose me. But because I never thought he would and because I had turned him down once before, I thought we just had each other so far in the friend zone that there was no changing that. Hell, I didn't even want to change it for a while. He fought for us. He fought for us in a way that you see on TV. He showed me what it felt like to be completely swept off your feet. And he still does it. There hasn't been a single day that's gone by where he hasn't made me feel like I'm everything he's ever dreamed of.

"My ovaries are exploding watching them do the daddy daycare thing..." Summer speaks again while Abby and I are both just drooling over our husbands.

"Don't we think it's about time that Chase stops inviting Kristen to holidays and birthdays? She hasn't showed up to a single thing... I think at this point, if I were her, I'd be afraid to. She has to know we're all here just wondering where the hell she is." I shake my head at Abby's question.

"No," I say. "As much as it sucks, I don't think he should stop asking. It's the only thing he can do. So fifteen years from now, when that sweet girl asks him, he can say he tried and even if she never shows up, he'll want to be able to tell his daughter that he tried."

"I just wish he would accept more help. I'm a nurse, for God's sake, he can trust me with a toddler," Summer complains, but something else shows in her voice too. Affection? I think we all have gained a soft spot for Chase over the last few years with everything, but especially Summer. I've watched her cry for Chase, for his situation. She's been more upset about everything Chase is going through with Kristen than anyone else.

"How are things going with Drew?" I ask Summer, changing the subject to something lighter.

"I really need him to be named something other than Drew," Abby chimes in with a laugh.

"Good. Fine. I don't know, actually." Summer shrugs as she looks at me but then turns her eyes back to Chase. He wipes his brow as his mom comes over and gives him a hug. He looks so defeated all the time, but he never shows it around his daughter. CeCe believes her dad is Superman. And she's right.

"He's too good to worry about Kristen. He deserves so much better. Someone who would appreciate him and love the hell out of them both." Summer's features soften as she sits back in the chair and my eyes move to Abby.

"Why don't you offer to nanny for him a few days a week? That way it helps him out, and he can have somewhat of a life again. Like you said, you're a nurse so you're already CPR trained..." I suggest, but Abby jumps in before Summer gets a chance to.

"He won't go for that. Right now, Chase is so hyper focused on his plan. He has a whole notebook with his daily schedules, his routines, his plans for literally everything. Being a dad is his only focus right now. It's honestly his own little playbook on how he expects things to go day in and day out... I think adding a nanny to that would throw it all off."

Before anyone else can say anything, Ford pops his head out to tell us they're about to sing "Happy Birthday" so we put a pin in our conversation and head back inside.

My husband is standing next to Liam, holding both of our sons in his arms as he softly sings along with everyone and my heart feels even more full than it did this morning. I have this wonderful life with a family I adore. Friends who might as well be family. My relationship with my sister is slowly on the mend and as for my dad, I still have faith in him… I still believe that there's hope for him.

Nate has proven to me that people can, in fact, overcome things that weigh you down. Admitting that you have a problem, no matter what it is, is half of the battle. Facing it… well, that's the other half.

Opening myself up to the things that scared me was the best decision I could have made. I think part of me was always in love with Nate Campbell.

It just took me years to let myself take the risk and say it.

ACKNOWLEDGMENTS

I have to thank the readers first and foremost. Your excitement for Nate and Mia's story has been a driving force in making this book into what it is. The messages and comments sharing your eagerness kept me going, especially on the days where their story seemed hard to write. And there were plenty of those. Forever grateful to you for allowing me to tell stories. I hope you enjoyed these two finally coming to their senses and getting together. Thank you for reading.

To my family and friends, you all always remind me of my abilities in the moments where I feel incredibly overwhelmed. I love you.

To Jillian Meadows and Lo Everett, thank you for reading my work and helping shape it. I admire both of you and truly appreciate your support, guidance and friendship.

My alpha readers, Wren and Mackenzie, thank you for helping me bring Nate and Mia's story to life with your feedback and suggestions. I will forever be thankful for the two of you. I live for your hilariously chaotic notes.

My beta readers, between your kind words, suggestions, hilarious comments and overall excitement over Nate and Mia's story, you all helped give me the confidence that this book had something special. Thank you all so much.

Caroline, my Editor, I'm always so appreciative of your time and effort that goes into my words. I'm also very thankful that you don't make fun of how many times I can misspell the word scrunchie. I probably lost count after the sixth time. Thank you, friend.

Cathryn, thank you once again for formatting this book so beautifully.

Mel (Mel D. Designs), another cover, another knockout. I've loved working with you again and cannot stop looking at the pretty blue cover on this book. Thank you.

To anyone who has struggled with their mental health, the world is better with you in.

COMING SOON

Follow me on social media for more information on book three of the *Out of Bounds* series—Summer and Chase's story. You can find me on Instagram and TikTok @erinmackenzie.author.

ABOUT THE AUTHOR

Erin Mackenzie is from a small town in central Florida where she lives with her husband and daughter. Her love for reading started at a young age and then was rediscovered after she became a mom and wanted something that was just for her. When she isn't reading or writing, you can find her trying out new recipes to cook or bake, spending time outdoors or rooting on her favorite sports teams.

Printed in Great Britain
by Amazon